THE BOY AND THE CROW

Brendan Walsh

Typefaces: *Cover title is ChunkFive Roman, courtesy of fontsquirrel.com, the copyright owner. Text typeface is Book Antiqua.*

Spelling: *American style.*

Cover Photo: *Brendan Walsh*
Cover Design, Retouching & Author Photo: *Brian Cockerton*
Crow illustration: *Montréal illustrator, Adam Duff*
Creative Direction: *Christopher "Chris" Walsh*

Conditions of Sale: *All rights reserved. No part of this publication may be reproduced, stored in a retrieval system, or transmitted in any form or by any means, electronic, mechanical, photocopying, recording or otherwise, without the prior permission of Brendan Walsh, the copyright owner and publisher.*

This book is sold subject to the condition that it shall not, by way of trade or other means, be lent, resold, hired out or otherwise circulated in any form of binding or cover other than that in which it is published without the copyright owner's and publisher's prior consent. Furthermore, these conditions shall be imposed on the subsequent purchaser(s).

Author's Notes: *While the author draws on real-life experiences in writing this book, the story is fictional. Except for the character, Banjo Bob Cussen, whose name is used with permission, any similarity to other actual characters, living, or dead, is coincidental. Likewise, the town of Noburg mentioned in the book is a fictional setting.*

© Brendan Walsh 2013. All rights reserved.
Montréal, Québec, Canada.
www.theboyandthecrow.com

Happy Reading

[signature]

For:

Bernadette, Christopher, Cormac, Kelly Ann, Lee-Ann and Tessa Marie.

Acknowledgments

I extend my heartfelt gratitude to the following people without whose help I could not have produced this work:

Heather Pengelley, Montreal writing teacher, editor and playwright who volunteered her precious time to review my first draft and offer her constructive critique. Her "brutally honest" feedback and encouragement were a joy to receive. I will always remember your generosity, Heather.

Canadian playwright and author, Colleen Curran who put me in touch with Heather in the first place. You chose a great challenger and mentor for me, Colleen.

My cherished childhood friend, Yves Saint-Pierre who challenged me to reconsider my storytelling "voice." Because you introduced me to the wonders of the wild during our teenage years, you helped me shape and hone this story.

Stephen "Steve" Jones, Montreal author, musician, translator and my first Irish fiddle teacher who shared his editing skills in reviewing the near-final draft.

Veteran Canadian journalist and long-time friend, Rob Bull, for providing valuable editing advice several times en route. Thank you, Rob, for never saying "no."

Richard Andrews and Elizabeth Jane Hirst, my teaching colleagues, for their review and critique of a much earlier draft. Thank you for your diligence and encouragement.

To the following who accepted to review a draft of this book: Anna Cockerton, Meaghan Gibbs and Leslie Macleod. Thank you for your constructive feedback.

And last, but not least, to Kelly Ann, for reviewing the first proof hot off the press. Thank you for your corrections suggestions and, of course, your challenges.

Special Notes of Appreciation

To Bernadette Duffin, my spouse and soul mate, for encouraging me to write a book that would appeal to younger and older readers. Thanks for being there, Bernadette.

To Lisa MacCallum who unwittingly inspired the idea for this book when she told me about her true encounter with a crow that had perched on her moving windshield wiper blade in Vancouver several years ago. Thanks for the spark, Lisa.

To "Chris" for the many times he challenged me creatively during the hectic year before publication. Thank you for encouraging me to rethink things, Chris — especially when I did not want to.

To Cormac for his encouragement along the way. Thanks for believing in me.

To Brian Cockerton for: his guidance in resolving technological issues; helping me with the cover design and production; retouching the front cover photo; supplying my photo for the back cover; and reviewing the manuscript. Thank you for your ongoing assistance and patience, Brian.

Prologue

WHENEVER I PUT PEN TO PAPER, as I do now, to write about familiar places of my past, memories roll through my mind like the frames of a silent-movie:

The quiet corner of the old neighborhood is six years younger as it cuts to a scene in which fellow gangbangers lurk in an alleyway, pigging out on pizza, pastries and greasy French fries smothered in barbecue sauce.

The headlights of a passing car dissolve to a lamppost, its light shining down on Melody, the first girl I ever kissed.

The screech of a city owl fades to the scream of an approaching police siren. Suspicious layabouts scatter like flies.

A kid on a bike cuts to one balmy early-June afternoon when I skip school and escape with fellow truant Neil McCutcheon to watch jockeys slumped in their sulkies, riding crops in hand, chasing after their quick-paced, poop-plopping horses as they race towards the finish line at Yonkers Raceway.

While the tennis court next to my old tenement is a more recent juxtaposition, it nevertheless triggers the most powerful memory of all: a court where I am making my final serve and I am about to learn the final score in one of the most important matches of my young life.

Chapter 1

THE JUDGE'S EYELIDS looked to me like they were glued shut, as her right hand crept across her bench and grasped the gavel. Then she opened her eyes and fixed them on me.

"Do you have anything to say before I pronounce sentence, Mr. Cagney?"

I lowered and shook my head several times, wondering what sentence I would receive this time around.

My heartbeat seemed to be racing against the pendulum of the nearby wall clock -- two beats for every tick-tock. My stomach turned and rumbled with nervousness, even though I was trying to look tough to the dozen or so noisy Crows I could see standing on the lawn outside the window. The judge had ordered the window open after the air conditioner croaked.

"Give me something!" she demanded, her voice echoing off the intricately carved oak wall paneling that covered the juvie courtroom's walls. "The charges are serious and this is the second time this year that you have appeared before me in this court."

I avoided her gaze by fixing my eyes on the antique brass calendar on the wall to her left. I had seen the bailiff roll the digit of the day forward by hand before the judge arrived. It read Friday, August 24, 2007.

"I deserve all you're gonna dish out, Miss." I said in response to my lawyer's shoulder nudge.

She raised her eyebrows.

"I mean Your Honor. I did the things they all say I did. Well, not me directly, but I was there all the same and I'm, well, you know, real sorry I stood by and did nothing."

"Finally getting somewhere, are we? Or, are you just mouthing your lawyer's words to impress me? Who knows for sure? Perhaps a long period of detention may be just what you need to cut the ties with that cowardly gang you belong to, especially since you won't identify your accomplices."

"Objection. He's only 16, Your Honor," Clinton Alliston, my lawyer said when he stood up. "He deserves a second chance."

"And what about the old lady who was knocked down when the Crows gang stole her purse?" she countered, signaling him to sit down with her down-turned palms. "Doesn't she deserve a second chance to shop in peace? She needs a hip replacement thanks to your client's despicable crime. And, yes, before you remind me, Mr. Alliston, I am well aware of the letter that she wrote to you and this court conveying her forgiveness upon Daniel Cagney, whom she called *a lost soul in need of prayer and forgiveness*."

The Crows outside cheered and cawed. They also flashed one of their signature slackings: two closed hands pressed against each other while their thumbs opened and closed sideways like bird's wings. The judge quickly drowned out the noise with her gavel and her voice.

"Get that riffraff off my lawn!" she commanded the bailiff. "And tell them if there are any more outbursts or disruptions, I'll hold them all in contempt and throw their sorry butts in jail where they belong."

"I would agree with the complainant's opinion," Alliston said, flashing a quick-to-order smile.

"Now why does that not surprise me in the least, Mr. Alliston?" she quipped.

The courtroom doors squeaked open. It was followed by the sound of heavy boot steps and a deep male voice.

"Sorry for barging in, Your Honor, but I've just arrived in town after a long drive. I came here in the hope that I could be helpful to you in deciding this case -- with the court's permission, of course."

I turned and looked at the old hippie standing in the aisle. He had long, grey, braided hair and a salt-and-pepper beard that looked like it had made a quick getaway from the nearest barber's chair. He wore matching light blue-denim jeans and shirt, sleeves rolled up to show off well-muscled arms. A knotted red neckerchief circled his neck and he was standing in soiled brown work boots, each loosely laced. In his right hand, he held a green baseball cap with a Vermont state emblem on its visor.

"Only close family members have standing in this juvenile court, sir," she challenged.

"I am family," he countered. He made for the defense table in long strides.

"This ought to be a good'un," I whispered to Alliston, as he was about to approach the bench. "I've never seen this old guy in my life."

"I'm Danny's maternal grandfather, Your Honor, and, as far as I know, his only living relative -- apart from his mother and my wife. With all due respect, I think that gives me standing in any court, given my limited understanding of the law, of course."

"Is this indeed your grandfather, Daniel?"

I scratched at the crow tattoo on my left arm, hoping none of the guys had heard her call me Daniel. They'd think it too soft and uppity a name for one of their own. I shrugged my shoulders.

"I don't know. Could be. I can't remember much about any of my grandparents. And I don't remember any of them with a beard and a ring in his ear."

"The beard's a recent addition, as is the earring, which was a present from my wife for crossing the International Date Line, a sailor's tradition. I'm sorry. My name is Mahoney. Tyler Mahoney."

He pulled out some documents from the back pocket of his jeans and handed them to the judge.

"The boy's mother is my daughter, Maire Mahoney. Of course, her married name's Cagney."

As the judge examined the papers, the sun peeked out from behind a cloud and lit up the name on the bronze plaque resting on her bench. The name Arlene, as in Hon. Judge Arlene Fisher, suits her I thought and I began to feel hopeful for the first time since being arrested two weeks earlier. I studied the deep lines on her careworn face as she perched on her bench. She was surrounded by her attentive brood of lawyers, clerks, and me, her latest societal misfit. This was her domain and her ears were cocked to register and digest the intent of every single spoken word, inflection or omission that disturbed it.

"These papers appear to be in order. Of course," she cautioned as she handed the envelope to the clerk, "we shall have to authenticate them. So exactly what solution did you have in mind, Grandfather Mahoney, given, as you say, your limited understanding of the law?"

"Deliver the boy to my care for a year, Your Honor, and I promise to make a man of him on my farm in Noburg, Vermont. His grandmother's a licensed teacher and she'll give him all the proper schooling the state requires and then some. And I'll make sure he gets the discipline and direction a boy his age needs."

"Why are you doing this, Mr. Mahoney? The boy, after all, appears to be almost a total stranger to you. You have been an absent grandparent most of his life, have you not?"

"He's my blood, Your Honor. Not seeing him was never my choice. Drugs and Maire's loser boyfriend were responsible for that."

"You didn't answer my question."

"My wife and I would like a second chance to do what we couldn't do before, if you know what I mean."

Her smile said that she did.

"We'd almost completely lost touch with Maire until she called from prison the day after Danny was arrested. She's serving time again for a drug offence. It was the first real news we've had of her in recent years. In fact, Danny was only about seven when we last had physical contact with him at our farm. When Maire was in jail those times since, she refused visitors even though we tried many times to see her. She felt too ashamed of her physical and emotional deterioration. At least that's what I think."

"Thank you, Mr. Mahoney, for your openness. Now, as I said earlier, I need to look into all this some more before I render my final decision on Daniel. In the meantime, if you would like a few minutes to chat with him now, I'll permit it, but only in the presence of a court-appointed officer -- and, of course, his legal counsel. Are you and Daniel agreeable to that arrangement?"

When we told her that we were, she picked up her gavel and tapped the bench twice. I knew in the interval, between taps, what her final decision would be.

"This court is adjourned until tomorrow morning at ten."

"Tomorrow's Saturday, Your Honor," Alliston objected.

"If I can make myself available, Mr. Alliston, so can you. If you cannot be present, don't. Delegate an alternate. I want to resolve this case as expeditiously as possible. I have a heavy docket next week."

Alliston was about to say something, but then thought better of it and shrugged his shoulders instead.

After she stepped down from the bench, the judge ordered the bailiff to "hang on a minute." Then she fixed her gaze on me.

"Daniel Cagney, there's just one thing above all others that puzzles me about you. Why on God's good earth would an obviously intelligent young man like you want to hang out with a band of illiterates like the Crows, many of whom have stood right where you are standing today? For the life of me, I just don't understand."

She shuffled through some papers that she was carrying and added, "It says here that you are a straight A student and that you won top prizes in English Literature and French at your school last year. Well, tell me. Is it me, or do you see a disconnect here, young man?"

I lowered my head to look for an answer on the well-shined wood floor, but I didn't find one there. And that bothered me.

Chapter 2

I WAS HAPPY ENOUGH not talking, but my newfound grandfather had to go and break the frigging silence as we drove north in his three-seat pickup truck, a Chevy.

"You've been fidgeting 'n' fumbling with that envelope since your release."

I shrugged and turned away to look at the stationary herd of cows whizzing by in the other direction at exactly fifty-five miles per hour, just like the road sign had commanded. Some of them were bent over grazing, while others stood and stared at us with dumb looks on their long faces as they chewed their cud.

"I'd be curious to read what's inside if the judge had given it to me instead of you," he said, nodding at the envelope in my hand. "I really don't think it's going to bite you. Do you?"

"What the hell," I muttered under my breath. "If it'll, like, make you *happy*."

I ripped open the envelope and removed a greeting card. "It's only a damn card," I said.

His eyes told me that he didn't like me damning.

On the front of the note, there was an embossed illustration of a mature black crow swooping down to land. Its piercing, blue-grey eyes glared right at me as it descended from a cloudless sky.

My grandfather smiled and looked at me as he downshifted on the steep hill we had started to climb.

"That crow picture is appropriate, don't you think? You being one I mean."

"It's only a stupid picture."

"Stupid, huh. That's what you think?" he challenged. "Like the crow you had tattooed on your arm? Now why would you want to become a Crow, if you thought they were just stupid birds?"

I shrugged. "It's just a gang name. Like Bloods or Scars."

"Well, crows are not stupid by any stretch of the imagination," he said. "In many ways, they're a lot smarter than some humans I've met. I have a great book on birds at the farm and I'd be glad to lend it to you. You'll see. They're not just garbage lovers like you see in the city."

I shrugged again.

"How long's it gonna take to get there, Mister? I'm tired and hungry and I need a piss."

His eyes told me he didn't like the word "piss" either.

"About two hours," he replied. "We eat right after chores, but we'll give you a break from them your first day. Oh, and you can call me Poppy, not Mister. I used to call my own grandfather that. Poppy I mean."

"Chores? So, that's why you spoke up for me in court. Sounds like you need a slave."

"Not exactly," he said with a chuckle. "Think of it as a character-building experience. Feeding and watering animals. Cleaning out their stalls. Fixing fences. Things like that."

"Well, I'm no slave. I ain't doing any of that."

"You don't work, you don't eat. It's that simple. Everyone has to do his own fair share on a farm. That's the way life is."

"Some life!"

"Hey, there's a gas station up ahead," he said, ignoring my remark. "Let's make a quick pit stop."

He stressed the word "pit" to tell me that he really meant, "piss."

He parked the pickup and retrieved the key from the ignition.

"Be honest. Aren't you just a wee bit curious to read what the judge wrote on her card?"

"Not really," I replied, fidgeting with it. "Words are cheap."

"I never got the impression that she spoke for the sake of speaking, did you? I think she genuinely cares about you and your future. I mean I'm sure she gave a lot of thought to that picture selection there. I think it's her way of encouraging you to fly in a better direction."

"So, she's a half above 13 and a half," I replied.

"Meaning?"

"Thirteen-and-a-half. That's gang-speak for when you're in court and you expect the worst. Twelve jurors. One judge. And a half-ass chance of getting off. No jail time is the extra half, if you're lucky."

He nodded understanding as he got out of the pickup.

"Let's eat. If you need it, the washroom's out back. I'll fill up the tank and see you inside."

I got out, too, and walked towards the diner. A middle-aged trucker was zipping up the fly of his dungarees as he exited the washroom and walked towards me. His enormous belly was flopping over what couldn't have been more than a 34-inch waist. He inhaled deeply and tightened his leather belt. He had a bushy white Santa Claus beard and a small wart on the tip of his nose, which twitched when he spoke to me.

"You dropped something, sonny," he said in a gruff smoker's voice. "Looks like a card. If it's your birt'day, happy birt'day."

As I picked up the card, I could hear him singing, "Happy birt'day to me. Happy birt'day to me. Happy birt'day dear whoever you are. Happy birt'day to silly me."

He was still singing his heart out as he climbed into the cab of his 18-wheeler and drove off with his arm resting on the open window.

I looked about me to make sure my grandfather wasn't looking and then opened the card slowly to read the judge's note. Her words sent a shiver up and down my spine and I shuddered when its journey ceased.

Dear Daniel,

Please accept this card, as an expression of the hope I have that you will make the right choices in your life from this day forward.

You have been given a precious gift, the gift of grandparents who care deeply about your wellbeing, as I do. I wish only for you to succeed in everything you do from this day forward.

I urge you to make wise choices with a clear head and good conscience, and to discover the true meaning of the word friendship on your journey through life.

I chose this card for you on purpose. It is my sincere wish that the image of the crow, one of the wisest of birds, will inspire you to think about making good changes in your life.

For your information, the artist is a renowned mouth painter who was paralyzed during a diving accident several years ago. She never gave up, despite the tragedy that befell her.

Hopefully yours,
(Judge) Arlene Fisher
August 25, 2007

• • •

We arrived at the farm in the evening.

"Welcome to the Mahoney Family Farm," the wood-burned headline on the sign at the gate said. The message below it read:

> FRESH FRUITS, VEGETABLES
> & DAIRY PRODUCTS
> YEAR-ROUND
> ALL ORGANICALLY GROWN
> FREE PARKING AHEAD 1,000 YARDS

"What's with the toy barn on the post?" I asked.

"That's our mailbox," Poppy answered. "It's a scale model of our real barn. Your mother made it."

"You're kidding!"

"No. She made it all right. It was her woodworking project in high school."

"Sounds like another one of her best kept secrets."

The laneway snaked its way cautiously around tall and proud stands of Scotch pine, cedar and maple on both sides, revealing no hint of the farm until it uncoiled in front of the house. To celebrate our arrival, the maples had rolled out a plush, fresh carpet of sweet, tobacco-scented red, yellow, and brown leaves, while white smoke puffed from the stone chimney. A border collie uncurled itself from sleep, wagged its tail, and ran towards us without barking.

"Sit, Milah," Poppy commanded as she jumped up at me. "Meet Danny."

I flashed a smile when she sat as ordered. I put it away when Poppy noticed it and flashed one of his own.

"You like dogs, I see. I think the feeling's mutual. She usually barks at people she doesn't know."

Milah seemed to have a smile on her face, too, and it made me think about how I was going to cope with all this unwanted attention. The Crows flew into my mind and I wondered what they were up to. "Stealing, selling or smashing heads probably," I whispered to myself. "They're having all the fun and I'm stuck all the way up here in Nofunburg or whatever you call this place."

Chapter 3

MY HEART FLUTTERED as we pulled up in front of a two-story log cabin that looked like it belonged on a wilderness holiday postcard.

As she walked from the front door towards us, Gran was wringing her hands on a long, flower-patterned apron that partially covered her white T-shirt and her blue jeans down to her knees. She smiled at me and primped her grey hair, which was tied back in a bun the size and shape of a calorie-rich Tim Horton's doughnut. I froze when she wrapped her arms around me and hugged me.

"Welcome home, Daniel. It's so good to see you. I never thought I'd see this day soon enough and here you are, in the flesh. You've grown into a handsome young lad. Did you find the journey long? You must be starving. Did you get Daniel something to eat, Tyler?"

"We stopped for gas and a quick bite after leaving the city, then drove straight through. By the way, he doesn't answer to Daniel anymore, Lee-Ann. Call him Danny. You fix him up and I'll get his bags."

She linked her arm in mine and half-pulled me towards the house. I took in a quick panoramic view of the farm before reaching the front door. Beyond the trees, there were plush, green fields surrounded by wooded mountains as far as I could see. Sheep, herds of cattle and horses grazed quietly in the distance beneath the setting sun.

I began to daydream of earlier times as a youngster. The sheer quiet of the images I saw seemed to be tempting me, like bait at the end of a fishing line, as I recalled bits and pieces of my childhood on the farm. Images of people, whose faces I could not make out, beckoned to me with outstretched arms and I wondered how many casts and strikes it would take to hook and reel me in. I took a deep breath and held the air in my lungs as long as I could, determined to resist being landed and becoming someone's trophy for as long as possible.

Gran looked up at the evening sky.

"It'll be one fine day tomorrow."

"How would you know that?"

"Red sky at night, a fisherman's delight. Red sky in mornin', fisherman take warnin'. It's an old saying, and a pretty accurate one, too."

The sky was red like she'd said. It blended in well behind the blood-red bricks of the chimney. Gran followed my gaze.

"Your mother helped me build that chimney from the foundation up. In fact, she took to setting and pointing those bricks like a Glaswegian brickie fresh off the boat, with the quick lip, but minus the accent."

I gave her a disbelieving look.

"It's true. That was 27 years ago. Your grandfather built the rest of the house himself using only hand tools and sweat."

I wondered what other surprises Mom had been keeping from me. Then I tried to imagine myself as an eight-year-old, building things. The trouble was that too many of my memories were destructive, not constructive.

"Come on in and make yourself at home, Danny," Gran said as she opened the door. "I hope that you will be very happy here."

• • •

They sure never had homes like this in the city, I thought. Everywhere I looked, I saw huge lacquered logs, all neatly butted together. A fieldstone fireplace was set in the far wall of the living room; floor-to-ceiling shelves of books on either side guarded it. Early American antiques and handcrafted reproductions graced the room. A long pine table surrounded by eight matching high-backed chairs occupied the center spot in the open living space. An oak staircase curved its way to the second floor. Family photos, oil-painted landscapes, an old musket, a weathered fly rod, and a dark-stained violin hung on the walls. The TV was conspicuously absent and I thought it must be in another room.

In one corner of the living room, a tiny light on top of a photo portrait caught my eye. There was Mom sitting on a horse. Her soft smile drew me towards her, like a moth to a candle flame.

"It was taken the day she turned 17," Gran sighed as she entered from the kitchen. "The chestnut was our birthday gift to her. She loved that filly so much. It's so hard to believe that she'd ever leave her behind."

"What was she like when she was my age?"

"Sweet, and sassy, but not in a disrespectful way. More high-spirited, I'd say, like her horse. Generous to a fault. Ever so gentle with people, especially youngsters and old folks. And, boy, did she ever love animals! Even insects! Once she spent a whole hour ungluing a fly from flypaper with a wooden matchstick to help it escape. She was a good girl, but no saint, mind you. She had her bumps, too, just like the rest of us."

"Bumps?"

"She could be moody and flare up like a firecracker if you pushed her too hard or told her to do something she didn't care to do. She wasn't the best of students at school either, but she could have been if she'd put half a mind to it. That was our Maire. God, I miss her so much, bumps and all."

"What about him, my old man I mean? Did you know him well? I have only faded memories of him. He was in and out of jail until he got himself killed dealing."

She looked up to collect her thoughts.

"Doug strayed into the farmyard like a lost puppy one day, hungry, thirsty and looking for a day's work in exchange for a place to stay. Your grandfather felt sorry for him and hired him on for the summer. He regretted that decision later when he heard Doug was selling drugs to local kids. By then, it was too late for Maire. He had her hooked on him first. Whatever he was selling followed. We helped her get dry for a spell before she got pregnant with you. I heard that he flew the coop after you turned seven and she slipped back into drugs shortly after that. They're such a curse. Drugs I mean."

"I hate him," I said. "He killed Mom as far as I am concerned."

"Hate only harvests more hate," she said. "Let it go before it eats you up."

"All I've got is hate and anger," I insisted. "It's what kept me going on the streets."

The kettle whistled, as if to scream, "Boy, that's a whopper!"

"Well you're not on the streets now, thank God. Why don't you freshen up?" she said. "Dinner's almost done. There's a bathroom over there," she added pointing. "And you'll find lots of towels in the linen closet right next to it. Help yourself."

My packsack was waiting for me outside the bathroom door. After I'd washed and slipped into a fresh pair of jeans and a T-shirt, I joined my grandparents at the table. A couple of logs crackled in the fireplace while soft country music came from the record turntable. My ears perked up when a violin soloist broke in with a slow air.

"You like music?" Gran asked as I sat down.

I nodded and she smiled. I picked up my spoon and began to slurp the hot vegetable soup. I stopped between mouthfuls when I noticed that Poppy and Gran had bowed their heads and clasped their hands in silent prayer. I put the spoon down and bowed my head, feeling self-conscious, I should add. A few moments later, as if on cue, they both blessed themselves with the sign of the cross and began to eat. Then Gran nodded to me.

"Dig in, Danny. Don't be shy."

I have to admit that her cooking was A-1, unlike the junk food that I was used to scoffing on the run back in the city. After I'd eaten a second mountain of mashed potatoes and gravy, Poppy spoke up.

"I noticed your ears perk up when you heard the fiddle playing, Danny."

"I thought it was a violin," I answered.

"A fiddle and a violin are one and the same. It's called fiddle when you play folk music and violin when you play classical. The fiddler is the great Tommy Peoples. He's probably one of the world's finest living Irish fiddlers, in my humble opinion."

"Do you play the fiddle?" I asked.

"Some. But, truthfully, I'm not a real musician, just a bit player. Tommy, on the other hand, he's the real McCoy. He seldom plays a tune the same way from one time to the next. I saw that for myself when I attended one of his fiddle workshops in Montreal a few years back. I was too intimidated to play a note for two weeks after seeing how good he was."

He sighed before sharing his afterthought.

"I have a spare fiddle collecting dust in the barn. I leave it there during summer and fall in case I want to bang out a few notes between chores. I'd be glad to teach you a tune or three, if you're interested."

"I'm tone deaf," I replied. "You'd be wasting your time on the likes of me."

"Now I don't believe that for one minute," said Gran. "If you appreciate good music when you hear it, there's no way under the sun that you're tone deaf. Now eat up young man. You'll need your strength when your grandfather gets you up early in the morning for chores."

"What time is that?" I asked.

"When the rooster crows," she laughed. "Except roosters crow any time they darn well feel like it. They sure know how to annoy us for stealing their lady friends' eggs."

"I'll wake you up at five," Poppy said. "We start milking at six sharp, then we feed and water the stock. Breakfast's at eight. You'll have worked up enough of an appetite by then."

"That early?" I protested. "I sometimes only crash at that time."

"You'll get used to it after a few weeks."

"A few weeks?" I muttered under my breath. "First chance I get, I'm out of here, big time!"

"Did you say something, Danny?" Gran asked.

"Er, not really. I'm just dead and I was wondering where my crib is."

Gran looked at Poppy for meaning.

"I think he means he's tired and wants to know where his room is," he said.

"My oh my, I didn't even show it to you. It's downstairs to give you some privacy. You have your own bathroom there, too. Would you like me to show you? Tyler, I mean your grandfather, already put your packsack there."

"Don't bother. I'll find it," I said as I was getting up from the table.

"Did you get your fill?"

"Yes," I replied. Then I added that it was "real good" when I remembered that Mom liked me to thank her whenever she cooked.

Gran smiled.

The grandfather clock chimed once as I reached the top of the stairs. By the time I reached the last step, it had chimed eight more.

• • •

The decor of my room matched the rest of the house with its log walls and handcrafted furniture. Antique farm implements decorated the walls. Books on all sorts of subjects filled two tall bookshelves: from agriculture and ecology to history and geography; from literature and history to music, child-care and wilderness living. Another collection of hardcover books was waiting for me on an old school desk near my bed. A note on the top one read: "Home Schooling Texts for Daniel."

"I guess my grandfather was serious about getting me home schooled," I said to myself.

I opened the doors of an imposing pine armoire across from my bed and discovered a hulk of a TV hiding inside. I used the converter to click through about a half-dozen channels tops and quickly realized that there was no cable or satellite hook-up on the farm. I switched off the set and allowed myself to fall backwards on top of the bedspread with my arms and legs outstretched. I woke up in a fetal position when Poppy rapped on my door the next morning.

He came back a few minutes later and shouted, "Last call, Daniel! We're running late."

I looked over at the door and saw the judge's greeting card sliding underneath it. Yawning, I stretched out and walked my hands towards it while my legs remained on the bed. I reeled in the card with my right hand and pushed myself back onto the bed with my left. I read the message again before flicking the card. It glided to the top of the dresser next to a wrapped gift box that I hadn't noticed before crashing last night.

Curious, I got up and reached for the gift box. It was addressed "To Daniel, from Gran and Poppy." I removed the gold wrapping carefully and found two gifts inside: a Swiss Army knife and a hard-cover Reader's Digest book, "North American Wildlife: An Illustrated Guide to 2,000 Plants and Animals."

After flipping through the pages of the book, I placed it back on the dresser, telling myself I'd read it later. I then pried open the Swiss Army knife to discover all sorts of miniature tools, including several different sizes of knife blades and screwdriver heads, a can opener, a combination corkscrew and a bottle cap remover, a file and a pair of scissors. The largest of the knife blades bore the engraved inscription, "To Danny, Grandparents Mahoney, 2007."

I collapsed all the blades, tools, and utilities, then slipped the knife into the side pocket of my jeans.

Chapter 4

"CAW...CAW...CAW," the crow beckoned as it kept vigil from its perch on the topmost branch of a giant cedar in the barnyard. "Caw...caw...caw," a second crow echoed as it landed to feast on grain that lay scattered on the ground. About 15 others soon positioned themselves on branches of surrounding trees close to the sentry who, like the prayerful mother superior of cloistered nuns, continued to keep careful watch over her charges from her lofty position.

For some reason, these feathered creatures had begun to fascinate me. This surprised me because I had never given real crows as much as a passing thought in the city. I considered them nuisances that could easily, and without warning, deposit their droppings on your head, or worse, your food.

"That's only a small murder of crows," Poppy said.

"Murder?" I replied.

"That's what you call a group of crows."

As soon as I got within 100 feet of them, the sentry cawed rapidly to its members and they all flew off in different directions, leaving the grain behind for dozens of hungry and braver sparrows that had been waiting their turn to feed.

Poppy chuckled when he saw me dragging my listless body towards him. He was holding two freshly saddled horses by their harnesses, one white, and the other jet black.

"Hop on," he said as he handed the white horse's reins to me. "Jessie's yours while you're here. Mine's called Lightning."

"I don't know how," I replied, now almost fully awake. "I can't remember being on a horse before."

"You'll learn easy enough. Jessie's as gentle as they come. Grab the reins in your left hand like this, stick your left foot in the stirrup, and pull yourself up with a swing of your right leg. Like this."

I copied him as best as I could. After two failed attempts, I found myself sitting in the saddle and, thankfully, facing the back of the horse's head instead of her rump.

"Good stuff!" he said. "You'll be rounding up strays in no time. Now watch everything I do like a crow with a small 'c' and try to do the same. I think there's no better way to learn than vicariously."

"Vicaria who?" I asked, ignoring his sneaky reference to my gang membership.

The horse answered Poppy's chuckle with a whinny and began to follow Lightning slowly with absolutely no help from me. She carried me to the barn, which was nestled next to the henhouse about 800 feet or so from the main house. All the surrounding buildings had matching log designs with freshly painted red tin roofs, including the two long-retired "His and Hers" outhouses, standing side by side, a woodcarving of an old man on one door and one of an old woman on the other.

"The locals call them crappers," he said.

We dismounted and wound our horses' reins around the barn's hitching post. At that moment, I heard cows mooing in the distance and I imagined myself as a cowboy in an Old West movie.

I followed Poppy into the barn and was immediately impressed by how high and massive it was, with its intricately laced wooden support beams and rafters. But the shape of the building itself struck me even more. Its three connecting sections formed the letter "Y."

"You built this barn, too?"

"With your grandma's help," he answered humbly. "And your mother pounded in more than her fair share of dowels, as I recall."

"What're they?"

He reached for one of the long, smoothly rounded wooden rods that were stored in a wooden barrel. It was about half of an inch thick and about three feet long.

"We used them instead of nails to bond wood wherever we could, even in the main house. I'll show you how to do it some time, if you like."

"A lot of good banging in dowels will do me when I'm back in the city."

He didn't react to my threat to leave.

"Well, we've got a lot of milking to do now. You can wash your hands over there in the sink."

He handed a towel to me.

"I'll show you how to clean the cows' udders and teats. We have 50 to do in all, cows that is. You can thank God for machinery. It would take forever for the two of us to milk them all by hand the way my grandparents did."

As I was washing up, he pulled an overhead lever to release cattle feed into stainless steel troughs that ran the full length of each intersecting trisection of the barn. Then, stick in hand, he left the barn and walked straight as a pin to a nearby paddock where his herd of hungry cows was waiting. And judging by their mooing, I concluded that they were waiting anxiously to be fed and milked.

Poppy whistled and Milah seemed to appear out of nowhere. She ducked under the fence, barking on the go. As if on cue, the cows crunched together beyond the stainless steel gate, which Poppy slid sideways on its rollers. He waved his stick in his left hand above his head while stretching out his right one to block any straying cow's path.

Milah barked and pretended to snap at the back of the cows' hind legs. Like a drill sergeant at assembly, she ordered her platoon to march obediently in single file towards the barn.

The cows stopped when they reached their feeding troughs. As soon as they started eating, Poppy pushed a button on an electronic control pad at the end of a cable that dangled from above, activating a steel bar that locked their bulbous necks securely in place while they fed.

"Watch what I do and repeat it," Poppy said. "It's not rocket science."

He used a soft cloth and warm water to wash the teats of a few cows.

"Here," he said, handing me the cloth and bucket. "You can clean the rest. Stay clear of their hind legs if you want to avoid any rogue kicks. These ladies don't know you yet and some of them may just feel a sudden urge to put a dowel-less city slicker like you in his place."

"Dowel-less," I thought. "So he hadn't ignored my remark about not needing dowels back in the city after all."

When I'd washed the last of the cows, Poppy began attaching what he called robotic milking machine units to each cow's teats. I watched him carefully as he almost absent-mindedly finished one and started another.

"Think you're up to the task?" he asked.

"I guess," I lied.

I felt relieved when I had actually attached my first one with almost no difficulty. The cow in question lifted its head from the trough and tilted it slightly as if to look back at my progress. She followed up with a moo of approval and a plop of smelly dung. Satisfied, she resumed feeding, paying no heed to my discomfort.

Poppy chuckled. He patted me on the shoulder and said, "Good job."

I flinched when he touched me because I was not used to compliments. Gang members are quick to shit all over you when you think you're on top of things. In fact, in my experience, they only praise you when you pull off a score that they can cash in on personally.

It took about an hour for all the cows to give up their milk without much objection, while devouring the reward in their troughs. The sucked milk traveled through transparent plastic tubes into a giant stainless-steel vat at the center of the barn and its scent blended with the odors of cows, hay and manure to form a surprisingly sweet odor.

"Eau de la ferme," I said to myself. "I should bottle it and send it to my high school French teacher."

The vacuum created by the robot made a dull, chug-a-chug sound to a distinctive dada-da-dah jig beat. I was soon rapping and tapping along with the tune and didn't realize I was doing so until I saw Poppy smiling his approval once again, which put a halt to my debut. He then began unhooking the robotic milking units and I did the same.

When we had freed the last of the cows from bondage, Poppy lifted the restraining gates and began herding the cows out to pasture with Milah's help. I couldn't help notice the coordinated teamwork and unspoken communication of master and dog. Poppy simply pointed his finger, nodded his head, or whistled in a certain way and Milah earned her keep by responding gladly and flawlessly every time.

"I'm hungry," I complained. "When do we eat?"

"As soon as we're done in the henhouse and we've checked on the bullocks in the top field."

It didn't take us long to harvest the eggs from the hens who squawked and flapped their wings to protest the intrusion. Following Poppy's lead, I nested a few dozen of the eggs carefully in one of the wicker baskets that had been waiting there for us to fill. They felt warm to the touch.

"They don't seem to like what we're doing," I said.

"That's understandable," he replied. "But they'll go on laying more tomorrow just the same. Kind of like people," he added. "We keep doing the same things day in, day out, not realizing that we are in the same old rut."

"Like me, you mean?"

"I mean us all, but if the shoe fits, as they say, wear it. And speaking of shoes, we'll have to see about getting you some good work boots with steel toes. You'll need them around here. Your footwear won't last a week with all the muck on the farm."

I looked down at my running shoes. I got them for almost a five-finger discount at a flea market before I got arrested. They were splattered with a curdled mixture of milk spots, mud and cow dung. The Crows wouldn't like that, I thought. Clean shoes and reverse-threaded laces, bowed at the bottom instead of at the top, were two favorite Crow rules. My laces were still reverse threaded.

"Last impressions are important when you're kicking someone's head in," Bongo Peters had told me the day I was initiated. "So make sure your shoes are clean and that they see the way your laces are tied before you kick them in the head. And your slingshot should always be sticking out your right ass pocket."

Crows always wore a slingshot's rubber band around their left wrists like a bracelet, and never on the slingshot handle itself. That way, the cops could hardly accuse us of carrying a concealed weapon. I never got mine back when I was released from juvie and I missed it.

• • •

Before heading back to the house, Poppy and I rode side-by-side to check on the beef cattle that were grazing peacefully in a meadow. They hardly moved from their chosen spots as we circled them. Poppy counted all of them and, when he was satisfied with their number, he pulled on his horse's reins to point her towards home. Mine followed without waiting for me to tug her reins.

Poppy and I stopped only once before reaching the gate to make sure that an old white enamel bathtub, which served as a cattle trough, was full of drinking water. Both horses were treading extra carefully and I wondered if they were trying to avoid breaking the precious cargo of eggs that their riders were carrying.

Hundreds of swallows, sparrows and crows, oblivious to the cares of the world around them, flitted, flapped and floated in the sky, expressing their delight for the gift of a new morning and the free bounty that had been provided for them. Only the crows appeared to be bothered by our presence and I began to have the feeling that they, like the rising sun, were making sure that I was not to be kept out of sight. It was a feeling that would continue to grow the more I had contact with them. In fact, whenever I worked around the farm or walked along a trail, I often had the eerie sense that crow sentries were monitoring my every move and reporting it to fellow members of their murder. I came to think of it as "The Caw Caw Report."

Later that morning, I thought of how the Crows, in the city, especially Bongo, behaved in a similar manner. Even when they weren't around, I had an uneasy feeling that they were always watching me, waiting for me to slip up.

Chapter 5

"CAW...CAW...CAW," Bongo mimicked as he delivered a hard kick to the side of the Blood's head. His prey lay screaming and squirming on the sidewalk, hands shielding his groin from a second kick.

"The next time you come on Crow turf, you won't get off so fucking easy."

Bongo nodded to Nipper, and Sammy, who grabbed the Blood and pulled him to his feet. He was bleeding from the side of his head. He was about a year or two younger than I was, and a lot skinnier. A fresh crop of pimples and blackheads sprouted on his face.

"Take him to the edge of our turf," Bongo commanded Nipper, "and give him a good hard kick in the ass goodbye."

"I'll take him," I said. "I gotta meet up with Melody anyhow and she lives around there."

"Okay, Karate," Bongo agreed. "But watch yourself. We'll meet you and Mel at MacPuke's for a burger in an hour. Be there!"

We formed talons with our fingers before shaping our hands into fists. We pressed our fists together, our signature greeting or adios to fellow Crows.

"Caw...caw...caw," Bongo squawked.

"Caw...caw...caw," the rest of us answered.

"Crows forever."

"Crows forever."

"All for one," they all shouted after me as I walked away with the Blood.

"One for all!" I replied, not looking back.

"Look. He pissed his pants," Nipper screamed with delight. "He pissed his pants. Caw, caw, caw, the Blood's pissed his pants and Karate has to take care of him."

Just like Nipper, I thought. She didn't like too many people and I was high on her list. One of the other girls told me that she found me too snobby because I didn't talk the same as all the other guys, which was true I guess. I was the only one still in school and, as far I knew, the only one who had ever read a book from cover to cover. Except for Playboy, Penthouse or Hustler. Even then, they never got much past the photo spreads -- not even the girls.

• • •

The Blood and I headed north to East 50th. I decided not to go past Bridlegate to avoid running into rival gang members. Several different gangs had cropped up in the area recently as the ethnicity of the 'hood changed. And members of the more traditional gangs were doing long stretches for everything from robbery to gunrunning, drug-dealing and even murder.

"What's your name?" I asked him.

"I'm a Blood. That's all you gotta know!"

"What's your fucking name?"

"Tiger," he replied in a more conciliatory tone.

"Well, you sure didn't act like one back there with my OG, did you?"

"What's an OG?"

"Man, how long have you been a Blood? Original gangster. Your gang leader."

"I'm not full patch. I joined a few weeks ago to avoid getting beat up again. They only use me to run errands and clean up the crib after they party.

"If you don't like being a bitch, don't act like one."

"They're all bigger'n and stronger than me."

"So?"

He shrugged his shoulders.

"I'm sorry," I said.

"For what?"

"I dunno. Because you got beat up some, I guess. Or, maybe you don't really want to be where you are, no more than I do."

"That's the way it's for you, too?" he asked with a puzzled look.

I shrugged.

"Don't come no further," he warned. "There's Bloods hangin'. You don't want to mess with 'em, 'specially when they see how banged up I am."

"Oh shit! I'm outa here!"

Two Bloods, squatting on the stoop of a nearby apartment building, scrambled to their feet and started running towards me. I ducked into an alleyway and ran as fast as I could, knowing that my life could very well depend on all the extra speed I could muster.

When I cleared the alley, I spotted a bus and made a mad dash for it. I managed to hop on just before the doors closed. As it pulled away from the curb, I looked back and spotted my two pursuers again. The bus was too fast for them and they stopped running. I smiled at their defeat and gave them the finger. One of them formed a gun with his right hand and his lips mimed, "Pow, pow!"

"Pay your fare and sit down before you fall down," the bus driver snapped. A big brute of a guy, he was wearing a ring with a U.S. Marine insignia and a "Death Before Dishonor" motto tattooed on his left forearm.

I did as I was told and half-sat down next to an obese black woman who occupied her window seat and a full half or more of my aisle seat. She wrapped her fat arms tightly around the shopping bag on her lap and dared me with her eyes to steal it, which right then was the furthest thing from my mind.

I looked away and spotted a funeral cortege approaching on the far side of the street. As the hearse crept by, I felt a twinge of sadness as I recalled how different Tiny Tommy "the Gun" Macleod's cheap purple coffin looked from the posh one in the passing hearse and how few mourners there were at his funeral a month earlier, compared to this one. Drive-by killers, out to make a name for themselves, had shot Tommy who had been a Crow for just six months. My gang coughed up the money for the burial after Aldo and Sammy had broken into the funeral home and stolen some of its embalming fluid, which they later sold to some Puerto-Ricans for big bucks. I knew one guy who liked to mix it with pot to get one hell of a high. At least that's what he told me anyway.

All the time Mom was doing drugs, she did her best to keep me from using them. Although I was tempted many times to do so -- I never did.

"Dope is for dopes," Mom preached constantly, often crying when she did. "And look at me. I'm the biggest dope of 'em all."

She tried to stop a few times, but they, the drugs, always won eventually. Each time she got clean, she'd always talked about going back home to the farm to see her folks and go riding. That would last a few weeks until the food stamps ran out and a new druggie boyfriend moved in to play hubby to her and daddy to me. I vowed to kill the last of them after he smacked her and me around when I told him he could fetch his own beer from the corner store. That was the day I became a Crow and the last I would ever see of him.

• • •

Three Crows stormed into the elevator that day before I could push the button for my floor. One of them, a junior boxing champ called Sammy "Wham Bang," shoved me hard into a corner and grabbed the two-by-four from my hand. "Caw… caw… caw," they all squawked as one.

Aldo, a.k.a. Aladdin "the Magician" Forlini, took a grease pen from his pocket and marked out Crow territory by writing tags all over the existing graffiti on the walls of the elevator. Like the other two Crows, he had a rubber-less slingshot brazenly staring out the right rear pocket of his baggy black jeans, which were worn in "plumber's bum" style.

"Who's head were you going to bash in with this toothpick?" the one called Bongo asked.

"None of your fucking business!" I shot back, trying to act tougher than I was.

He removed the rubber band from his wrist and stretched it across his slingshot. He placed a ball bearing in the patch and aimed it at me

"You were saying?"

"My mother's new boyfriend," I replied.

"That's better. "

"Time for the boyfriend later," he said, lowering his slingshot. "We been watching you cause we're looking for new Crows and we wants to see if you got enough piss 'n' vinegar to be one. Push the top one!" he ordered Aldo.

When the elevator reached the twelfth floor, Bongo gave me a nasty grin. Two gold-capped teeth sparkled in the center of his mouth, one on top, one on bottom, which only made his grin nastier.

"Now we're going to beat the shit out of you. If you're still alive when we reach the first floor, you're a Crow. If you refuse to join, then we beat the living shit out of you some more. Okay?"

Without waiting for an answer, Bongo pressed the first floor button and it answered with a buzz, the signal to start the match I didn't ask for. He clenched the huge fist at the end of his well-muscled right arm and took a wide swing at me. I ducked and immediately adopted a Kung Fu stance. In the thirty seconds or so it took to reach the first floor, I managed to block most of their punches and kicks with defensive maneuvers without having to resort to counterattacks. And I thanked my first martial arts teacher, my sifu, for teaching me how to defend myself, and Mom for insisting that I take lessons when I'd rather read books.

"Look at Karate Kid go," Bongo shouted.

The elevator doors opened when we reached the ground floor and the three Crows stopped fighting.

"You're in," Bongo beamed. "You're now in the Crow family. Accept or die."

I shrugged. "Accept, I guess."

They let out a loud cheer, followed by three stretched caws, and lifted me in the air in celebration. I had to duck to avoid hitting my head on the elevator's ceiling.

"Don't you be worrying no more about your old lady's boyfriend," Bongo said. "He don't live here after today. Aldo,

Tommy, you come back tonight and give whatshisfuckingname his 'viction notice."

"Deano," I said.

"Deano? He a wop or a spic or something?"

"I never asked him. I just want him gone."

"You hear that guys? Karate just wants the prick gone."

He picked up the two-by-four from the floor and handed it to Aldo.

"Here's his going away present."

"Caw...caw...caw," Aldo and Sammy said.

"Caw...caw...caw," I echoed and we all laughed.

"What's your 'partment number?" Bongo asked.

"Basement nine," I replied.

As we were leaving the building, I felt beads of sweat trickling down my forehead and I began to feel scared -- scared that Aldo and Sammy would kill the bastard. I realized that I didn't want them to go that far.

"Can't you just scare him into leaving?" I asked. "You don't need to beat him up."

"That depends on him," Aldo said.

Chapter 6

AFTER I'D DEVOURED A HUGE BREAKFAST of ham, eggs, and home fries, Poppy suggested that I go for a ride around the farm by myself "to get acquainted."

"Be good to Jessie," Gran said. "She's the daughter of your mother's favorite horse. You couldn't ask for better stock. Lightning's the father and Jessie's the last of his line."

She started cleaning off the breakfast table.

"Unfortunately, your Poppy had to have him gelded."

I looked sideways at Gran before responding.

"You mean you cut his balls off?"

"That's one way of describing the procedure," Poppy grinned. "A bit primitive, mind you, but it does the trick."

"What did Mom call her horse?" I asked to change the subject.

"Slán," he answered. "It's pronounced 'Slawn' and it means farewell in Irish."

"Slán," I said as I got up to leave. "I like the sound of it."

"Slán," I repeated as I opened the back door to leave.

"You say Slán leat," Poppy said. "That means farewell to someone who is actually staying."

"Oh." Said Gran, "I see you decided to bring your gift."

"Gift?" I asked with a grimace.

"The Swiss Army Knife. It's poking out of your back pocket."

"Oh," I said uncomfortably. "I should've said something about that. I found it and the book this morning."

"You always need a good knife around the farm," Poppy said. "It'll come in handy, you'll see. And the book will help you identify the flora and fauna around these parts."

"Flora and fauna?" I asked.

"They're fancy Latin terms for plants and wildlife."

"You speak Latin?"

"Used to speak a bit. When I was studying to be a…priest."

"A what?"

"Don't looked so shocked," Gran said with a smile. "It was before I de-collared him."

"Mom never told me that!"

"Maybe it was because we never made a fuss about it."

"That's the truth," Poppy added.

"I'll get going," I said and made for the door.

Gran called after me.

"Danny, I am going to put the final polish on a step-by-step lesson plan for your home schooling today. It's mostly self-directed and should only take you about three or four hours a day to get through. Of course, I'm always available if you run into difficulty or have a question."

"Okay," I said.

I let the door's closing have the final say.

• • •

Gran appeared on the porch while I was hitching the horse.

"When I get back from doing my mobile library rounds in a couple of hours, we'll take you into Noburg, Danny."

"I've got nothing better to do," I said, immediately regretting my tone.

She pretended not to notice.

"It's not much of a town in terms of size," she said. "But it's full of decent folk. We'll pick you up some things at the General Store. You'll need good gear around here. Just don't expect the latest fashion. For that, you'll have to head on down to Burlington or Plattsburgh, or better still, Montreal."

I walked the horse slowly down a long winding concrete path. It led to a meadow that stretched as far as I could see in all directions. After I had unlatched the gate and closed it behind us, Milah darted under the fence, her tail wagging, and her tongue lolling as she looked up at me. Except for the chirps of birds and crickets, the silence was a far cry from the incessant car honks, siren wails and people chatter of the city, a cacophony of sounds that I hardly ever noticed when I was there but found myself missing, just a bit, now.

Milah chased after some Canada geese. They flew away and landed on top of a far hill. I mounted the horse very carefully and we trotted slowly towards the big birds. When we arrived at the top of the hill, Milah was waiting for us while a hot sun climbed out from behind a dark cloud and shone down on us.

Milah barked at the geese. They honked back before flying away.

"Here, Milah! You'll never catch them now."

Milah stopped in her tracks and cocked her ears. She turned and scurried towards a young girl who was sitting reading a book under the shade of an enormous oak tree. The girl's horse, a gold palomino, with a white mane and tail, and white shins that looked like knee-high stockings, was tethered to a nearby bush, chomping on sun-dried grass.

The girl was beautiful. She had straight, shiny chestnut-brown hair that fell down to her shoulders. She wore a tight white T-shirt, black shorts, and a pair of blue and white Nike running shoes. She had red marks on her thighs, which, I would learn later, were hard-won saddle sores. She was deeply engrossed in her book and was about to take another bite from the sandwich that she was holding in her right hand. Milah had a different idea. She snuck up, snatched the sandwich between her teeth, and then ran off. The girl screamed at the four-legged culprit and then fixed her blue eyes on me.

"Don't you know how to control your dog?" she yelled as she stood up. "It scared the bloody hell out of me. It stole my lunch right out of my hand."

Milah was already devouring the sandwich.

"I'm sorry," I stammered. "She's not exactly my dog and I didn't know that she'd do something like that."

"Just what do you mean by not exactly?" she said sarcastically, her hands on her hips.

"It belongs to my grandparents. This is their land."

"The Mahoneys? You're their grandson? And that was their dog?"

"Yes, yes and yes," I answered with a half smile.

She laughed and extended her hand.

"I'm sorry. Sometimes I talk too fast and don't wait for answers when I'm upset. I'm Jane Calloway. I live at Cross Keys Farm, three farms over, just past the old Quaker church and graveyard."

"I'm Danny," I said, shaking her hand. "Danny Mahoney. I'm from New York. The Bronx."

She smiled and let go of my hand. She began to turn away, but then stopped herself.

"Big city boy, eh? Hey, would you like to ride a bit with me? My palomino hasn't had a good run today. I don't want him to get fat and lazy."

"I guess. But I'm not very good at it yet. I'm just learning. This is only my second time on a horse, and both times today."

"No sweat. I'll go easy on you. Well, maybe not too easy since you're half responsible for my lost lunch."

"I'm real sorry about that," I lied.

"Forget it," she replied. "I didn't like it anyway. Cucumber and cheese is one of my ma's *eat it, it's good for you* favorites – not mine."

She clutched her horse's reins and mane with her left hand, placed her right one on its rump, then pulled herself up and onto its bare back effortlessly.

"You don't use a saddle?"

"Only when I'm roping steers," she answered. "Most times I just like the freedom of riding without one. Especially on Goldie. Goldie's my horse's name."

"Hi Goldie," I said.

"I don't talk much," Jane said on Goldie's behalf in a high alto voice.

"She sounds just like you."

She laughed.

"What's the name of yours?"

"Jessie."

I realized then that that was the first time I had called Jessie by name myself.

"Well, how about you and Jessie head over to Paddington Pond with Goldie and me? It's lovely there. There's a waterfall and a heronry worth seeing."

"Heronry?"

"A colony of herons to city boys like you."

I smiled at her teasing.

"Sounds good to me, but I have to go into town with my grandparents in a couple of hours. Noburg I think it's called."

"We should be back well before then."

She pulled Goldie's reins gently to the right. The horse's head followed and she trotted off.

"Hey wait up," I shouted.

I chased after her, but not as fast as I would have liked. My behind bobbed high off Jessie's saddle and crashed down, again and again. Jane's butt seemed to absorb Goldie's trotting gently, stride for stride, without complaint.

We headed for a circular stand of sugar maple on the far north side of the farm. It was set below the face of a small mountain with fir trees growing out of its rock crevices.

"Hey, watch out for the chickens," I shouted to Jane.

"They're not chickens, city slicker. They're Northern Bobwhites," she added, laughing. "They belong to the quail family."

The two small birds made a distinctive whistling sound as they scooted away from us along the ground towards the pond, warning other kin that intruders were invading their turf. Milah snuck out from beneath some brush and chased after them, barking as she went. Each of the birds had a stripe that ran across the eye to the back of its head.

"I call them bird pirates," Jane said. "The one with the dark-striped eye patch is a male. The lighter-striped one is a female. Where she goes, he follows. People around here love to hunt them in the fall. They make good eating, but they keep their wild taste if you don't cook them right."

We both dismounted and tied our horses' reins around saplings. As we did so, our two bodies touched slightly and a shiver of excitement shot up and down my spine.

"You okay?" she asked.

"Sure," I lied. "Why?"

"I dunno. Like, you know, you look kind of surprised all of a sudden."

"What's that big bird doing standing still in the water?" I asked, to change the subject. "At first I thought it wasn't real. It looks like it's standing on a stick."

"That's a blue heron," she said. "It's waiting for a fish to swim by. Wait until you see how graceful it looks when it spreads its wings and flies off."

Jane lowered her voice. It had a teasing tone to it.

"Feel like joining it for a swim?"

"I, er, didn't bring a suit," I stammered.

"Who's going to see us here?" she laughed. She crossed her arms in front of her and pulled her T-shirt over her head, exposing a green bra that only partially covered her breasts. She hung the T-shirt on a bush and ran down to the water shouting, "Last one in's a rotten egg."

The heron extended its large wings and flew off as gracefully as Jane had said it would.

"Wow, look at it go!" I exclaimed, undressing as quickly as I could.

I ran down to the pond in my boxer shorts, leaving my clothes and shoes in a heap on a springy carpet of green moss. I jumped in and swam towards Jane as she treaded water. The pond was crystal-clear and felt colder in some spots than in others.

"Do I make you feel uncomfortable?" she asked.

"No," I lied. "Well, maybe just a little," I added, showing her the tiny space between my thumb and index finger to express how much. "I'm not used to girls being, like, as free-spirited as you."

She pushed her body up slightly and floated on her back, her lovely breasts making eye contact with the lucky sky.

"I thought girls in the city were all so daring, doing anything they want, when they want."

"Some are. Some aren't. It's just, like, in the gang I run around with, girls all pretty much act the same. They dress and talk the same. It doesn't pay to be too different."

"Gang? You mean a real gang or guys you just hang around with?"

"A real one."

She yawned and raised her arms and let them fall sideways into the water with a splash, suggesting to me that she really didn't care what type of gang I belonged to. Then she caught me completely off guard.

"Why are you staring at my boobs?"

"I wasn't. Was I?" I stammered. "I didn't know I was. I mean."

"I don't mind. I'm just razzing you. I mean: if God didn't want guys like you to stare at them, I figure he wouldn't have made them."

She stopped floating on her back and treaded water again.

"I bet I know your gang's name," she said, pointing at my tattoo. "Either the Birds or the Ravens. And judging from your all-black clothes and shoes, I'd say…Ravens."

I fidgeted with the black rubber band on my wrist. "Clever and close. Crows, not Ravens."

We were both smiling when, suddenly, she threw her arms around me and kissed me hard on the mouth. Just as quickly, she pulled away with a shocked look on her face and covered her mouth with the palm of her hand.

"Oh, my God, I can't believe I just did that! I don't even know you. I've never done anything like that before, I swear to God. I don't know what came over me!"

She lowered her eyes and slowly raised them again before turning and beginning a fast swim crawl to shore.

"Wait up!" I pleaded. "Please don't go!"

She picked up her T-shirt from the bush and made a dash for Goldie. She jumped onto her back from behind with the practiced finesse of a rodeo rider. Then, she leaned down and untied the reins.

"I'd really like to see you again," I shouted after her when I reached the edge of the pond.

She looked back when I stood up on the pond's pebbled shore.

"I don't know if that's such a good idea."

She tugged Goldie's bridle and dug her heels into her ribs. She headed south towards Cross Keys farm. I kicked a rock in frustration only to hurt my big toe.

"Why do girls always think like girls, Jessie?" I said. "I just can't ever figure them out."

Then I imagined dozens of identical Janes flitting, unpredictably, like birds, from one perch to another.

As if to reinforce my point, a murder of a dozen or so crows cawed repeatedly in response to my outcry and flew up and away in the same direction as Jane.

I watched the departing images of horse, rider and crows fade to pixels in the distance. It was a mournful scene, witnessed by a legion of couldn't-care-less cliff swallows, darting to and from their lofty nests, their distinctive faces glistening in the sun.

Jessie and Milah were waiting for me patiently in the clearing and I sat down on a rock next to them to dry off when a forked branch of a maple tree lying on the ground caught my eye. I picked it up. I then took my Swiss Army knife out of my back pocket and, as automatically as Poppy had prepared his cows for milking, I began sawing and carving it into a slingshot handle. I used the knife's file to smooth away any rough spots. I then removed the rubber band from my wrist and stretched it across the slingshot's arms.

The weapon felt good in my right hand, like the reassuring grip of an old friend. I picked up a round pebble from the ground and inserted it into the center of the band, which I then cocked, pulling it back slowly with my left hand as far as my nose. I aimed and fired at a solitary black spot in a willow thicket 100 yards or so away and about 15 feet off the ground, not thinking for a moment that I would actually hit it. To my surprise, the spot flapped its wings and flew directly into the path of my airborne missile before falling like a lump of spent coal to the earth. I ran towards it and saw that it was a rather smallish black crow with traces of white feathers on its wings. It made a weak gargling sound as it lay on its right side, its right eye completely closed, while its wide-open left eye, finding no one else to blame for its misfortune, stared at me and only me. When I saw the bone of its left leg piercing its skin, I dropped the slingshot.

The thought flashed into my mind that, except for the odd cockroach, fly or mosquito, I had never killed anything in my life before. I picked up the bird and stroked its warm belly, hoping to revive it somehow. A tear rolled down my cheek as I realized that this beautiful creature would never fly again, thanks to my stupidity. This rather surprised me because, back in the city, the sight of a dead crow on the street was just that, well, another dead crow.

I set the still bird down gently on a boulder and used my knife to dig a small grave. I picked up my slingshot and removed its rubber band, which I tossed into the brush. I then stuck the slingshot's handle in the ground at the head of the hole and, lowering my head, managed to say, "I'm sorry."

I lifted the bird with as much reverence as I could under the circumstance. I was about to lower it into the grave when it stirred and made a cry that was a cross between a gargle and a feeble caw. It was a joyful sound because it meant that it was still alive. Then and there, I swore to do all that I could to help this wounded creature stay that way – alive I mean.

I removed my shirt and wrapped it snugly around the body of the bird, taking special care to avoid any sudden stabs of its beak. I needn't have worried. It didn't stir even when I trekked back to Jessie with it. Somehow, I can't remember exactly, I managed to hold it securely in the cradle of one arm as I mounted.

When I arrived back at the farm, Poppy and Gran were ready to head into town. I am sure that, as I approached in the distance, they must have wondered why Jessie was carrying me towards them so slowly, especially when Milah had probably arrived a good 15 minutes ahead of us. And they must have wondered why I was shirtless, and what I was holding in the crook of my arm.

Chapter 7

I PLACED THE CROW ON THE WORKBENCH beside Poppy's MacBook in the tool shed, which was about 50 feet from the house. I covered it with an old piece of terrycloth Poppy had found inside a wooden trunk that he said he had made using only hand tools.

"Its real name is tack box," he said. "We used to keep all the horse bridles, reins and grooming accessories in it."

It looked to me like it belonged more in an art gallery than in a shed or a barn. About three feet long and two feet high, its wood-grained finish on all visible sides was an artist's palette of stains and dabs of old paint that had been splashed on and scraped off over many years. It had two black wrought-iron hinges and matching lock and key. A gold-painted anchor emblem accentuated each of its two polished-brass handles.

"I made it when I was a medic in the navy," Poppy said matter-of-factly. "I can teach you how to make one some day, if you show an interest."

I couldn't bring myself to show him any at the time, even though, deep down, I think I was interested.

He reached into the tack box again and removed what looked like a wooden Popsicle stick.

"This tongue depressor ought to do the trick once I split it," he said.

He set himself to making a splint for the bird's limp leg.

"I'll rub some analgesic cream over it before setting it."

49

We heard a rattling sound outside the tool shed and Poppy shouted, "Is that you, Lee-Ann? Did you fetch the surgical tape?"

"Yes to both questions," she replied. "And Chuckie's old cage, too. I rescued it from its hiding place in the attic. I just don't know where all that stuff up there came from."

"Who's Chuckie?" I asked Poppy.

"Our long departed pet parakeet. Requiescat in pace."

Gran's timing with the cage was perfect, I thought, as the young crow was beginning to show more signs of life. After flapping its wings weakly, and blinking its good eye a few times, it opened its beak and uttered a faint caw from deep in its throat. In the meantime, Poppy connected his MacBook to his cell phone. He then clicked his way to a website dedicated to the well-being of crows and ravens, including injured ones raised, reluctantly, in captivity by their care-givers.

"There's lots of useful info here," Poppy observed

Gran entered the shed. She set the cage and tape on the bench in front of us.

"There," she said with a sigh of exhaustion. "I've got to run. Things to do in the house."

As the door closed behind Gran, Poppy shouted after her, not forcefully, but loud enough for her to hear.

"Lee-Ann, any chance you could scrounge up a pair of good-sized tweezers to use as a feeding tool? No sense in getting our fingers pricked for being good 'crowmaritans'."

"Would you like me to bake a nice apple pie while I'm at it?" Gran quipped. "All this fuss over a bird that will eat our crops down the road!"

Poppy opened the door and looked out at Gran.

"The pie would be a bonus. Oh, for its food, we'll need some oatmeal, nuts and beef heart. I'm sure worms will do, if we don't have hearts. I'll get Danny to pick through the cow manure for some," he added with a bit of a chuckle.

"Thanks a lot. I've always wanted to be a shit-kicker."

"Did you know that crows belong to the corvid family?" he asked.

"So my gang buddies back in the Bronx are corvids? Wonder what they'd think of calling themselves that. Too snotty I bet."

He scribbled a few notes down on the back of a brown paper bag. I found it a bit difficult to read his scrawl at first and had to eyeball it two or three times to make out the words, "Estimated age."

"You really think he's about ten months old?" I asked. "Assuming it's a he," I added.

"Well, I'm no expert, but the site says, if the tail feathers are four inches or more, the crow's full-grown. That'd make him a teenager -- like you. I'll get a tape measure from my tool section in a minute to make sure, but for now I'd say, they're almost three inches, no more. You?"

"I guess," I said, holding up my right thumb and forefinger and examining the gap I'd opened up between them to make sure.

The bird's eyelids trembled. He opened them slightly and stared at us through tiny slits.

"We could weigh him," I suggested. "The site also says a full-grown one is between 14 and 16 ounces and that an adult's eyes are brown. His eyes are more bluish-grey. Oh yeah, if the mouth is pinkish, he's not a year yet. His mouth is sort of rusty. I think it's getting ready to turn brown. You?"

"Right on the mark there on all counts, Danny. There's an electronic scale over there behind those upright milk cans, if you want to weigh him to be sure," he said pointing. "It's pretty precise. I use it to weigh medication for sick animals."

He was shaving a block of cedar with a hand plane when I brought him the scale.

"That should be enough to make our young friend comfortable," he said as he sprinkled shavings on the floor of the cage.

I lifted the crow and placed him gently on the scale.

"Thirteen ounces on the nose," Poppy observed. "I'd say that does put him just shy of a year."

Gran arrived with the tweezers and a small plastic bag filled with food.

"I mashed up some chicken liver and left-over porridge. I don't have any fresh ground beef. Here, Danny, it's time to feed your baby."

"I've never done this before!"

"Neither've we," she said. "There's a first time for everything. Besides, you're the only Crow here."

They laughed. I didn't.

I pried open the tweezers' jaws and grabbed some of the mashed-up food with it. I then touched the tip of the tweezers to the crow's beak, which was now opened wide, and I released the food. He continued to snap up food, while keeping his good, but ever-wary eye focused on me. Occasionally, he stopped eating for a beat or two and pecked instead at the foreign object that was holding his broken leg in place.

Poppy surfed the web again while Gran and I looked on.

"It says here that stroking its throat will help the swallowing process."

I tried doing that and it seemed to do the trick.

"Don't be too kind," Poppy warned. "The last thing we want to do is overfeed him."

"Do you think we should do anything special to keep him warm since there's no heat in the shed and we don't have a bird's nest for him?"

"We're in luck there," Poppy said as he reached under the workbench and retrieved a fish tank that had seen better days. "I used this as an incubator a couple of years ago to keep a baby rabbit warm after its mother was killed by a fox. It uses a small 7-watt light bulb. It'll give off just enough heat without burning him."

He unclipped the light fixture from the fish tank and handed it to me.

"Do you want to clip it to the bars of the cage before putting him inside? Oh, and you'll find an old bird bottle feeder in one of those drawers over there. It'll let him drink any time he feels like it."

I kind of liked the way he asked me to do things. It was as if he were offering me a choice to do it or not. In gang territory, no one asked you. There, it was always a case of "Do it my way -- or else!"

"Have you given any thought to naming your crow?" Gran asked.

I hesitated for a moment before placing him in the cage, and then said, "Paddy. Because, well, I near killed him at Paddington Pond."

"That's a real nice name," Gran said. "But, hey, don't be too hard on yourself. What's done is done."

"I'll second that," Poppy agreed.

"I hope Paddy does, too," I said. I stroked his stomach and broken leg with an index finger, and then switched on the

53

light bulb, which barely lit one corner of the cage while projecting shadows across the rest of it.

"I'll check in on him in a couple of hours," I added, closing the cage door.

"Good idea," Poppy replied. Gran nodded.

"Under the circumstances, we can put off going into town until tomorrow, if you like."

"Sounds like a plan," I said.

I looked back at Paddy in the cage. He was looking out the cracked windowpane and I smiled at the thought that he had a bird's eye view of the farmyard.

I followed Gran and Poppy out of the shed. As I closed the door behind me, I could hear the hum of an approaching engine while images of the day flashed through my mind. Most were of Jane before, during, and after our swim. I realized that I was beginning to have strong feelings for her. I had never felt quite that way about any girl before. I wondered how long it would be before I would see her again, and would she talk to me when I did.

I didn't have to wait long to find out, as it turned out. A beat-up Ford pickup truck pulled up outside the tool shed. Jane was sitting slumped in the passenger seat with her eyes barely peeking over the dashboard. The driver, a portly man in his fifties, was hiding much of his face behind a bushy white Santa Claus beard and handlebar moustache. He was chewing tobacco on one side of his mouth. His long and stringy white hair almost touched his hunched shoulders. The look on his face when he glared my way through the opened driver's side window told me that he was not here to drop off early Christmas gifts, especially to a "less than" like me.

The man didn't bother to kill the poorly-timed engine when he got down from his cab, but he looked like he could kill me. His eyes continued to bore holes in me through his smudged, wire-framed spectacles that sat somewhat lopsided on his sunburned nose under the peak of his Ames Feedstore baseball cap. I avoided his stare by focusing on the "Jesus Saves" and "The wages of sin is death" stickers on the rear bumper of his pickup.

I wondered if Jesus would save me from whatever this man was all riled up about.

Chapter 8

HE ROLLED HIS EYES, showing their whites, and then he removed his baseball cap and threw it on the ground. It landed between Gran and Poppy.

"You keeps that stud of a grandson away from my Jane, then," he shouted, spitting yellow tobacco juice at the ground; some of it landed on his cap. I found his voice high-pitched for a man of his build. "She's not yet 17 for crying out loud."

"Danny's just shy of that, too, Abe," Poppy replied calmly. "Now what seems to be the problem *today*?"

"One of my Mex summer hands spotted the two of 'em swimming in Paddington Pond a couple of hours ago. And they weren't exactly decent then, if you knows what I mean."

"Decent?" Poppy asked with a shrug.

"Let me finish my piece and I'll tell you. Me and the missus are God-fearing folk as you well knows, Tyler, and we brung all of our eight kids up to be just as righteous, too. Jane's our youngest and the only one that's not married off. We means to do good by her on her Christian walk then and I don't want whatever-his-name-is defiling her."

Poppy looked my way.

"We didn't do anything wrong," I protested. "We met, went for a ride and a swim. The only bad thing is in his imagination."

"That's good enough for me."

"What does Jane have to say about all this?" Gran asked.

"Never mind her, Lee-Ann" Abe said. "I'll do her talking for her."

"Well then, there's nothing else to say, is there Abe? We'll just have to take Danny at his word and leave it at that."

Abe picked up his cap. Holding its back with his left and the peak with his right, he pulled it down hard on his head, almost completely covering his glasses.

"Just you keeps him the heck away from her then, hear? The next time I won't be dropping by with my lip. I'll be sporting my over-and-under 12-gauge for some serious hunting, if you knows what I mean."

He wagged his finger at me. Then, with his head half turned towards us, he walked back to his pickup.

"Stay you the heck away from her then, or by the good Jee-sus in me, you little whippersnapper, or whatever the heck your name is then."

"It's Danny and I'm no whippersnapper, mister." I said with my right fist clenched and ready to strike. I took a big step towards him. Poppy grabbed my shoulder to restrain me.

"And you can watch your smart mouth while you're about it, then" he answered as he climbed into his truck.

As he drove off, the hand that had held mine at Paddington Pond dropped a scrap of paper out of the passenger window before reaching into the air and giving a quick, backward wave. When the truck had disappeared around the bend in the laneway, Poppy picked up the note and handed it to me. I unfolded it slowly and read it:

"*Dear Danny,*

Meet me tomorrow at nine at my reading tree.

Jane.

P.S. My dad will be at the cattle market."

Gran slipped her arm gently around my shoulders and said, "I don't know what's in that note, Danny, and it's none of my business. But you won't want to be having any more run-ins with Jane's father. He's always been a slice or two short of a full loaf when he gets all riled up. And it's usually over little, or too much."

"I'll second that," Poppy agreed. "I sometimes think he would have been better off living in the Dark Ages. Apart from a phone and a radio, you won't find much modern in his home. No TV that's for sure. And Internet? Forget it. He thinks they're all the work of the beast."

"You mean that fucking control freak doesn't even let Jane watch TV?"

Once again, his eyes reacted to my foul mouth, but Gran didn't say anything.

"Sure she does," Gran said. "Every time she visits a friend's house, I hear. The rest of the family, too -- including her mother. Some say they're starved for it. Of course, I'm quite sure Abe doesn't know."

I shook my head.

Poppy gave me a gentle punch on the shoulder.

"Hey, why don't we go check out that old fiddle in the barn?"

"Do you mind if we do it some other time?" I replied. "I'd like to hang out in my room for a bit."

Poppy's quick smile told me that he didn't mind.

• • •

I lay on my bed staring at the ceiling. I began recalling the many detours my life had been taking for some time: from coping with Mom's drug habit to her latest stint in jail; joining the Crows to being arrested and sent to my grandparents' farm; meeting Jane to striking Paddy; then being told to back off and take another road or else by Jane's old man.

As if to agree those roadblocks were indeed a big part of my life, the pre-programmed clock radio on the nightstand beside my bed clicked on and another Crow, Sheryl, was singing a verse from her hit song, *Every Day is a Winding Road*. Even after I had switched the radio off, two of the lines kept on playing in my head:
Everyday is a winding road
Everyday is a faded sign

I thought of how much I had wanted Mom to hold us together as a family; how wound up I had felt before, during and after her brushes with the law; how many winding roads I had traveled to fit in and feel loved; how often I had got close to thinking everything would turn out all right and it didn't; how many opportunities I had chased only to see them fade as easily as gold dust slipping through a prospector's worn fingers to become lost in a beach of worthless sand.

I looked around the room for something to distract me. *Book of North American Birds* was lying open on my dresser. I reached for it and discovered that it was opened to a section on crows. I knew that I had not left the book open myself and concluded that Gran might have done so on purpose when she was vacuuming the room.

After I'd read the last entry on the America crow, I realized that, since joining the gang a year earlier, I had not read one book or written a single word in my journal. Before my initiation, words and writing had been a passion of mine -- a welcome escape from the pain around me. As long as I could remember, I liked making up stories about all sorts of make-believe characters and reciting them to anyone who'd listen. Melody, my first girl, was my best encourager until she moved to Canada with her mother when her father, an air force test pilot, was killed during a training flight.

I made several trips to the tool shed that day and evening between chores to check on Paddy and play *Poppa Crow*. I used the tweezers to feed him tiny morsels of food. I got a kick out of the way his beak opened and closed like a pair of agitated barber's scissors.

As I was giving Paddy one last morsel of food, my mind drifted back to one bitterly cold winter day when I was nine. I had arrived home from school with sore, frost-nipped hands and fingers after forgetting my gloves in my locker. Mom had been drug-free for about six weeks, I think. She was trying very hard to make up for her poor child-rearing efforts. It had been a good time and a frustrating time. On the one hand, I delighted in the newfound attention. On the other, her efforts to compensate did seem to be a bit overdone.

This particular day was different. She grasped my bare hands and massaged them vigorously between hers, bringing them back to life. Then she made me a hot mug of delicious hot chocolate, encouraging me to hold the mug between my palms to warm my fingers. Soon the numbness gave way to stinging pain and tingling, and then welcome normalcy, hugs, laughter and talk of a better future for both of us. I wished and wished that feeling would last forever. Of course, life's twists and turns had other ideas; they had a habit of getting in the way of the best-sown hopes and dreams of mother and child.

I draped a cloth over Paddy's cage, said goodnight, and switched off the shed's light. I latched the door behind me and looked up at the night sky. Venus was staring down at me through a peephole in the dark clouds that completely covered the rest of the sky. A northeast wind began to blow and, as its power increased, it pelted hard drops of rain against my face. I scrunched my shoulders and ran as fast as I could towards the house. I was anxious to shed the loneliness I was feeling all of a sudden.

In the near total darkness, only shadows of memory danced in the night and I could not wait to reach the sanctuary of my grandparent's porch. I thought of Milah and longed for her company, but immediately realized that, like one of those good or bad memories, she, too, had a habit of disappearing and reappearing whenever she darn well felt like it.

• • •

The constant patter of rain pelting the tin roof of the house and the occasional claps of thunder kept me awake most of the night. It seemed like I had only slept a few minutes when Poppy rapped my door to wake me for chores before dawn. I decided to drag myself on foot through the rain to the barn rather than saddle up Jessie because my rear end and inner thighs were still sore from all the riding yesterday.

Poppy did his best to ease me into casual conversation during milking, but I only answered with yeses or noes between flashes of lightning that made the lights flicker. He soon realized my mind was elsewhere and let me be. When we had finished gathering eggs from the henhouse, he asked me what plans I had for my free time. I had a feeling that he knew what my answer would be before I had framed it.

"Jane Calloway wants me to meet her."

"Think that's a good idea under the circumstances?"

"Her old man will be at the cattle market."

"I see," he said softly, nodding his head. "Just remember what Gran told you about Abe. He can fly into a rage for the least little thing. With him, everything is black or white, good or evil, with no allowances for in-betweens. And he can hold grudges until hell freezes over with his "eye-for-an eye, tooth-for-a-tooth" views. That's the Abe Calloway I've known much of my life. Be careful is all, for the sake of everyone involved."

"I can't explain why. I just have to see her again."

"I understand. Let's wash up and have breakfast. You can head out right after."

"Thanks, Poppy."

"For what?"

"For not being pushy, I guess -- and for not expecting me to behave, well, you know, your way. Oh yeah, and for standing up for me when that lunatic accused me of stuff I didn't do yet."

His eyes and his smile told me that he appreciated the sentiment and I was struck by his softness of heart. My stomach was churning and I felt like a wuss -- like some pussy who was planning to settle down here. That had to remain the furthest thought from my mind, because I was still determined to get back to the city as soon as possible. Wasn't I?

Poppy and I returned to the house gripping baskets of warm eggs in our hands and a case of silence in our hearts. He, too, had decided not to take his horse that morning; I found out a few days later that it was, ironically, because the slightest rumble of thunder easily spooked Lightning.

"By the way," he said. "Thanks, too."

"For what?"

"For calling me Poppy before. That's the first time you called me that and it felt kind of good to hear it."

I straightened my shoulders and walked faster towards the house ahead of him. I felt like I was carrying his gaze on my back and I didn't like that feeling one bit.

"Caw...caw...caw," the warning call in my head crowed. "Caw...caw...caw."

Chapter 9

I FED PADDY and cleaned his cage before setting out. I was glad to see that he seemed just as hungry as he had the previous evening. I took that as a good sign.

Jessie and I arrived at the reading tree around nine, but Jane was nowhere in sight. I looked for any telltale signs of hoof prints in the surrounding fresh mud, but found none, only human footprints leading from the trail directly to the tree. Puzzled, I pulled Jessie's reins gently to the right and circled the tree until a quick burst of tittering from above caught my attention. I looked up, but could not spy the titterer. As Jessie and I circled the tree again, I heard Jane yell, "Here I come, ready or not!"

I caught sight of her out of the corner of my left eye as she jumped down onto Jessie's rump and wrapped her arms tightly around me. She grabbed the reins from my hands and dug her heels into Jessie's sides, sending her into a fast gallop away from Paddington Pond to the seclusion of the wooded mountainside to the west.

"Are you crazy?" I asked her. "You scared me shitless. Dropping out of nowhere like that!"

She laughed and dismounted. She had a small packsack on her back.

"I didn't exactly drop out of nowhere, silly. I dropped out of the tree."

"How did you get here? Where's Goldie?"

"I hiked. I told my folks I was going to a friend's house. I figured if I didn't ride, my dad would be less suspicious. It's a good three-mile trek cross-country, you know, and my feet are sore. So, be kind to me."

"All that way on sore feet just to see me? I'm flattered."

"Where's Milah?" she asked, pretending not to hear my remark. "I don't want her stealing my lunch again."

"She started to follow me, but then chased off after a squirrel. She'll show up soon enough when she remembers she can't climb trees."

Jane hopped onto Jessie's back again and wrapped her arms around me. We followed a narrow trail for a few minutes, from the foot of the mountain to an abandoned A-frame log cabin in a wood clearing. Scotch pines towered above us on all sides. The metal chimney on the cedar-shingled cabin roof leaned to one side and was rusting. Most of the glass in the windows was broken or missing. A circular piece of wood, the size of a dinner plate, had been nailed to the front door long ago, judging from the rusty nail that pinned it there; an enormous rainbow-colored spider was busy spinning its web over the name "Tom Mullins" that had been wood-burned onto it.

We dismounted and I tied Jessie's reins to a post on the nearby well. I noticed a bucket lying on the ground. It was splattered with tiny holes.

"Haven't you ever seen bullet holes before?" Jane quipped as she watched me staring at the bucket. "Some of the locals use this place for target practice since appendicitis did Trapper Tom in a good five winters ago. The same Tom whose name is on the cabin."

"I didn't think people died of appendicitis anymore."

"You do, if you don't get help right away. Old Tom didn't have a phone or electricity up here. Cops figured he actually died from the cold because he was too ill to keep the wood stove fed. Some snowshoers found him frozen solid weeks after he died. Apparently, both his hands were stuck to his sides and he had a look of terror on his face. Molly Tomkins told me it took nearly a week to thaw him out before her mother, the medical examiner, could do the autopsy."

"Sounds creepy."

"Nothing to be afraid of. Old Tom was a gentle old cuss. So, if his spirit is still about, it'll be a good one. That's what my Gran says anyways and she's an expert on all that stuff. You know tea leaves and Ouija boards and horoscope charts."

"What does your old man say about that, him being a born-againer and all?"

"He thinks Satan is waiting for her in hell, but that's okay, because she's my mom's mom, not his. She just lives with us. It makes for some pretty good theatre sometimes, with dad and Gran playing opposite one another -- like Archie Bunker and Meathead reruns."

"Your dad seems to have just about everything figured out, doesn't he?"

"You can say that again. He has his good points, but sometimes. Well, you know what dads can be like."

"You're wrong about that."

"How come?"

"Do you mind if we change the subject? I don't want to talk about him right now."

"I don't mind." She clasped my hand in hers, gave it a reassuring squeeze, and then looked up at the sky.

"Those clouds look like they're going to pee their pants any second. Let's go inside before we get soaked. I packed us some cold drinks and snacks, and we can hang out some."

An old Vermont Castings soapstone stove stood at attention inside the cabin's single room, which was sparsely furnished with an unpainted knotted-pine drop-leaf table and two wood-stained chairs with weak legs and shredded wicker backs. A hutch on the wall near the stove showed off a battered coffee tin, two rusted metal mugs, a trap with a mouse skeleton pinned to it, and a beer bottle with a one-inch red candle stub stuck in its throat, with overlapping layers of different colored wax streaming like lava down its neck.

"Be it ever so humble, there's no place like home," I said, blowing dust off the table.

"It may look humble, but Old Tom Mullins sure didn't die broke."

"What do you mean?"

"He used to be a big city something or other. About 30 years back, his family was killed in a fire while he was on a business trip. They say his hair went pure white from shock overnight. He came to Vermont to heal and never looked back. He never did heal though. He became a bit of a hermit and, except for the odd skier or backpacker who passed by, he hardly ever spoke to anyone. He just 'yepped' and 'noed' and nodded. Your grandfather composed a fiddle tune in his honor after he died. He plays it at the country fair every year. It's called *Ole Tom Mullins Jig*. Hey, you want to go?"

"Where?"

"To the fair. It starts in two weeks. It'll be a lot of fun."

"Sure, if you're going, I'll go. But what about your dad?"

"Chances are he won't spot us in the crowd," she said as she removed her backpack. "Want a drink?"

I grabbed her gently by her shoulders and kissed her gently on the mouth.

"What was that for?" she asked, feigning surprise.

"Payback for yesterday," I replied, and kissed her again.

She kissed me back and then pulled just as quickly away.

"Don't be getting any big ideas just because we're alone here," she warned. "Let's take things slow. Like turtles, okay?"

"Okay...if that's what you want."

She uncapped two cans of spruce beer and smiled impishly. "This'll help you cool down."

"Don't count on it."

She clinked her can against mine and winked.

For the next two hours, we sat across the wobbly table on equally wobbly chairs, sharing bits and pieces of our wobbly lives growing up in two totally different worlds. I was as fascinated about her upbringing in the country as she was about mine in the big city. I told her that the characters of her life story, for the most part, seemed to be more grounded than the stressed-out characters of mine.

"I'm not so sure about that," she said. We have our share of takers and crazies around here and you don't have to look too far to find them. You just haven't been here long enough to notice."

"At least you don't have to worry about gangs and turf wars around here."

"Are you kidding? Have you ever seen farmers fighting over an inch of land? Believe me, it can turn just as ugly and the feud can be passed on to future generations who only have a fuzzy idea of what the original fuss was all about."

The hands on Jane's wristwatch signaled to me that I had to get going.

"I've got to drive into town with my grandparents," I said. "We didn't make it yesterday and they want to pick up some work clothes for me."

She pressed her lips together and sighed.

"Do you really have to?"

"Yes. I promised I'd be back by one and I have to take you home. Well, at least almost all the way home in case your dad shows up."

I took her hands in mine across the table. Our eyes met.

"Jane, I really like you and I want to see you again soon."

"Me, too," she said. "I feel like I've known you all my life and we've only just met."

"Me, too."

She squeezed my hands and my arms stiffened.

"What's wrong?" she asked.

"I want this feeling to last, I guess. I'm, well, scared that something will happen to take it away — like it always does."

"If you mean my dad, he'll grow on you, if you give him half a chance."

"You think?" I answered, releasing my grip on her hand. "He sure has one funny way of showing it."

We stood up and walked towards the door. I held it open for her and she kissed me on the cheek as I closed it behind us. It was a kiss of reassurance, I think -- her way of telling me that she was there for me, no matter what.

Jessie whinnied and raised her head, which was already pointing towards home. I clasped Jane's hand and walked slowly towards Jessie, wishing to prolong, just a little, the momentary feeling of belonging. It was replaced by a feeling that someone was recording my every move in this new place. I looked up and there, on the tallest branch of the tallest tree, a lone sentry, black as coal, was fixing watchful eyes on us, but especially me. Moments later, he cawed rapidly and birds of his feather flocked by the dozens and landed on the branches of surrounding trees to watch, too.

An image of the tool shed sprang to mind and I imagined Paddy cawing back boldly, as if to say to his friends, "He once was lost, but now he's found."

"I can't believe it," I said under my breath. "I need help. I'm hearing voices."

Chapter 10

THE FRONT DOOR of our apartment was ajar and I could hear Mom sobbing in the kitchen. I pushed it open wider and saw that the place was a mess. A chair and a coffee table had been upturned. Broken dishes and glasses, as well as some of my favorite books and torn pages of my writing journal were scattered across the floor.

"What the hell happened?"

"Deano left me."

"After he ransacked the bloody place! All I can say is good riddance!"

"He was all bloody when he came in and he just went crazy. He started breaking and throwing anything he could lay his hands on. He said two punks beat him up in the elevator and he blamed you."

"Me?"

"He said they dropped your name when they were hitting him. Did you have anything to do with it?"

There was no anger in her voice, just defeat.

"I just got here. I didn't see a thing. Anyway, I'm glad he's gone. We don't need a prick like him in our lives."

"Please don't swear, Danny. At least he had a job. How're we going to survive now?"

"You mean how're we going to support your drug habit *from now on*."

She lifted her hand to slap me across the face, which would have been a first for her. She stopped herself in midair.

"You've got to get clean, Mom. This is no life for you or us. Look at this place and you."

"I've tried. I've tried. God knows how I've tried."

"That's because you always think you can do it cold turkey on your own. The family therapist at Nar-Anon said that you need a support group."

"They don't know what it's like."

"The lady I spoke to said that five years ago she was in exactly the same space you are now -- except much worse. She sold her body on the street to pay for her drugs. Is that your next step?"

"How dare you talk to me that way! I'd never do anything like that. "

"You wouldn't, but your addiction would. Get help damn it! I can't take this life anymore, if you can call it a life."

She sobbed harder.

"I'll give them up next week. I promise."

I felt a knot in my stomach as I studied her contorted face. At that moment, she looked a lot older than 35. Her face was pale and drawn, and she was so skinny. Her dyed blond hair with its dark streaks gave her a tired and rough edge. Hesitating at first, I reached out and gently touched her shoulder. She looked up at me, trying hard to make her quivering lip smile.

"We'll get through it somehow," I said. "I'll clean up and then I'll go and get a take-out for supper."

"You always take good care of me. I don't deserve you."

I was about to tell her that the Nar-Anon therapist had told me that I was part of her problem. An "enabler" she called me, because I was always picking Mom up and trying to fix her. She told me I needed to find the courage to let go.

I cleaned up the place as well as I could and scraped up our last 15 dollars for the take-out. She was sleeping when I left. When I returned about 30 minutes later with a large all-dressed pizza, she was gone.

I looked for Mom the rest of the evening and night. I went to all her old haunts: O'Reilley's Pub where her dealer conducted business; Darlene's Diner where she often spent the night with sister and brother druggies; Old Mill Mission where she sometimes begged a free meal; and even the always dangerous back alleys where pimps, prostitutes, heroin addicts, winos, and aspiring-to-be-no-place-else also-rans hung out. I tried the hospital and neighborhood clinic, but no one recalled seeing her. As a last resort, I dropped by the local cop shop the next morning and spoke to a duty sergeant. He had a robotic, monotone voice and a Bronx accent.

"Oh yeah, I remembers her. The skinny dyed blond with the long legs and a peddle-ass skirt creeping up well past her belly button."

His tone didn't change when I reminded him that he was talking about *my mother*.

"We brought her in for assaulting a police officer and dealing drugs. She's looking at some hard time. You better get her a good lawyer, kid. She's gonna need one."

"We don't have money for a lawyer," I protested.

"Then, if I was you, I'd tell her to cop a plea and throw herself on the mercy of the court. Unless you wants to take your chances with legal aid. Good luck with those piss-ups!"

He said that I couldn't see Mom until after her arraignment the next day. The phone rang and he picked up the receiver.

"Hi Honey," I heard him say. "Yeah, it's been a busy night. The usual crap, you know. Nothing special."

"Nothing special," I grumbled to myself. "We're nobody in your eyes, that's for sure."

We were merely another case. An entry in the asshole's fat log that would be crossed off as a win for the cops as soon as Mom was found guilty and shipped off to prison. And the prick didn't care whether she got five years or life. It was all the same to him. Another tick-mark of success in a conviction ledger, another erasure of the chalkboard. He would go home to his family and never again give Mom even a passing thought, except for her short skirt, of course. That would be one to tell the boys at the local cops' watering hole.

• • •

Mom's case was one of the first on the docket the next morning. She was shaking so badly from withdrawal that her legal aid lawyer had to help her remain standing. When the judge asked her how she wished to plead to the two charges against her, the prosecutor jumped to her feet.

"If it pleases the court, we have a plea agreement with the defendant. The state has reduced the dealing charge to possession of a controlled substance and the criminal assault with intent to harm charge to simple assault in exchange for her guilty plea."

"Is that so, Counselor?"

"Yes, Your Honor," the legal aid lawyer replied.

"Sentence recommendations? You first, Miss Tubbs."

Miss Tubbs's name belied her physical appearance. An attractive black woman in her early thirties, she weighed no more than 100 pounds soaking wet.

"Three years and, hopefully, somewhere the defendant can come to terms with her drug habit, Your Honor. She's been in and out of jail during the past 15 years, and always for drug-related offences. Any lesser sentence I'm afraid would send the wrong message to society."

"Mr. Humphreys?"

The defense attorney buttoned his checkered sports coat and approached the bench. I wondered why they always did that -- button their jackets before speaking, I mean."

"Stay back, Counselor. I can hear you from over there."

He walked backwards to the defense table.

"Time served would be nice, Your Honor."

"One night in jail? Dream on."

"Can I say something, Miss? I mean Your Honor?"

The judge's eyes bored into me. So did those of the prosecutor and her legal aid lawyer. Mom's just opened wide in surprise.

"And you are?"

"Danny Cagney. Mrs. Cagney is my mother."

"Speak and be quick!" the judge ordered.

"I just want to say that Mom isn't a bad person, Your Honor. If it weren't for her drug habit, she wouldn't be here. She needs help, not prison. Please do what's right and help her get clean."

"Thank you, young man," she said, managing an unofficial smile. Then she turned to face Mom.

"You should be very proud of your son, Mrs. Cagney. It took a lot of courage for him to speak up in court on your behalf. Unfortunately, I have to respect sentencing guidelines. However, I will take the prosecutor's advice and see if we can arrange to send you to a minimum security facility where you can get the help you need."

She paused for a moment to think and then consulted her notebook.

"Do you like cats, Maire?"

Mom nodded her head to say that she did. I was happy that the judge had called her by her first name.

"Good, because I may have just the place for you to spend the next 18 to 24-four months. This court is adjourned until 10:00 a.m. tomorrow morning. I need to confirm whether or not the detention center has a place for you in its rehab program, and if the Bureau of Prisons will accept my recommendation to serve your sentence out of state."

When the bailiff escorted her away, Mom gave me a fleeting smile.

"Young man," the judge said to me. "Can you meet me in my chambers at 9:45 tomorrow morning please? I would like to talk to you one-on-one."

"Yes, Your Honor. I'll be there."

"Good. Just don't be late. I want to confirm a few points with you."

I knew I wouldn't be late, even if it meant having to camp outside the judge's door all night. After all, as the Nar-Anon guy said, I was an enabler and hard-won habits are hard to break.

Chapter 11

"DON'T BLINK," Gran said with a chuckle as we drove along Main Street. Poppy, who was doing the driving, just smiled in agreement.

"Huh?" I replied.

"Because, if you do, you'll see no Noburg."

"Hasn't grown much since its founding," Poppy shared. "It's over two centuries old. Your home state of New York is just down this road a piece to the left at the fork in the road, after you cross the bridge over Lake Champlain. If you take the road to the right, you'll be almost spitting distance to Canada. Actually, it's only a five-minute drive or less to the border and less than hour to Montreal."

"We're that close? They speak French there, don't they?"

"That they do," Gran agreed. "And about 70 or 80 other languages I'm told. It's a very cosmopolitan city. We'll take you there soon, won't we, Tyler?"

"Sure thing. Here we are!" he added as we pulled up in front of Noburg General Store. "I'll leave you in Gran's capable hands. I have to get a new water pump in Champlain and I might nip into the Legion for a quick pint with the guys. What say I meet you back here in about an hour-and-a half?"

He counted out $200 in twenties and handed them to me. "Here, this is an advance on your pay."

"I'm getting paid?"

"Slavery ended a long time ago," Gran said. "Now let's see if we can find some goodies for you to spend it on. See you, Tyler."

Gran and I disembarked and waved at Poppy. He gave the pickup's horn two quick honks and made a U-turn before driving slowly north on Main Street. One of the daylight running lights was flickering and Gran sighed.

"I've been after your grandfather for weeks to fix that darn headlight."

The store had a homey, country feel. It was stocked with floor-to-ceiling shelves of merchandise: from groceries to fishing and hunting gear; from all-weather clothing and footwear to home and garden accessories; from tools and mousetraps to souvenirs and medicines. There was also the friendly chat of sales clerks. For the less talkative and calorie-conscious customers, it even boasted a delicatessen counter and an ice cream bar, offering nutritious and not so nutritious snacks. A lot of stuff stood out on barn-wood hutches and on top of an old wood stove that looked like it had not been fed or stoked in years.

"Good morning, Mrs. Mahoney. How are you?" the smiling girl behind the counter said. She couldn't have been more than 15 or 16, I thought. She wore her long black hair in a braided ponytail.

"Good morning to you and fine, thank you, Tessa. And how about you and the folks?"

"No complaints, thanks. Everyone's doing just fine."

"This is my grandson, Danny," Gran said rather proudly. "He'll be staying with us for the next while or so. Longer, if he wants to."

"Hi Danny."

She tried unsuccessfully to hide a full set of braces by moving her lips as little as possible when she spoke, like a ventriloquist.

"Hi," I said.

"What can I get you?"

"He needs some good work boots, a warm jacket with a removable liner, a cap, lined and unlined work gloves, a couple of warm shirts and sweaters. Oh, yes, and a poncho."

"You're in luck," Tessa said. "We're having a back-to-school sale. Everything is 20 to 40 per cent off."

"Well you can point the way then. Oh, and put everything on our tab please."

"But Poppy gave me 200 bucks," I protested.

"That's your pay. This is our welcome home gift to you."

"But..."

"No buts now. And Tessa, if you think he needs anything else, you tell him and stick it on the tab, too. He won't be attending regular school this fall, but he'll need school supplies all the same."

"You home schooling him then?"

Gran nodded.

"I wish you could home school me, Mrs. Mahoney. My mother said that you were her best teacher ever."

"That's sweet of you to say, dear, but I know there were lots of good teachers in that school."

Tessa responded with a gentle smile, and then nodded for me to follow while Gran turned her attention to a dress that had caught her eye.

"Don't tell my boss," Tessa whispered as we walked to the men's section. "But the best deals are, like, always in the back. We keep the more expensive gear up front for tourists who always seem to be in a big hurry. Impulse buyers my boss calls them. Hey, I hear you've been seeing Jane Calloway."

"Boy, news travels fast around here. Who told you that?"

"I dunno. It just came up in customer chat I guess. So, you seeing her?"

I pretended not to hear her question.

"I like that jacket there. Do you have it in a medium-tall, with long sleeves?"

She removed a black one off the rack and handed it to me. I tried it on and it fitted me like a glove.

Within the next 15 minutes, I had everything that Gran had suggested and more. She said that she couldn't believe I'd finished shopping already, even though my arms were packed high with bags and boxes.

"You're obviously a buyer rather than a shopper to outfit yourself so quickly," she said. "We'll have to kill some time before Tyler comes for us. Why don't you leave all that with Tessa and I'll show you around town on foot. Hmmm, come to think of it, that'll only kill 15 minutes or so, if that, but I'll think of something else. Hungry?"

"I'm hungry most of the time."

"Spoken like a true teenager." She chuckled. "Those hormones of yours are sure to be in constant need of fueling. Let's pick us up a hearty sandwich at the deli counter. We can order one for your grandfather, too."

"Okay, but only if it's on me."

"A deal. You lead the way."

Afterwards, we sat together on the front porch and enjoyed our sandwiches, exchanging nods and quick hellos with passers-by and shoppers entering and leaving the store, and observing an occasional local going in or coming out of the red-bricked courthouse across the street. Gran caught me looking at the sky above the World War II memorial monument in front of the courthouse steps.

"A penny for your thoughts, young man."

"I was thinking about Paddy," I said. "I'd like to buy some wild bird seed and nuts for him before we head back."

"My, my, there's true thoughtfulness in you, Daniel Cagney, and I wonder if you realize it just yet. The seeds are a good idea."

"I'll be back in a minute," I replied as I stood up, "I'd like to get a little something for Jane Calloway, too."

Gran just smiled. I didn't tell her that the thought of buying something for Jane was merely an excuse. I really wanted to buy a long-distance calling card in case I felt like calling Bongo. I didn't want her to know that I was going against the judge's order not to contact gang members during probation. I purchased a saddle-tooled brown-leather belt for Jane and a five-dollar phone card.

"Oh, she's going to love that," Gran said when she saw the belt. "Look at the images of galloping horses all around it. It looks like a roundup. Whoever crafted it didn't have a train to catch."

The familiar putter and whistling of Poppy's Chevy pickup caught our attention as it made its way down Main Street towards us. Its brakes screeched as he pulled up behind an old black Toyota pickup.

Gran greeted him as she always did, like he was the most important person in her life. Then again, come to think of it, she always did her best to make me feel that way, too.

"I guess I'll have to replace the front brakes *and* the water pump," Poppy said through the open truck window. They sound like they're on their last legs."

A sign on the back of the Toyota announced that it was a 1995, four-wheel-drive manual, and that it was for sale for $1,250 or best offer. That made it 12 years old. It had some rust on it, but it purred like a kitten when its owner, a muscular-looking black man in his late thirties, started it up. A magnificent cedar canoe sat on the roof rack and extended a good six inches beyond the vehicle at both ends.

Poppy and Gran exchanged hellos with the man; he had the broadest of smiles and a full set of brilliant white teeth.

I half-listened to their conversation as I made a tour of the vehicle, stooping down occasionally to inspect the underneath.

"Hey Tyler and Lee-Ann. How's it going? I've been traveling a fair bit and I never got a chance to thank you yet for all the fine tutoring you gave to my Emma last spring. She did so well that she earned herself a full scholarship to Vermont State."

He turned off the engine.

"It includes a living allowance. It's good news for the family all 'round because Judy and I could never have afforded to send her there on our tight budget. Emma will be the first of our family to attend college. We're mighty proud, thanks to you."

"I'm delighted to hear your good news, Jake. All I did was point the way, remember. Emma did all the hard work. She's the one who deserves the praise."

"Well, you both had a hand in it then."

He paused for a moment. Then he looked up to catch a happy thought.

"Hey, Judy and I are planning a barbecue send-off for her Friday night. I'd like you and Tyler to come. Tyler can bring his fiddle and play in the jam session. It'll be a fun time. Blue grass. Celtic and, if they let Yves Lafortune across the border, Québécois, too. Oh, yeah, Banjo Bob Cussen from up Montreal way volunteered to drop in for an hour or two before he heads down to Burlington for a gig with his group, Swift Years."

"Okay by me, Jake. And once Tyler hears Yves and Banjo Bob will be there, he'll be warming up all those favorite old tunes they play before you can say 'rosin the bow.' I'll call Judy and see what she'd like me to bring."

"No need to bring a blessed thing," Jake replied, "only yourselves."

"Now, now, Jake, you know I don't believe in going to a get-together with both arms the same length. I'll be calling Judy, if it's all the same. And I'll bring my drum, if that's okay with you."

"Whatever you say, Lee-Ann. Hey young fella," he shouted as I was kicking a tire. "You interested in buying my beautiful Toyota?"

"Maybe," I replied cagily while Poppy and Gran studied me curiously. "Is it in good shape?"

"The best for its age," Jake said confidently. "There's just a squeak or two over 200,000 miles on her, but I reckon she's good for that again. He work for you, Tyler?"

"In a manner of speaking. He's our grandson. Danny. Maire's boy."

"Sweet name of Jesus, you don't say. Maire. My, my, my! Come to think of it, I do see her in him. Tell you what, Danny. Maire was a good friend of mine growing up. I'm asking anyone else twelve-fifty and I think that she's worth every penny of it. But, if you're interested, I'll let it go for a thou'. I'm buying a new second-hand one next month and I'll need the cash for the down payment."

"I have six hundred saved in the city and I can spare a hundred from the money I have on me," I said. "If I can get the money in time, can I give you seven hundred down and a hundred a month for the next three months?"

Without hesitation, he held out his hand to mine and squeezed it firmly. "Done, if you and Lee-Ann don't have no objection, Tyler."

Poppy shrugged and Gran raised her arms in surrender.

"Well," Jake said, "I'll get it all spruced up for you and wait for your call. He paused for a second or two and laughed. "The price includes driving lessons, if you want. She's a standard shift, you know."

"Thanks, but I already have my license," I said. "I got it after I turned 16. And I learned on standard."

"It looks like you've got all your bases covered then. Call me when you're ready to make the transfer. Your grandparents have my number. Hey, maybe you'd like to come to Emma's going-away, too. We can square things up there and then, if you're ready."

"Okay by me."

"Looks like you and Jake Saulter have both made yourselves a good deal, Danny," Poppy said.

"Hope so."

As soon as I said that, I began to worry about how I was going to convince Bongo to send me the six hundred I had coming before getting myself arrested.

• • •

I waited a good hour or so after Gran and Poppy had gone to bed before calling Bongo. I tiptoed to the front porch with the portable phone in hand, but let go of the screen door too quickly and it banged hard behind me. I took a deep breath and listened for a good minute or two to see if Gran or Poppy had heard the noise, too. When I was sure that they hadn't, I punched in the calling card number and its PIN, then dialed Bongo's cell phone.

Hey, Karate!" Bongo exclaimed. "What's been happening, my man? Where the fuck is you anyway? No one's heard shit from you. You know I get pissed when guys don't check in."

"I'm in upstate Vermont, a place called Noburg. The judge sentenced me to probation on my grandparents' farm for a year."

"Hey, guys, can you believe?" he shouted. "Karate's a fucking farmer in Vermont!"

Whoops and catcalls in the background answered him.

"Everyone's got to keep quiet about where I am, Bongo. If the judge finds out I'm talking to any of you, it's off to juvie for nine months I go. My record gets wiped, if I stay clean."

"No sweat, Karate. Who's gonna find out? You need anything to get you through? Some uppers maybe."

"No thanks. You know I don't do uppers. But, I do need some cash. I need the six C-notes you owe me in a hurry."

"No fucking way, man. We're all short. The cops are all over us every chance they get since you got busted. I can let you have maybe three tops."

"I'll take the three," I replied, not bothering to mask my disappointment. "How do you want to send it?"

"The only way I ever do. Give Nipper your address and I'll slap her fat ass over to Western Union right away. You can thank me later for my generosity. Hey Nipper, get your boobs out of my chink food and take down Karate's address!"

The phone went silent. I could hear paper shuffling and music in the background. I smiled as I imagined the cleavage that Nipper always seemed to get a kick out of showing off. I think I was the only gangbanger who hadn't been with her, even though she had a rep for being "free and easy."

Nipper didn't offer me as much as a "how're ya doing?" or a hint that she was otherwise pleased to hear from me. She kicked right in with "Okay, like, what do I have to scribble?"

When I told her my full name and address, she asked me if "Daniel was spelled with two "As" and two "Ls." When I told her the correct way, she wanted to know if "Noburger was, "like, one word or two" and, in a failed attempt to be funny, asked "did I want fries with that?" She had better luck spelling Vermont, but I had to repeat the zip code three times before she got it right. Then I heard Bongo's voice screaming, "Get his fucking number. I'll call him back with the details when it's done!"

"I can't give you the number," I said quickly. "No one can call me here." I'll call Bongo later."

"He said he can't, like, give you his fucking number 'cause no one's allowed to..." Her voice trailed off and the phone went dead.

Without thinking, I set the receiver down on a small table made from white birch branches and crept back to my bedroom as quietly as I could. I woke up next morning to the sound of the screen door opening and closing, and Gran's concerned voice.

"Hey Tyler, you left the phone on the front porch again and the battery's dead."

"Couldn't have been me," he protested. "I didn't call a soul yesterday. Must have been you."

"Maybe I did. I know I called Judy about Emma's party. And Sadie called to tell me that my Sears catalogue order had arrived, and we caught up on family stuff. That's it. Oh well, my mind must be slipping."

I pulled the covers over my head for a guilt-filled minute; this brief vanishing act was interrupted by a gentle knock on the door and Poppy's voice.

"Time to get up, Daniel. Cows are *a-mooing* and hens are *a-cluckin.*"

• • •

After lunch, when Gran and Poppy were taking a nap, I made another quick call on the sly to Bongo to get the wire transfer details, including the transaction number. I made sure to set the phone back in its cradle this time before nipping out to the shed to feed Paddy.

Paddy screeched so much when I entered that I thought he would wake up Poppy and Gran way back in the house. "Caw…caw…caw…caw," I mimicked.

"Ah, that's why you're excited. Looks like Poppy bought you an automatic seed-feeder. Now you can feed yourself when I'm not here."

I made a mental note to thank Poppy for the feeder, and the nuts and raisins he'd stored in it.

As Paddy pecked away at the seeds, he continued to make that weird throaty cry of his, even after I left him there. It sounded like wailing and I wondered if he was doing that to be set free from his cage. Then it struck me that the two of us had a lot in common, because I was a captive on the same farm, too. The difference was I could fly away any time I felt the urge. All I had to do was walk past the front gate. I wondered why I didn't, and that thought bothered me long after I had left Paddy behind in the tool shed.

Jessie was all saddled up and waiting for me outside for the ride to town. I rode her along a quiet back road that Jane had told me about the last time we'd met.

"It'll take you longer to get there," she had said, "but you won't have to worry about traffic jams. It used to be a wagon road and the only way into town before Noburg went modern when my folks were kids -- if you can call the olden days modern."

The road was everything that Jane had said it was and I could swear that Jessie knew every plod of it. I loosened Jessie's reins and let her take me all the way at a slow pace. We were in no hurry because we had hours to kill before supper, and it gave me time to study my new surroundings.

After we left the farm, we began to climb a long, steep hill. The sound of Jessie's hooves changed pitch as they clip-clopped against the stones packed into the sandy path. An old weathered signpost at the foot of the climb said that the road was called *Big Hill*.

When we reached the summit, Jessie jerked her head abruptly to the left and sneaked a look back over her shoulder as if to make sure that I was still there. Then, just as quickly, she jerked her head forward and whinnied as we passed the ruins of the "O'Neil Mansion."

I patted Jessie's mane and said, "It looks like you want to make sure I don't miss seeing that big old house, Jessie. Is that what you're all fussed up about?"

Much of the mansion's roof was long gone and what remained was now covered in green moss with tree branches sprouting out of some sections. Intricately-woven Scotch stone walls, some two-feet thick were still standing their ground, surrounded by five outbuildings that were still in a state of fairly good repair. I began to get a sense of how majestic and full of life this building must have been once, and I imagined different generations of owners and servants moving about the huge estate.

I thought about dismounting, but Jessie had other ideas. She picked up her pace, trotted over to a stream that was bubbling down the side of the hill and lowered her head. While she drank her fill, I began to rob a prickly bush of its juicy blackberries. As I reached for a second handful, the rustling of leaves startled Jessie and me. I could not see the source at first until it jumped up and barked. Jessie reared her front legs slightly and I found myself almost sliding backwards off the saddle; she settled down when she saw that the culprit was her friend, Milah.

"What the hell, Milah, you silly mutt! You could've killed me."

Milah barked again and chased off after a rabbit until it disappeared down a burrow in the short grass as suddenly as it had first appeared. Not one to give up easily, she tried to widen the hole with her front paws, but the hard-packed soil refused to surrender more than a few sprays of dry clay.

Milah soon became bored and decided to join us on the rest of the trek to town. En route, farmers on tractors and in pickup trucks, along with their hired hands looked up from their work in the fields. Some of them smiled and waved at me; others simply nodded their heads or, more accurately, moved their chins to the left in one quick abrupt movement, causing the tops of their heads to move just as quickly in the opposite direction. I tried to imitate this chin-head-chin greeting but found it too awkward.

"I guess head hellos take years of practice, Jessie."

On the outskirts of town, we approached a long covered bridge with a red tin roof. A chorus line of warbling pigeons on its rafters and bubbling water in a hurry to negotiate the rapids below greeted us. The blue type on the metal signpost at the bridge's mouth announced that its name was "The Doon Covered Bridge," and that Thomas Doon had built it himself in just eight weeks during the hot, dry summer of 1888.

Milah was the first to enter the bridge, scaring away dozens of pigeons. I looked up as bits of fluffy white feathers floated down like soft snow upon Jessie and me, but she didn't seem to care about them one bit. Like Poppy's barn, the beams and rafters were all neatly butted, jointed and doweled together with not one single nail in sight. The craftsmanship was impressive and I felt like I was in the sanctuary of a church, rather than the inside of a covered bridge.

The road beyond the bridge wound its way slowly towards Noburg, hugging several shale rock formations during its steep descent, before unwinding itself in the final stretch. A sign pointed the way to Saint Dominic's Episcopalian Church, the tallest structure to catch my eye. The bells of the church's whitewashed tower chimed our arrival at two exactly.

As Jessie and I made our way along Main Street, it was empty of people and felt even hotter than the weather reporter on the morning radio had said it would be. I hitched Jessie to a post outside Western Union and went in to fetch my cash.

The old man behind the counter wasn't in any mood for arguments when I protested that I was supposed to receive three hundred.

"That's all it says on the paper, sonny. Two hundred. Not a penny more."

"Fucking Bongo," I said under my breath.

"What?" the old man replied.

"Nothing."

I took the money, thinking of two scenarios. Either Bongo had decided to short-change me or Nipper had pocketed the difference. I settled on the second, which gave me a problem. If I told Bongo, he'd beat the crap out of her and the rest of the gang would come down on me hard later for squealing. And there was no sense confronting her directly. She would just deny it and tell me to go fuck myself. I stuffed the money in my pocket, swallowed my anger and my loss. I then left to find water for Jessie, Milah, and myself.

I noticed a hose on a sidewall of the Western Union office and used it to spray off the thick lather of sweat that had stuck to Jessie's body like white carpenter's glue. I then curled my left hand into a scoop and filled it several times for her to drink, which she seemed pleased to do. When Milah slinked towards us begging for her fair share, I got down on my knees and gave her a few scoops, too. I only stopped when her eager slurps transformed into a growl, then barks. I looked up to see a tall and broad teenage boy with shoulder-length black hair standing over me. A smaller guy about the same age stood beside him; he had carrot-red hair and a pointed chin.

"Your name Cagney?" he snarled from one corner of his mouth, ignoring Milah's barking.

"What if it is?" I asked as I began to stand up.

He answered me with the toe of one of his work boots, digging it into my shoulder and sending me sprawling onto my back, cutting one of my elbows and a cheek on the hard ground in the process. He then placed the same boot on my chest and pressed down hard. Milah barked louder.

"Stay away from Jane Calloway. She's my girl and I don't want some city slicker coming between us, understand?"

"That's for her to decide, scumbag. Not you."

"He didn't hear me, Billy. What do you think I should do to improve his hearing?"

"Make him understand, I guess, Wade," Billy shrugged.

"Good idea. A good kick in the side of his head should help him do just that."

Wade lifted his foot off my chest and cocked his leg. Milah barked even more at him. I waited until the moment he was ready to release his kick and rolled sideways out of the way. With only empty air between him and the toe of his boot, he lost his balance and knocked against Billy. The two fell as one, with Billy on top of Wade's back. I stood up quickly and pushed Billy out of the way. I then grabbed Wade's ankles and pulled his legs up to his rear end, crisscrossing one over the other in a judo hold I had learned from a school friend. He groaned in pain.

"I think your friend here said to fuck right off, Billy, unless you want me to break his leg."

"What do you want me to do, Wade?" Billy whined.

I pulled down hard on Wade's scissored legs again.

"Do what he says, Billy! He's killing me!"

Billy hesitated until his eye caught a rock beside him on the road. He looked at me out of the corner of one eye and moved slowly towards it.

"Don't even think about it, Billy, if you know what's good for you and him. I'll snap his leg in two before you even touch that. Then I'll take care of you."

I watched Billy back away slowly and then run off down the street shouting, "I'll go get some of the guys."

"How're we going to play this out, *Wade*? We can stay here all day if you're bad, or I can let you go, if you promise to be a good boy. What's it going to be?"

When he didn't answer me, I applied more pressure to his legs.

"Okay," he yelled. "We'll call a truce for now. Let me up. I'm in so much pain."

"If you say so, but next time I won't be so gentle."

I knew his legs would feel shaky from the pressure I was putting on them and he'd be no more threat to me. I released my hold and watched him scramble first to his knees and then to his feet.

"You haven't heard the last of this," he warned, as he struggled to regain his balance. "I'll get you for this, you dirty bastard!"

"Caw...caw...caw! Do I look scared of *you*?"

Milah barked at Wade and he backed away. I mounted Jessie and rode slowly down the street, trembling in the saddle. Jessie jerked her head back a couple of times to let me know that the bit was hurting her mouth, while Milah ran in protective circles around us, as if she were herding prized stock home.

Wade shouted after me.

"I'll get you for this, Cagney. I swear to Christ I will. And when you're least expecting it, you son-of-a-bitch!"

• • •

The trip home was longer when a bull broke out of its pen and ran wildly down Big Hill Road. It took three farmers and a sheepdog almost half an hour to round it up.

By the time I rode into the farmyard, I found it a little cooler. The sun was playing hide-and-seek with some mischievous dark clouds that refused to stay in one place for more than a few seconds at a time. Moments later, the clouds burst open and soaked us from head to toe, hoof, and paw.

"The weatherman was talking out of his ass when he forecasted hot and sunny all day today, girls," I said to Jessie and Milah.

Milah barked, but Jessie didn't let on she'd heard me. She made for the barn and her dry stall, where I unsaddled her and dried her off with a towel.

When I stepped outside the barn, I saw Milah jump onto the porch and shake unwanted rain from her body before curling up into a furry ball next to a rocking chair. She closed one of her eyes and squinted at me with the other. I hurried to the shed to take care of Paddy whose signature screech I heard before I had even opened the door.

"I guess I'll have to teach you how to caw properly soon, Paddy," I said. "That noise you make is getting to be a right pain in the ass."

Chapter 12

"WHAT ON EARTH have you been up to?" Gran asked.

She made her way from the kitchen to the top of the basement stairs and stared down at me as I was going down on tiptoes.

"You're all cut up. And look at the state of your clothes!"

"It's nothing," I replied, lowering my head to hide my facial wound. "I got into a bit of a scrape with one of the locals in town is all. He accused me of stealing something from him."

"What exactly?" Poppy chimed in as the side door to the backyard closed with a bang behind him.

"It wasn't a 'what' exactly," I replied. "It was a who."

"Let me guess. Jane Calloway."

I nodded.

"I see. So, you met him, did you? Wade Simmons. I expected that would happen sooner rather than later. And no doubt, his shadow, Billy was right there cheering him on or waiting to do his bidding. Billy, as in *follow the leader* Billy Cross."

"I never got their last names," I said. "But the first ones are right on."

"You'll want to stay away from that pair," Poppy suggested. "When they're together, they're trouble with a capital 'T'. Alone, you'll hardly ever hear a peep out of either one of them."

"I'm not looking for trouble, even one with a small 't'."

"Sometimes trouble has a way of finding you regardless of best intentions," said Gran. "Troublemakers like that are always up to one thing or another. I should know. I taught both of them during my last year. All I'll say for now is that apples don't fall far from their trees."

"I'll be careful. Don't worry."

"Well, you weren't so careful today. You look like a dog's breakfast," Poppy said with a hint of an amused smile. "How'd they fare?"

"Billy ran off to find his pals. I didn't wait around for them."

"And Wade?"

I managed a smile.

"That's what I thought," Poppy said with a proud look on his face. "Just don't turn your back on any of them, okay?"

I nodded that I understood. I ended the discussion when I said, "I'll go clean up."

When I got to the top of the stairs, I turned to face him.

"Poppy, I hate to ask, but do you think you and Gran could spot me a $300 advance on my pay?"

"For?"

"I came up $300 short for Jake Saulter's truck."

"What do you think, Lee-Ann?"

"Fine with me."

"I'll go to the bank tomorrow then."

"Thanks," I said.

• • •

I had just finished washing up when I heard Jane's voice upstairs.

"Hi, Mrs. Mahoney. Tessa called and told me what happened in town. Is Danny all right?"

"Why don't you ask him yourself, dear?" Gran answered when I reached the top of the stairs. Then she went into the kitchen.

Jane ran to me and hugged me. She stroked the band-aid on my cheek and then stood back to look me over.

"Did he hurt you much?"

"Not too bad," I replied nasally, like a seasoned boxer with a many-times-deviated septum. "You should-a-seen da udder guy, Miss."

She laughed and shook her head.

"I'm sorry. I knew I should have warned you about Wade. He's so possessive and controlling. I only went out with him for about a month, and that was one too many for me."

"Hopefully, he won't bother either of us again."

"Don't bet on it. Wade Simmons has to win at everything, just like his father, Edgar. Sheriff Edgar Simmons. He used to own a lot of land around here until the recession hit him hard. My dad said he had made some bad investments and now takes it out on everybody."

"Well, I'm not looking for trouble with Simmons, but if it comes my way, I won't run from it."

She pulled back the sleeve of her blue denim shirt to peek at her wristwatch.

"I have to get home before my dad gets back from his prayer meeting. I'm not supposed to be out. Can we meet up tomorrow?"

"You bet. I'm free after chores and feeding Paddy.'

'Who's Paddy?"

"My new friend. I wanted to surprise you."

"Friend as in girl...or boy?" She looked jealous.

"Boy. You'll meet him soon. Promise. How's about ten tomorrow?"

"Okay," she said as she made for the front door. I followed her.

"It's supposed to rain cats and dogs, so how about Tom Mullins's place? I'll bring lunch for three -- you, me and *your mystery friend*."

Instead of answering her, I grabbed her by the shoulders, spun her around, and kissed her gently on the lips. I told her that I wanted her to be my girl and that I wanted to hear her say she was.

"It's all a bit quick...but, yes, I'd like that. I would really like that."

After we sealed the deal with more kisses, the thought suddenly hit me that Wade Simmons was going to like the new arrangement even less than he did before. Reasoning with the likes of him was, for sure, a no-go. For the time being, I resolved to avoid him, if I could. But, if push came to shove, I knew the old Crow in me would be sure to push and shove right back. After all, as Gran had said a few minutes earlier about the apples not falling far from the trees, I didn't exactly leave the old Danny back in the city, did I?

There was a mountain bike leaning against a tree and Jane got on it. I called to her as she started to peddle away.

"Hang on a sec, Jane! I have something for you."

I dashed downstairs to my room. I returned a minute or two later with a gift box and handed it to her.

"I see you used expensive wrapping paper," she laughed.

She ripped open the comic section of Saturday's newspaper that I had used to wrap her gift.

"Only the very best for you."

"A belt with horses. I love it. I'll wear it tomorrow."

She leaned over her bike and kissed me on the cheek.

"I'm glad you didn't get too beat up." She smiled.

"Me, too."

I watched as she pedaled down the path towards the front gate. She waved at me without looking back, but I knew that she knew I was watching her every move as she rode.

Chapter 13

JUST AS JANE HAD FORECAST, it was raining hard the next morning. I woke up before Poppy and decided to tend to Paddy before anyone else got up. I heard Poppy snoring as I opened the front door to go out.

Paddy greeted me with two low caws when I entered the shed and I echoed them as closely as I could.

"Hey, Paddy, boy. What've you been up to? Getting better, I hope. Your cawing's improved some."

I slipped on a pair of canvas work gloves and reached for the tweezers that were lying waiting on the bench beside the cage. I opened the bag of seeds and nuts that I had purchased in town and used the tweezers to grab some bigger ones for Paddy. He snapped them up eagerly with his beak as quickly as I offered them. After topping up the bottle feeder with fresh water, I opened the cage door and grabbed hold of Paddy despite his protesting caws and pecks, and flights to nowhere because his leg was still in a sling. I was happy to see that the tape Poppy had rolled around the sling was still intact and I remained hopeful that the leg would mend within the anticipated two-week healing period.

I completed my examination and set Paddy down gently in the cage. He used his outstretched wings as stabilizers and hobbled to a far corner where he turned to face me. He cawed several times in quick succession. It was as if he were telling me to get the hell off his crow turf and leave him alone.

"Okay," I said as I closed the cage door. "Hang on to your feathers. I'm going. But, before I do, I am going to find a larger food dispenser for you. I think you can feed yourself completely from now on."

Paddy turned his back to me as if to say, "I am not listening to you, Danny Boy." However, I could see that it was all an act on his part because his head was turned slightly to the left, just enough for him to watch me warily out of one corner of his eye.

I rummaged through a drawer and managed to find a Tupperware container. I filled it with worms I had dug out of the pile of horse shit the day before, slicing them in wiggling pieces first. After placing the container inside the cage, I made for the door, pitching three low caws to Paddy who twitched his head slightly in response.

"See you later, Paddy. From one crow to another, I hope you'll be thinking of me as much as I'll be thinking about you. Remember, I'm just as caged in as you are."

I made up my mind then and there that I would utter two short caws whenever I entered the shed and three upon leaving. Paddy, I was sure, would come around eventually and learn that I was not his enemy.

"As a matter of fact, Paddy, *my friend*," I said. "How would you like to tag along with me today?"

"Caw," he replied. "Caw…caw…caw."

"Let's go then," I replied, lifting him in his cage.

Chapter 14

I TIED THE CAGE TO JESSIE'S SADDLE HORN before setting out in the rain for Old Tom's to meet Jane after chores.

Milah ran ahead of us, disappearing, reappearing, and barking whenever she felt like it. Paddy, on the other hand, didn't make a sound during the half-hour ride.

I was beginning to feel a bit cocky as I rode along the trail. I thought that a casual observer might even think that I was a real pro, holding the reins in my left hand and the saddle horn in my right.

By the time Jessie, Paddy and I arrived at the cabin, the rain had stopped. A doe was grazing quietly on wild grass while her two fawns munched nearby on fallen leaves and pine needles. The doe didn't hear me at first because, as Poppy would explain later, I was probably downwind from her. I tugged gently on Jessie's reins and we both watched the hungry family in silence. However, Paddy and Milah had other ideas. Paddy belted out four quick caws while Milah sprang into the clearing like a circus barker who was determined to grab everyone's attention.

Startled by the commotion, the deer raised their heads and cocked their ears before they had even spotted the canine intruder. They leapt into the camouflage of the woods. The two fawns were glued to their mother's rump, mirroring her movements in scale: prance, hop, and jump for prance, hop, and jump. With Milah, of course, in hot pursuit.

I dismounted carefully, still holding the cage. I fastened the reins to a spruce sapling, giving Jessie just enough slack to sample the surrounding vegetation.

I was about to sit down on a tree trunk when Jane arrived, driving an old two-wheeled horse cart pulled by Goldie. The cart looked like one I'd seen in one of my favorite, Irish movies, "The Field." It was packed with several planks of weathered timber, plastic sheets, tarpaper, all sorts of tools, and the promised lunchbox for three.

"Hey, Danny," she said. "Nice to see you made it on time."

"You, too," I replied. "Except you're two minutes late."

"Traffic," she quipped. "Rabbits everywhere along the trail. And the potholes those groundhogs keep making."

Paddy's cage rested on the ground at my feet. He looked up and cawed.

Jane looked down at him and smiled.

"This is Paddy, your feathered competition. I brought him along as you suggested."

"I'm curious. Why didn't you tell me about him before yesterday?"

I shrugged. "Waiting for the right moment, I guess."

"He looks pretty tame."

"He seems less and less nervous the more I have contact with him."

"Are you thinking of keeping him as a pet?"

"At first I thought it would be sort of neat to, but I don't think it would be fair. He was born wild and he should stay wild, with his own kind. Besides, it's against the law to keep him."

Jane laughed.

"What's so funny?"

"You, the big city gang member. I didn't think you guys worried too much about breaking the law."

"Well, I don't have much choice in the matter."

"How come?"

I told her why I had been sent to my grandparents' farm and my first encounter with Paddy. She listened without saying a word until I had finished.

"Wow, what my dad would do with that news!"

"And you?"

She shrugged her shoulders. "I'm glad."

"Of what?"

"Glad the judge sent you here to do your time. The rest of the story doesn't matter. Let's change the subject."

She stood up in the cart and pulled her top up, enough to expose her waist.

"Like it?"

I looked down at the belt I had given her.

"It looks great on you, but then even a dishcloth would."

She smiled at the compliment.

"Hey, what's all this stuff for?" I asked, pointing to the cart's contents.

"They're all second tools from one of our barns. No one'll miss them. We're going to patch up Tom's place to make it rainproof. It'll be our little hideaway. What do you think?"

"Besides the fact that you're a bit crazy?" I laughed.

"Crazy?"

Laughing, she grabbed the axe and jumped down off the cart. She raised it above her right shoulder and pretended she was going to strike me. She sunk its cutting edge into a tree stump instead.

"I'm crazy. Crazy about you."

She threw her arms around me and kissed me hard on the mouth. I started laughing in response and, after stammered attempts to tell her why, all I could manage was, "I don't know. Happy I guess."

Then it hit me in a flash. I had not laughed as heartily since I let myself go in the third grade.

• • •

The school bully, Mickey Snide, a fat ten-year-old loved to pick on my best friend, Nick Marsh. He would often push Nick down and sit on him to prevent him from moving. Then he would punch him in the face and head.

Although I was a year younger and 40 pounds lighter than Snide, I promised myself I'd do something the next time he went after Nick who was too chicken to fight back himself.

One day, a Friday I think, I got between Snide and Nick outside the lunchroom. When Snide put his hands on my chest and started pushing me instead, I remembered a move from my judo class. I used his weight against him. Instead of pushing back, I grabbed his arms, pulled him towards me, turning at the same time. He landed hard on the ground with me on top of him. I was no match for him, however, and he quickly flipped me onto my back and sat on top of me. He then punched me the same way he had punched Nick the day before.

Thankfully, the principal, Mother "Dearest" St. Agnes broke up the fight before it got worse. She was furious when she saw that my elbow was bleeding. What she didn't know was that the blood was coming from a week-old old scab, but I never told her that.

"Get off him this minute, you big brute!" Mother Dearest commanded.

"He started it, Mother," Snide complained.

She pinched and tugged his right ear until he was on his feet. I got up by myself and looked at Snide. He was a head taller than I was.

"You big liar!" she screamed. "Look at the size of you compared to him. And I suppose he bled all by himself without any help from you? Get you down to Mother de Lourdes's detention room. Tell her I'll deal with you myself later."

She touched my cheek and smiled. "Go you on upstairs to my office, Daniel. I'll be up soon to tend that wound for you. I'll have to call your mother and tell her what happened."

She called to Snide when he reached the down staircase.

"And I'll be calling your parents, too, to be sure, Michael Snide. Hopefully, they will punish you at home after I'm done with you here."

When Mother Dearest was out of earshot, Nick and I laughed. Then I chanted, "Me and my old scab beat that scab. Me and my old scab beat that scab. Serves tub of lard, Mickey Snide fair and square. Serves tub of lard, Mickey Snide fair and square."

Nick joined in the chorus, "Serves tub of lard Mickey Snide fair and square."

• • •

"Earth to Mars. Come in, Danny. Where'd you drift off to?" Jane said.

I told Jane the story about Mickey Snide.

"Serves tub of lard, Mickey Snide fair and square," she chanted.

"You've got a neat voice."

She smiled at the compliment. "Can't say the same for you. But I'll teach you how to hold a tune during clean-up."

"You're too kind."

She pushed me playfully. I pretended to resist. I reached down and picked up Paddy's cage as we inched towards the cabin door. Once inside, I set the cage down on the table.

It took us nearly two hours of non-stop work to de-clutter the cabin while Paddy watched our every move. We removed unopened food cans, bottles of all kinds, mouse and rat traps, mounds of moldy books, paper and everything that was beyond easy repair. I insisted on keeping some of the less damaged books and magazines and Jane, my cleaning boss, reluctantly agreed. She suggested placing all the burnable items in a pile at the center of the clearing.

"One evening we can come here and light a bonfire, just the two of us," she said.

"Sounds romantic."

"You think? Do you want to eat something or start patching up things first?"

"I'm not hungry. How about work first? I want to see how good you are."

"I can bang a nail and saw wood as good as any guy. Been doing it since I was ten."

She grabbed my right hand between her two, looked at my palm, shook her head, and frowned.

"What?" I asked.

"I should've brought a first-aid kit because those soft city hands of yours are sure to be all blistered up before the day's done."

"Well don't count my blisters before they've popped," I warned. "I might just surprise you."

I took back my hand and walked outside to the cart, leaving Jane at the front door. Goldie was munching on some wild grass and was too preoccupied to notice me. Milah poked her head out from underneath the cart and barked once.

I retrieved two planks, a hammer, a saw and some nails from the cart. I stuffed handfuls of nails into the pouches of the tool belt I'd fastened around my waist. Then I slipped the roofing hammer and hammer-stapler into the belt's stainless steel holding rings. I carried the planks to the cabin and leaned them against the wall.

"Hand them up to me when I'm on the roof."

"Hey, who made you my boss all of a sudden?" she asked, her hands on her hips.

"Me. You can be the boss of the inside. Me outside."

"I guess that's fair."

I had noticed a hand-made wooden ladder at the side of the cabin earlier. After checking it for sturdiness, I placed it against an eve of the roof and climbed up, saw in hand.

"You've done this before?" she asked.

I looked down at her and smiled. "Last summer, I worked for a city roofer. At first, I was the go-fetch-it, but after a while, the foreman started to trust me. He wanted to make sure that I wasn't afraid of heights and was comfortable walking around the roof. I was I guess because he upped my pay. And yes, I did earn lots of blisters the first week, too, you'll be happy to know."

"Okay, Superblisterman," she replied, "Here's your wood. Just be careful up there. There could be lots of rot and you won't see it until you're falling through it."

"Okay, Mom."

I took the wood from her and laid it down near me, within easy reach. I then crawled around on my hands and knees to spread my weight while inspecting the roof for damage. Finding only three or four weak spots, I set about removing broken cedar shingles and the damaged boards underneath.

It felt good to be working with my hands again and, after an hour of pulling, tugging sawing, banging, and a few "ouches" and "oh shits," I'd repaired the more noticeable damage. I was about to climb down the ladder to get some tarpaper and new cedar shingles from the cart when I spotted them lying near the edge of the roof.

"Thanks, Jane," I shouted. "I didn't see you carry all that stuff up."

The clashing of pots and pans in the cabin told me that she didn't hear me. When Paddy cawed from the kitchen, I wondered if he had.

I stapled tarpaper in place where needed and nailed cedar shingles to it, making sure to match the existing shingle pattern as closely as possible. I felt proud of my work as I gathered up my equipment.

After I had climbed down the ladder and placed the tools back in the cart, I noticed that the lunchbox was missing. I turned and saw whiffs of wood smoke puffing out of the chimney; I found its sweet scent delightful and imagined that its puffs were curled letters spelling, "Welcome to Danny and Jane's Place."

Jane was standing over the wood stove stirring the contents of a steaming pot when I entered the cabin. She had already swept the floor clean and dusted everywhere and it was starting to feel cozy and warm.

"Smells good, Jane. I'm ready for it," I said, as I pulled up a chair. "Caw…caw…caw, Paddy."

Paddy didn't answer. He was staring at the back of the closed door, watching fresh red paint dripping down it from a message that warmed my heart:

Daniel Cagney and Jane Calloway
Our Special Place, September 2007

"Nice brush strokes," I said, smiling. "I'm glad you wrote that."

Jane blew me a kiss, as she carried the pot to the table. She poured piping hot soup into two tin cups. We ate in silence, exchanging the gazes and smiles. I think we were both feeling good about "us" and what we had done. During one passing moment, as I blew on my spoon to cool the soup, goose bumps ran a race up and down my back. I shivered when they crossed the finish line at the nape of my neck.

"What's wrong?" she asked.

"Nothing," I answered. "I was just thinking."

"Of what?"

"You, and how happy I'm feeling to be here, with you, at this moment."

She reached across the table and touched my arm. I pulled my hand back slowly. Paddy looked at me and cawed.

"And...?"

"I don't know what got into me," I replied. "I think I'm feeling happy and sad again -- at the same time -- if that's possible. It'll pass."

She got up from the table and walked over to me. Then she wrapped her arms around my neck, crossing her hands on my chest.

"I've also never felt happier than I do now, Danny. But, when I see you tune out sometimes, I get afraid, too. It's kind've like you're here one minute and then you're not!"

She lowered her arms and waited for me to answer.

"I'm still scared, too. That something's going to happen to steal my happiness away -- like a thief in the night. The way it always seemed to do back in the city."

I kissed her, first on the forehead, then on the bridge of her nose.

"I'm gonna do everything I can to make sure that doesn't happen. Jane. I promise."

Paddy let out two soft caws and Jane laughed.

"Do you think Paddy believes you?"

"Yup. He just told me so."

She planted another kiss on my lips and I kissed her back. I wanted to make love to her then and there, but she killed that hope when she looked at that darn watch of hers.

"We'd better get going. I'm already an hour later than I said I'd be."

I was disappointed, but I didn't push it. When the last log in the stove had burned to ashes a few minutes later, we packed up and closed the cabin door behind us. We left, feeling that Old Tom's belonged to us, now that we had given it a good facelift inside and out. I kissed Jane and helped her up into the cart. Then I mounted Jessie, holding Paddy's cage carefully in one hand as I did.

"Do you know the Saulters?" I asked.

"As well as can be expected," she replied. "My folks don't take to mixing with black people. Emma Saulter goes to Catholic school. We're Protestants. Nazarenes."

"How about you, Jane? Do you have any problem with black folks?"

"I don't know too many real well, but I guess not. I've never really given it much thought."

"Well how about coming with me to Emma's party Friday? I have to see Jake about a pickup he sold me."

"You never said anything about a pickup!"

"I was going to surprise you when I picked you up."

She frowned, prompting me to ask why.

"I would love to go with you, but if my dad finds out."

"Don't you think you should start living your life on your own terms, instead of his?"

"I guess."

"That settles it then. Can you call me tomorrow and let me know where to meet? I'm guessing not your place."

"I'd better meet you there, at the Saulters I mean."

I told her that my grandparents and I would show up around six. We then went our separate ways.

Except for occasional low-pitched caws, Paddy stayed quiet on the trip home. When I looked down to check on him one time, he was in a world of his own, preening his feathers and flexing his wings. When he was done, he began picking at the tape on his leg splint.

I noticed that my fingers were tapping on Paddy's cage to the beat of Jessie's hoof clops on the hard ground. I stopped tapping when the sound of cawing crows in flight caught my attention. I looked up and watched hundreds of them following their leader as they flew southward. I thought of Mom and wondered, at the speed the crows were flying, whether or not she would soon see them above the women's prison where she was serving out the last stretch of her sentence. I wondered, too, whether or not she would stay clean this time and whether or not I would have the courage to be kind to her either way -- without enabling her.

Jessie whinnied, jolting me back to reality. I then wondered if it would be a good time to start leaving Paddy's cage door open so that he could feel free to move around the tool shed, as he got stronger in the days ahead. I made up my mind to do exactly that when I got back to the farm.

Jessie whinnied again and I imagined Mom bathing in the farm's morning sunlight with Paddy flying around and around her head until he tired and landed gracefully on her shoulder. I saw him look into her eyes and make a sound like a cat's purr. She imitated it. Then the two flew off together into the distance, he flapping his wings, she flapping her arms until my daydream faded to black like a movie ending.

Chapter 15

THE PARTY WAS IN FULL SWING when I arrived at the Saulters with Poppy and Gran. We could hear music playing when we were a block away from the house even though the pickup's windows were closed. A banjo was belting out a neat tune and every second part seemed to me to be an answer to the preceding one.

We parked on the street outside the Saulter house, a modest two-story structure, with a gabled, cedar shingle roof, wood-framed dormer windows and freshly painted white stucco walls. We got out and walked towards the backyard garden. Poppy was carrying a fiddle case, Gran an Irish drum she called a bodhrán, which she spelled for me, stressing the fada, the accent on the 'a'. I was asked to carry the piping hot pies Gran had baked.

"Banjo Bob is playing up a storm as usual, Lee-Ann," Poppy said.

"How can you tell it's him, without seeing him?" I asked.

"All great musicians leave their own unique musical fingerprints on a tune when they play."

"And we've heard him render that same tune many times before," Gran said. "Did you ever see the film, *Deliverance*, Danny? It was the theme song."

"Oh, yeah. *Dueling Banjos*. I thought I recognized it. I saw the movie with my gang once. We used to hum the parts to each other. We got off on the threatening feel of its beat."

"That's what he's playing, but with his own twist," Poppy said.

When we entered the backyard, he waved at the musicians on the makeshift stage.

"And there's Banjo Bob Cussen himself."

Bob, a man in his forties, was wearing glasses and a bushy white beard, a baseball cap and a welcoming smile. Amazingly, he and a mandolin player were carrying on a conversation while building the tune up to a crescendo. They ended the music on a dramatic and abrupt short note. Bob extended his picking hand when he spied Poppy and Gran.

"Tyler, Lee-Ann! It's great to see your instruments, and the two of you, of course."

"Good to see yours and you, too," Poppy replied. He shook Bob's hand firmly and nodded to the fiddler sitting to his right. "Bonjour, Yves. Bienvenue."

Because Yves had already started to play a fast jig, he simply smiled.

"You guys keep playing," Poppy suggested. "We'll belt out a few tunes after we say hello to the Saulter family and their guests."

"Hi Lee-Ann and Tyler," a lady shouted and waved from across the garden. "I hope you brought an appetite. Hiro Hasimoto is on barbecue duty."

Poppy and Gran smiled and waved back. Gran massaged her tummy with her hand.

"The tune's calling," Bob said and immediately his fingers began to pluck his banjo strings in time to Yves's bow strokes. The bow was moving so fast across the strings that it looked like it was going up and down at the same time.

About two dozen or so toe-tapping people were gathered around the Saulter family, chatting and enjoying the moment, and the unusually warm evening for that time of year. There wasn't a tie in sight. They were all dressed in jeans or shorts, open-necked shirts or T-shirts. Half were black. The rest were white except for Hiro and another middle-aged, brown-skinned guy who was tuning up an erhu, a Chinese two-string violin.

The voice of an older male guest rose above the din. I heard him talking to a younger man and woman about Hiro.

"He saved a young girl from drowning in the Connecticut River a while back."

"Is he the Japanese man who owns that Chinese restaurant east of Noburg?" the woman asked.

"That's the one, *Hiro's Place*. He donated all the party food and his cooking skills to the Saulters. They're close friends. You'll never guess what the headline was in *The Noburg News* the day after he saved the girl."

He answered his own question. "Hiro a Hero!"

The young couple got a kick out of that.

Poppy and Gran seemed proud as they introduced me to some of the guests. It made me feel a little awkward – like I was their prodigal grandson. Without the fatted calf. Although there were a few cooked steaks on the table next to Hiro and he was flipping raw ones onto the barbecue.

I was starting to worry that Jane wouldn't show up when Jake Saulter slapped me on the back and tried to sound like James Cagney in an old black and white gangster movie I saw once. "Did youse bring the loot like I tolds ya kid?'

"I did. I have the seven hundred."

I handed him an envelope. He folded it and stuffed it into his back pocket.

"Aren't you going to count it?" I asked.

"No need to. You're a Mahoney, aren't you? That's all the counting I need do."

"But I'm also a Crow," I thought. "Maybe you should count it."

Say, how about going to the DMV Monday morning to make the transfer," he suggested.

"Okay by me."

"Great. Pick you up at your place around ten. You might want to call them first to find out how much it's going to cost to do the paperwork. I can't remember what it was last time."

"Sounds like a plan," I replied.

Then I thought about his reference to *my place* and it struck me that I didn't even think of the city when he did. I thought of the farmhouse.

"Hey, I've a better idea," Jake said as he threw a set of keys to me.

"What this for?"

"You can take the truck now. It's all tuned up for you. You can drive it to the DMV yourself and I'll meet you there."

"But..."

"No buts. It'll save me time Monday, if we do it this way."

"Thanks. I'll take good care of it until it's officially mine."

"Jake," a woman shouted. "We need some more cold beer and soft drinks."

The voice belonged to Judy Saulter, a stunning black woman with short hair. She looked to me like she was in her late thirties. I could not help notice her soft smile and welcoming brown eyes. She was wearing matching yellow jeans and running shoes.

A younger and just as pretty girl, who had been talking to Tessa a few feet away, walked up to Judy. She touched Judy's elbow and whispered something in her ear. Judy nodded. Then they both walked over to me. Judy extended her hand as Jake went to get the beer. Tessa waved hello and smiled without her braces, which the dentist must have had removed since I last saw her.

"You must be Danny. I'm Judy, Jake's wife."

"Hi, Mrs. Saulter."

"Call me Judy. Everybody does. And this is Emma."

"Hi Danny." Emma said. "I'm glad you came."

"Me, too. Congratulations on your scholarship. You must be pretty smart to win that."

She lowered her head bashfully and stuck her hands in the pockets of her tight blue jeans.

"Oh, I don't know about that. I have to work extra hard for every mark I get. I'm not one of those gifted students."

"I have something for you."

"You do?"

I reached into the side pocket of my jeans and retrieved a small maple-wood carving of a crow in flight for her. It hung from a leather lanyard.

"I made this pendant for you."

"Thank you. It's so beautiful. My best friend, Tessa told me about the crow you're caring for. Is that what gave you the idea to make this?"

"I guess. Crows are now my favorite bird. They're pretty smart students, too."

Emma looped the lanyard around her neck.

"I love it!"

"Oh, there's Jane Calloway," Judy interrupted.

Judy exchanged waves and a smile with Jane who was walking towards us. Emma waved and smiled, too.

"You never said she was coming, Emma."

I invited her," I said. "I hope you don't mind."

"Everyone's always welcome at our house. I just hope her dad doesn't mind."

Emma and Judy exchanged small talk with Jane before excusing themselves to mingle with the other guests. Jane seemed a little fidgety. Her gaze shifted from me to the street several times. She had a scroll in her right hand; a red ribbon tied in a bow kept it rolled up.

"What is it, Jane? You seem uptight."

"Same old. It's my dad. He didn't want me to come and we had a big fight. I ran out and took off on my bike. I'm afraid he'll show up here any minute and all hell's going to break loose. And now I'm afraid to go home."

"Do you want to leave then?"

"Yeah, but we should stay for a bit. Mrs. Saulter will understand. I'm sure she knows how all riled up my dad can get. Everybody does."

She handed me the scroll. "This is for you."

I unfurled it and was surprised to see a full-color sketch of me standing on the roof of the cabin, hammer in hand. I was amazed at the fine detail and the perspective. She had drawn me smiling as I prepared to patch up the roof. The drawing was so realistic that, at first glance, I actually thought that she had taken a photograph of me when I wasn't looking. She had captured my six-foot frame with all of its idiosyncrasies and imperfections: my pug nose; blond hair; blue eyes; the faded scar on my left cheek, the result of a boxing injury; and even the sprinkling of freckles on my cheeks, which I'm sure she had counted to the very last one before drawing them. My T-shirt sleeves were rolled up and she had made my biceps look a bit larger than they really were -- wishful thinking perhaps. Maybe she had an unconscious thought of wanting me to work out. It was signed, "Jane Calloway, 2007, 1 of 2."

"Wow, you are full of surprises, Jane! I didn't know you were an artist."

"I don't know about artist. I just like to draw. I've been doing it for as long as I can remember. It's a good escape when I feel down, like writing is to you, if you ever get back to it."

"What's with the numbers, one of two?"

"Yours is number one. I made an exact copy for myself. It's two of two. Of course, I have to hide it. If my dad saw it, he'd freak."

Tears rolled down her cheeks.

"I can't take much more of him, Danny. I'm thinking of running away. I'm so scared that he'll hurt you if he finds out I am still seeing you. All I need is for someone from church to spot us and… "

She snapped her fingers in the air.

"We'll figure out something," I promised, squeezing her hand. "For now, let's just enjoy ourselves. Let's eat."

Hiro lived up to his reputation as a fine chef. His burgers and barbecued vegetables were the best I'd ever had. I managed to eat two all-dressed burgers and a whole side plate of veggies.

The Saulters didn't object to Jane and I leaving early. Jane, as she had promised, told Judy the real reason why and Judy said that she understood. I told Poppy and Gran that I might be late, but that Jane and I would swing by the farm to check on Paddy before heading off for a few hours.

Jane and I held hands as we headed for my unofficial new pickup. We were just about to drive off when Jane said, "Wait! Can you hear it?"

"What?"

"Ole Tom Mullins Jig. Your grandfather's playing it now. He's pretty good, isn't he?"

I looked back to watch him playing the super catchy tune. Bob and Yves accompanied him. By the time Gran had added her bodhrán to the mix, people were clapping the beat.

A boy, about ten years old, soon accompanied them on his keyboard and played with impressive skill for such a young age. His father took a seat beside him and pumped out the music on his accordion. A few braver souls began dancing and trying to keep up with the feverish pace, with some shouting, "Go Gareth Go. Go Gareth Go!" to the boy and "Hit those buttons, Steve" to his dad.

Poppy and Gran played their hearts out and I felt included in their happiness. However, that thought quickly disappeared when the memory of what a high school teacher once said to me, when he found out Mom was in jail, flashed through my mind.

"Blood, like still water, runs deep," the teacher had said. "How well you tread that water is what makes the difference between staying afloat or going under."

"Why would I think of that right now?" I thought. "Am I afraid of drowning? If so, where? Here, or back in the city?"

Then I thought of Abe Calloway. He wouldn't mind where I'd drown, as long as I kept away from his Jane.

Chapter 16

JANE SHOWED ME a shortcut back to the farm and we pulled up to a five-bar gate that I had not noticed before. She got out and opened it and I drove through. She then closed it behind her and hopped back into the truck.

As we approached the tool shed, we could see her father's pickup truck speeding away from the house, its tires screeching on the tarred path, leaving a mixture of dust and tire smoke behind.

"Stop!" Jane ordered. "That's my dad!"

I stepped hard on the brake and waited until the truck was out of sight before driving on to the shed.

"Phew! That was close. He'll probably head over to the Saulters now, unless he's already been there. I don't know what to do."

"Do you want to go to Old Tom's?"

"Then what?"

"We can talk about what to do when we get there."

"Okay. I'm game, if you are."

"I'll get Paddy. I'd like to bring him with us."

I left the truck in neutral and headed towards the shed.

"Caw...caw," I sang as I entered the shed.

"Caw...caw," Paddy replied in a slightly higher tone. He was perched on a nearby shelf. He stared down at me.

After sprinkling a handful of nuts on the floor of the open cage, I stood as far back as I could and waited. Paddy kept a wary eye on me. After a few moments, he flapped his wings and flew the short distance into the cage, wobbling slightly as he placed weight on his injured leg. I closed the cage door when he started pecking at the nuts.

I returned to the truck and handed the cage to Jane. We then drove off slowly towards the back gate. When we approached a crossroads about a mile down the road, we both saw them at the same time: Wade Simmons and Billy Cross. They were climbing into Abe Calloway's pickup. I eased my pickup to the side of the road and hid it behind some bushes. We waited there until Abe's truck was out of sight. Then we headed off in the other direction towards Old Tom's place.

"That's all I need," Jane said." Wade Simmons and his constant shadow with my dad. My dad thinks the world of him because he and his family attend our church. He didn't believe me when I told him that I stopped seeing Wade after he slapped me across the face."

"Wade hit you?"

"I didn't want to tell you."

"I'm glad you did. I won't let that happen again."

Paddy cawed.

"Does Paddy still agree with everything you say?" she asked.

Rain pelted the pickup, gently at first, then forcefully.

"Maybe you should ask him yourself."

Lightning flashed in the distance and thunder followed. Jane moved closer to me and stayed that way until we arrived at our destination.

• • •

"Someone's been here," Jane said before we'd even stepped out of the pickup.

"Now don't go getting paranoid on me," I replied.

"I'm not being paranoid, damn it! Someone's been here. Something's just not right. Can't you see it?"

We left Paddy in his cage on the front seat and walked cautiously towards the cabin, following the strong beam of the flashlight I'd found in the glove compartment. I watched Jane as she explored every inch of our surroundings, making a complete circle on her heels.

"What?"

"Lots of stuff. That bucket over there has been turned right side up. I left it upside down so that rain wouldn't get in. And look at the axe lying on the ground. I was the one who used it last. I stuck it in the stump with a plastic bag covering it to prevent it from rusting. I thought about it when I got home because we should have left it inside the cabin."

"Are you sure?"

"Yes, I'm sure. I have an artist's eye when it comes to detail. At least that's what my art teacher once told me. Look around you. What do you see different?"

I shrugged my shoulders, but then I saw a difference and pointed.

Slivers of wood from the obviously pried-open cabin door lay on the doorstep.

Jane picked up the axe and handed it to me.

"Careful," she warned as we crept closer to the cabin through puddles of rainwater. When the cuck-cuck-cuck sound of a squirrel in a pine tree pierced the silence, we both froze in our tracks. Paddy answered the treed rodent with three quick caws. I had no idea whether he was trying to warn us to beware or assure us that all was well. Jane followed closely, with one hand on my shoulder.

I inched open the door. Its rusty hinges creaked and groaned for oil.

"Hello? Hello?"

When no one answered me, I pushed the door open half way and waited until I was sure I heard nothing. Summoning a little more courage, I gave it a stronger push, opening it all the way. As soon as we stepped inside, we were jolted by the agonizing shriek of a creature above us and the creepy touch of its paws when it dropped down from a rafter and ran across the back of my shoulders and then Jane's before jumping onto the floor.

We both breathed a sigh of relief when we saw a black cat run out the front door towards the woods.

"Phew! That scared the you know what out of me," Jane whispered. "I'm glad it wasn't human or a ghost."

"Me, too. But someone human has been here for sure. Look."

Three plastic soft drink cups, Hiro's take-out food containers, and beer cans were scattered on the table. Kitchen drawers and cupboards had been left partially open.

A black tag on the door of an open kitchen cupboard caught my eye and made my tummy flutter. It was a warning that I knew well: our secret hideaway had now been claimed as Crows territory. The crowfoot symbol was a warning for all, but especially for me I thought. When I saw my name circled in red paint on the back of the door, I knew for sure that the gang was looking for me.

Jane said, "I told you someone had been here. I know it wasn't my dad, so my question is who?"

I shrugged, then felt guilty not telling her that I knew who the intruders were.

"I don't think we should stick around," I suggested. "Until we know who it is."

"You're right. We can sneak back tomorrow when it's light and maybe watch from the woods."

"Good idea. I just hope whoever it was hasn't had the same idea."

"Now you're really beginning to freak me out. Let's go now."

"What do you think we should do about the door? We can't just leave it like that."

"Oh yes we can," she replied. "We don't want anyone to know we were here. Do we?"

"Good point."

As we returned the door to the position we had found it, the rapid cawing of many crows caught our attention. I aimed the flashlight's beam at the pickup truck. Talk about a murder! About 50 crows were perched all over the truck's hood, as well as its cab and cargo area, and in surrounding trees. They seemed to be communicating with Paddy who was cawing back at them from his cage.

A white spot crowned the head of one of the larger crows. All six of his toes, three on each foot, were wrapped tightly around the driver's side windshield wiper blade. He cawed furiously at Paddy as if to say, "Get the hell out of there this minute!" Three other crows swooped close to Jane as we approached the cab of the pickup.

"They're dive-bombing us," I shouted and we started running the rest of the way. All of the crows, except the one clutching the wiper blade, flew, like pellets from a shotgun blast, in different directions, some to the safety of nearby trees, others to the cabin's roof, and well beyond. We were soaking wet by the time we entered the cab. I started the engine and turned on the wipers. As the rain cleared from the windshield, we could see it, the crow with the white crown, still clutching the arm of the wiper blade, riding along with it -- left to right, right to left -- casting evil-looking eyes at us, cawing, expecting us, perhaps, to understand his crow-speak and what he was all riled up about.

I drove away slowly, determined to do my best not to hurt our feathery hitchhiker in any way. The road ahead was really nothing more than compacted soil, lined with deep tractor tire ruts, and I hardly had to steer as the pickup moved along them like a passenger train on rails.

"I've never seen anything like that in my life," Jane said.

"I've been reading up on crows and all I can tell you is that no one knows everything there is to know about them. They have their own personalities and they're not as predictable as you might think."

"How're we going to get it off?"

"That's up to him or her."

"Do you think it knows Paddy?"

"That's what I was wondering."

"See what happens if you stop quickly."

I slammed hard on the brakes as Jane suggested, but still the crow didn't budge from the wiper arm. It stayed with us for a good five minutes or more, staring at us, like a hypnotist attempting to induce a trance. Then, suddenly, it flew away without so much as a caw.

"I'll say it again," Jane exclaimed. "I've never seen anything like that before!"

"Ditto!"

What we did see were the headlights of an approaching vehicle. They lit up the night on the other side of the hill ahead of us. I quickly pulled into a farm laneway and switched off the pickup's engine and lights.

"Think it's my dad?"

"No sense taking a chance, is there?"

We ducked as the vehicle passed and breathed a sigh of relief when we saw that it was an ATV and not her dad's pickup.

"Phew," she said when the ATV's roar faded to silence down the road.

"We got all worked up for nothing."

"Danny?"

"What?"

"Let's run away together! Far away where no one'll find us!"

I took another breath, turned, and stroked her hair gently with the tips of my fingers. It felt soft and inviting.

"Then what? The cops will hunt me down for breaking probation. And where would we get the money to live on?"

"It's not fair."

"I know, but we both have to work things out before we can leave. Look, maybe you should try to get home before your dad does. Let your mother intervene for you."

I paused to let my suggestion to sink in.

"He won't hurt you, will he?"

She shook her head. "Only with words, and I sure have heard enough of them! But, I guess another day won't make much difference."

I leaned over and parked a kiss on her forehead. She ran an index finger around the spot after I did.

"Okay, let's go before I change my mind and run away for good," she said.

I could almost hear the silence as we drove slowly to the Calloway farm.

Even Paddy had the smarts to keep his mouth shut until the house was in view. He cawed when I braked the pickup about two hundred feet away from the house, as if to say, "We're here!"

"Wish me luck. I'll call you tomorrow to let you know if I'm still breathing," Jane said.

She shut the passenger door, walked slowly and deliberately towards the house, as if she were counting her paces. When she was about half way, she turned and blew a kiss, letting it travel along the pickup's headlight beams to me.

At that very moment, my lips produced words with absolutely no help from me and I had no idea what they would be until they reached my ears.

"I love you Jane Calloway," I whispered. "I really do."

I felt a knot in my stomach when she entered the house and the door closed behind her. I waited for about ten minutes and then drove at a snail's pace past the house, hoping to catch one last glimpse of her as I did. I looked into the rear-view mirror until the house disappeared into darkness, leaving an even bigger knot in the pit of my stomach.

• • •

By the time Paddy and I got back to the farm around 11:00, the clouds had migrated north to Canada, leaving millions of stars behind in a clear sky. Paddy couldn't care less about the stars. He had fallen fast asleep on the perch of his cage. He woke up when I killed the engine outside the tool shed. After I had him safely inside, I switched on the light, opened his cage door, and watched him fly up to the rafters. I switched on an old shortwave radio that had been gathering dust on a shelf and toyed with the tuner until I managed to coax a New York station to life. The signal faded in and out at first but, eventually, I could hear the transmission quite clearly, except for the occasional bits of static that smothered musical notes here and there.

U2 was singing one of my favorite protest songs, *Sunday Bloody Sunday*. While I sang along, I prepared some food for Paddy. However, instead of placing it in his cage, I tried something new. I slipped on a work glove to protect my left hand and sprinkled bits of chopped-up worm in its palm. I waited for a few long minutes, but he refused to leave his perch until I had pretended to close my eyes. Suddenly, like a pilot scouting for enemy soldiers, he circled my head a few times before landing softly on my shoulder.

I squinted and watched him hobble on his still weak leg along my outstretched arm towards the prize that awaited him. He paused on the way to study my crow tattoo on my partially exposed forearm. I tried to remain as still as possible while he devoured every last bit of worm. When he was done, he cawed. I reached out my free hand to retrieve more for him while he waited patiently. I placed the food carefully on my gloved palm again and he quickly polished it off, cawing when he had done so. I interpreted the caws as a polite "thank you."

I waited for his next move, this time with my eyes wide open, staring into his. He alternated between several stares and slight turns of his head as if he were trying to make up his mind about me. Then, without warning, he flapped his wings and half-hopped slowly up my arm until he reached my shoulder where he stood relaxed, like a friend who had just popped in for a visit. This time he was the one who pretended to close his eyes, but I was onto him. I could see a hint of blue as he squinted at me out of the corner of his left eye. I noticed, for the first time, that there was a slight reddish tint to his feathers. He lifted his head up when the music faded out and was replaced by the upbeat voice of a radio announcer.

"Welcome back. This is JJ. Joyce Jamieson. And that was U2 singing their internationally acclaimed hit song, *Sunday Bloody Sunday* on W3NY, New York's favorite alternative music station."

A few bars of dramatic solo trumpet music blasted in, followed by the pre-recorded voice of a male announcer: "This is a W3NY News Alert."

Joyce Jamieson took up where the pre-recorded alert notice left off.

"Police are still searching for four teenage gang members suspected of gunning down a member of the rival Scars gang in a battle over turf last week. The four, three males and one female are thought to be members of one of New York's fast-growing street gangs, the Crows. They are alleged to have shot and seriously wounded a 17-year-old male Scar in a drive-by shooting early yesterday morning. The suspects were last seen driving a stolen 2007 Toyota Camry north of the city. Police are asking witnesses to come forward as they fear an escalation in violence if the alleged killers are not apprehended quickly."

"Stupid bastards," I shouted to myself. "Bongo's been itching for a showdown with the Scars, but this. And then coming here!"

A cold feeling ran through me as the thought of the intrusion at the cabin earlier flashed into my mind. I dismissed it just as quickly, not wanting to deal with any such reality. I already had enough on my plate: I was still a prisoner, even though I had been sent to do time on my grandparents' farm. And I was a prisoner of my heart, thanks to Jane Calloway.

Paddy stayed on my shoulder until we heard a vehicle pulling up to the farmhouse a few minutes later; he then flew back to perch on one of the rafters, freeing me to look out the window. I could hear muffled voices as Poppy and Gran got out of a delivery van that I remembered seeing earlier outside the Saulters' house. The colorful bowl-and-chopsticks display on the van's roof was a dead giveaway: it definitely belonged to Hiro Hasimoto's Restaurant. I cupped my ear to eavesdrop on their conversation.

"We appreciate your kindness, Hiro. You're a great neighbor to have around," I heard Poppy say.

"My preazure!" Hiro replied.

I waited until Poppy and Gran were inside the house before saying goodnight to Paddy, sealing it with my customary low-pitched caws. He waited until I had closed the door behind me and cawed three times in matching low tone.

Chapter 17

POPPY AND GRAN WERE DRIVING THEIR ROCKING CHAIRS to nowhere in front of the fireplace when I got home. A lone log was smoldering in the hearth.

"Welcome home, Danny. You're back safe and sound, I see. It's too bad you had to leave early. You missed some great music. And your grandfather was in fine fettle. Not one missed or swallowed note."

"You just didn't notice," he said with a wink.

I plunked myself down on the sheepskin rug between them.

"We heard you playing *Ole Tom Mullins Jig* as we drove off, Poppy. Jane told me you wrote it. It was real cool."

"Oh, I don't know about that, but thanks anyway. I think I should have written a simpler version. I put in a few tricky parts that are still quite a challenge for me at my level of playing. Believe it or not, I tend to tense up just before I get to them."

"Well I never noticed and I bet no one else did."

"My offer's still open if you want me to teach you what I can on the fiddle."

"Maybe one day soon," I said. "I don't want to say yes and not mean it."

"That's a good answer," Gran said. "No sense pursuing something if you're not committed to the end goal, is there?"

"Before we put our heads down for the night," Poppy said. His smile was gone. "There are a couple of things we need to address with you, Danny."

I felt my tummy muscles tighten up.

"I hope it's nothing serious."

"Nothing to get your drawers in a knot about," Gran said. "First off, we love it that you're here. You are helping to fill an awful void in our lives that we've felt ever since Maire left."

Poppy leaned over and stoked the dying log. It came back to life.

"Gran and I are happy to see you trying to settle into a place that's very different from the one you left behind."

"The trouble is," Gran said, "you tend to keep your feelings to yourself. We're not sure whether you feel the same way we do – about wanting to be here, I mean."

I chose my words carefully before answering.

"To be honest, I miss the city sometimes. I know I have to make it work here to avoid doing time, so I'm doing my best to stay away from trouble."

"Remember what I told you before about trouble," Gran said. "It can easily find you despite your best intentions. That's why you have to always be on your guard. As my mother and her mother before her used to say, 'Show me your company and I will show you who you are.'"

"Is this what you really wanted to talk to me about?"

Poppy and Gran looked at each other and she nodded to him. He bit the bottom of his lip before continuing.

"I don't want to make things bigger than they need be, but it looks like you've found yourself a few enemies in the short time you've been here. Through no fault of your own, I might add."

Poppy adjusted the fireplace draft to draw more smoke up the chimney.

"You mean Wade Simmons and Billy Cross."

"Wade certainly. Billy not so much. I was thinking of Abe Calloway. He stopped by the barbecue twice tonight. Once, just after you left, then just as we were leaving. He was looking for you and Jane. The first time he was alone. The second time, the other two brats were with him."

"Jane and I saw the three of them together on the back road around nine, but we managed to stay out of sight."

Gran nodded. "Thank God for that. No sense butting heads with Abe again. Where's Jane anyway?"

"I talked her into going home. I guess I made her see that she didn't have much of a choice. She would like to run away but, as she told me, she'd only be running away from his words. He's never hit her or anything."

Poppy stoked the log with the poker again and it broke into pieces.

"That was a smart decision, Danny," he said.

"I sure hope so, but I have no idea what else to do. Her dad's the one with the problem. His imagination is in four-wheel overdrive. I'm trying hard not to hate him. Jane and I aren't doing anything -- except hanging out."

"Keep trying with the no-hating bit," Gran encouraged. "Hate only breeds more of the same and solves nothing."

"Maybe I should have a chat with his pastor to see if he can do anything to get through that thick skull of his," Poppy said.

"Just don't hold your breath," Gran cautioned. "They're both cut from the same cloth, *and* they probably think us Mahoneys are all damned to the fires of hell because we're not *saved*."

"All I know is Jane doesn't deserve to be treated the way he treats her."

"Unfortunately, she does have to try and respect his rules as long as she's living under the same roof," Poppy conceded.

"Could she stay here?" I pleaded.

"That would only make things worse for everyone, I think," Gran cautioned.

"Let's all sleep on it," Poppy said. "Nothing beats the light of day."

I stood up and started walking towards the basement stairs. I stopped half way and turned when a thought struck me.

"I've been thinking about a couple of things myself. Since I took Paddy home, I thought about keeping him as a pet. But then I got to thinking about Mom in jail and what it must be like to be behind bars day after day. It made me think about setting Paddy free before I drive down to see her."

They both nodded agreement.

"Would you like us to go with you?" Poppy asked.

"If you don't mind, I need to do this by myself."

"We understand."

Gran, as cautious as ever, added, "Just promise us one thing."

I nodded.

"Promise you won't be too disappointed if she refuses to see you, too."

I nodded again.

"We'll have to run this by the court first, Danny," Poppy said. "Your going on your own I mean. I'll call and see if I can get Judge Fisher's okay directly."

"Yeah, I figured as much. I'm still under farm arrest, aren't I?"

Gran exchanged glances with Poppy, and then looked me squarely in the eyes.

"Well that may be so as far as the court is concerned, Mr. Daniel Cagney. But, your grandfather and I have been hoping you will wake up one morning and discover here the space you need to be who you really..."

She stopped herself in mid-sentence and shook her head, "Oh, dear, I didn't mean to sound so, so..."

"Pedantic or school-marmish?" Poppy chimed in. He laughed. "You slipped back into your old classroom head for a moment there."

"No, I didn't, did I? Hmm, yes, I suppose I did." She laughed.

Right then, a warm shiver shot up my spine and whispered a simple message to me. I felt that Gran and Poppy knew what the whisperer was saying. I just shook my head in quiet denial.

We exchanged goodnights and I began making my way downstairs to bed. By the time I reached the third step, Paddy flew through my mind. I wondered if he had been receiving similar "feeling right at home" messages, too.

"I'll go ask him in a minute," I thought.

As soon as I heard Poppy and Gran shuffle upstairs to bed, I sneaked out to see Paddy, the only crow I now cared about.

• • •

When I switched on the shed light, my mouth dropped open. Paddy was nowhere in sight. I knew that I had left his cage door open to allow him to come and go freely, but I had expected to see him in such a small building. The only sounds I heard were my own footsteps, my breathing, the movement of objects that I pushed out of the way to see if he were hiding behind them, and Paddy's cawing, which sounded only in my headspace.

"Where are you, Paddy? Where the hell are you?"

After a few seconds that seemed more like minutes to me, I heard a gentle *rap-a-tap-tap, rap-a-tap-tap* on the windowpane. Paddy was perched outside on the sill, grappling with a triangular piece of glass that lay half in and half out of its mooring in the frame. I recalled noticing that crack the first day Paddy arrived in the tool shed. I imagined that he had managed to push the top of it forward with his beak and escape through the opening. He now seemed bent on making his way back in with less effort by making the entry larger. He succeeded with one last tug of his beak and the shard of unwanted glass crashed to the ground outside. Satisfied with his accomplishment, he poked his head in through the opening, fixed his eyes squarely on mine, and cawed twice. The rest of him followed and he hopped onto my shoulder and cawed twice again. I cawed back.

I reached into my pocket, being careful not to startle him. I took out a bag of Trail Mix and scooped up a handful of nuts and raisins. I presented them to him on my opened palm, a little wary that he might prick me with his pointed beak since I was not wearing a glove for protection. I need not have worried, however, because he dined on his prize with the deliberate, appreciative savoring of a gourmet -- one tasty morsel at a time.

I was filled with a feeling of joy as I realized that Paddy was bonding with me and, maybe, had forgiven me for wounding him at Paddington Pond.

"Caw…caw," he said.

"Caw...caw," I replied. I could have sworn on a bible that he was smiling at me and that he had a mischievous twinkle in his eyes.

I imagined that Paddy had decided that there was no need to patch up the opening in the broken glass. After all, he now seemed fit enough to come and go -- or leave for good -- as he pleased. That thought made me feel sad.

"You and I have a way out, if we want it, Paddy, don't we? You the window, me the gate."

Then the open window in Judge Fisher's stifling hot courtroom flew into my mind. I saw the Crows on the lawn, cawing and cheering me on. I saw the judge's gavel pounding hard on the bench. And I saw my doppelganger hanging by his fingertips from a wood beam of the courtroom's ceiling, before dropping to the floor and making a mad dash for the open window to join *his* once fellow Crows. When he pulled himself up onto the sill, the window dissolved into bars of steel and all the Crows were behind them -- *including me*.

Chapter 18

I FINISHED MY CHORES in record time the next morning because I wanted to be home when Jane phoned. Poppy had a breakfast meeting in town with his lawyer and took off as soon as we had checked on the cattle in the upper fields. I rushed into the kitchen and placed two full baskets of fresh eggs on the table.

"Any calls, Gran?"

She peeked over her eyeglasses at me like a cross schoolteacher.

"That's an impossible question to answer, young man, without so much as a 'how do you do' to your grandmother while you're traipsing cow dung all over the floor I've just cleaned and polished."

"Sorry. I wasn't thinking. Morning."

"Well, that's a start."

I retraced my footsteps and removed my boots on the back porch and left them there. I walked back to the kitchen in my socks.

"If by calls, you mean Jane Calloway, then no, she hasn't phoned yet. Why don't you wash up and I'll have breakfast on the table for you in about 15? Jane will probably ring soon."

"I'm not hungry, Gran. Really."

"Nonsense. You need to fuel your body after all your hard work this morning."

I washed and changed before sitting down to pick at my food. The portable phone was lying on the table near a mug of coffee. I stared at the phone, daring it to ring.

"Gran? Does the lawyer Poppy's seeing in town have anything to do with…with me?"

"Heaven no, Danny. Why would you think that? We have some legal work to do with our property line. We've got a usufruct problem."

"A usu what?"

"…fruct. Usufruct. Our lawyer said it means the right of passage on someone's land for enjoyment or profit. It seems there was once an old cart road running through our property from here down to Paddington Pond and thereabouts."

"I saw traces of it when I was out riding with Jane. There are still some flat stones on some parts of it, enough to make out that it was once a wagon road."

"That'd be the one. Well, some of the locals still trek along it when they're out hunting. Your grandfather doesn't object to them being there as long as they don't mistake our cattle for deer, which more than one nervous city-bred nitwit has done over the years. He just wants to make sure we're not liable if someone gets hurt, particularly when our bull is hell-bent on mating. If we're liable, we'll have to erect a fence on both sides of the trail. And that would be one costly and time-consuming undertaking we don't need after the recent jumps in feed and fuel prices."

I was just about to pierce the yolk of my poached egg with my fork when the phone rang. I picked it up before the second ring had ended.

"Jane?"

"No, it's not Jane, asshole," Wade Simmons snarled. "I'm just calling to say that I have a nice present for you and I'm going to give it to you when you're least expecting it. That is if Jane's old man doesn't get his fucking hands on you first."

The line went dead before I had a chance to respond.

"What is it, Danny?" Gran asked.

"It was Wade Simmons, threatening me again. He said Jane's father is after me, too."

"I'm going to phone Tyler at the lawyer's. We're going to have to put a stop to those bullies before someone gets seriously hurt."

"Could you do something for me before you call, Gran?"

Her smile told me she would.

"Call Jane for me. You have a better chance of getting through than I do."

"Do you know her number to save me looking it up?"

I shook my head.

"No worries. I'll get it."

Gran found the number in her personal phone book and called it. She covered the mouthpiece and whispered to me. "We're in luck. It's Martha, Jane's mum."

She uncovered the mouthpiece. "Martha, it's Lee-Ann. Lee-Ann Mahoney."

Although Mrs. Calloway was whispering, I could hear her voice clearly because Gran had pressed the speaker button on the handset. Intentionally or unintentionally, I can't say.

"Hang on a minute, Lee-Ann. Abe's just leaving, and I don't want him to hear us yapping."

The next few seconds seemed like ridiculously long minutes as we waited anxiously for Mrs. Calloway to return to the phone.

"He's gone to town," she said, still whispering, as if she were afraid he might hear her above the roar of the engine as he drove away. "I'm sure I know why you are calling. It's about our Jane and your grandson, is it not?"

"It's more than that I'm afraid, Martha. It seems Danny is being threatened not only by Abe, but by Wade Simmons as well."

"Why does that not surprise me? Wade is a problem kid, I know. Jane wants nothing to do with him or his friends, but they just won't stay away. The trouble is Abe has taken a shine to the boy and he's blinded to anything he does or says."

"So then, what are we going to do about Jane and Danny?" Gran asked politely. "Neither of them deserves to be treated this way."

"I know, Lee-Ann, but I am quite powerless when it comes to Abe. He lays down the law around here. I tried to speak to him when he got home last night, but all I managed to do was convince him not to bother Jane as she had already gone to bed. He said he would speak to her in the morning."

"And did he?"

"If you call a shouting match speaking when Jane threatened to leave home."

"We have to find a solution," Gran said. "As I said before, I don't want anyone getting hurt. Where's Jane now?"

"She hiked on over to Paddington Pond after chores. To sort things out, she said."

I didn't wait for the rest of the conversation. I exchanged waves with Gran and rushed to the porch to get my boots, then to the barn to saddle up Jessie. Milah, who had been sleeping outside Jessie's stall, decided to come with us and lead the way.

I rode to Paddington Pond as fast as I dared. As I passed Jane's reading tree, I looked up, half-hoping that she would jump down from it again, but she wasn't there. When I arrived at Paddington Pond, I saw no sign that anyone had been there that morning either. No footprints. No hoof prints. No Jane.

"Where is she, Milah? Where's Jane?"

Milah nodded her head and barked.

"Follow me," she seemed to be suggesting.

I tugged on Jessie's reins and pointed her nose after Milah. Overhead, a murder was flying in the same direction. I recalled reading that crows had a symbiotic relationship with wolves; the latter were known to follow the crows' cawing to deer hiding miles away in the woods. The crows feed on their remains after the wolves have eaten their fill, following the kill. I wondered if they were now leading me to one I held dear, or into a trap in which I, myself, would become the prey of two species of human predators: *Noburgers and/or Crows*.

When I arrived, the clearing was eerily quiet, except for the occasional calls of whippoorwills. Their calls sounded a lot like their name, "Whip-poor-will...Whip-poor-will...Whip-poor-will."

One crow was perched stoically on a branch of a maple, its black body superimposed against a flourish of yellow leaves that were starting to free-fall to the forest floor. I realized it was Paddy, himself, when I recognized the distinctive white marking on his neck.

"Caw, caw, caw, caw" he warned as he swooped from the tree towards me. He flew so close to my head as he passed that the air he displaced made my hair quiver.

"Caw, caw," I called after him. He disappeared into a thicket.

"Caw, caw, caw," came another reply from the cabin porch. Milah stopped in her tracks, growled, then barked.

The Crows tag I had spotted at the cabin earlier flashed into my mind and I felt uneasy. I turned to face the cabin, anticipating the sight of Bongo and his Crows, and a one-way ticket back to juvie court.

"Caw…caw…caw," the human caller taunted again.

Other members of his human murder joined in, but none of them turned out to be a member of the Crow gang; they were the local species of troublemakers in the form of Wade Simmons, Billy Cross, and a third guy. Billy, as usual, was stuck to Simmons's side like cow dung and grass. The two glared up at me from the porch. The third guy turned out to be Pauly Pendleton. He stood bare-chested in the door well, hanging onto one end of a taut rope with his right hand, while picking snot from his big nose with the crooked index finger of his left. A good six inches taller than Wade Simmons, he had a body-builder's chest and biceps, and a "six pack" abdomen to boot.

"You don't look happy to see us, prick-face," Simmons mocked. "What you think, Billy?"

Billy shrugged and walked a few steps away and stood beside three dirt motorbikes that were resting on their stands.

"What're you doing here, Simmons?" I asked.

"What's it to you? You ain't got no special rights to this place. Nobody lives here no more."

"What do you want?"

"You got lucky in town. But that won't happen again, will it Billy?"

Again, Billy shrugged his shoulders.

"Billy's the quiet type," Simmons said. "But Pauly there makes up for it. Show him what you caught in the woods, Pauly."

Pauly tugged on the rope and pulled Jane into the doorway; its other end was looped around her neck. Her mouth was duct-taped and her hands were tied behind her back. I could not be sure if her eyes were pleading with me to leave while I could, or to do something miraculous to free her.

I decided on the miraculous, despite the two-and-a-half-to-one odds. But, when I made a move to dismount, Pauly tugged harder on the rope with one hand while grabbing Jane's hair in his other. She tried to say something, but the duct tape refused to let her words pass. Meanwhile, Milah was growling and barking and snapping at Pauly's legs.

"Better stay on your horse and take your dog with you, asshole!" Pauly warned. "But, don't worry, we'll take good care of Lady Jane here after you're gone."

He released Jane's hair and began fondling one of her breasts. She tried to kick him to make him stop, but she was too close to deliver enough power to her leg.

"Get your filthy hands off her," I shouted, inching Jessie forward.

"Or you'll what exactly?" Pauly taunted.

Surprisingly, Simmons piped in. "Let go of her!" he ordered. "She's not part of the deal. And take that rope off her."

"Fuck you," Pauly spat back, moving his hand to Jane's other breast. "You can have her when I'm done with her. Billy can get sloppy thirds."

Billy lowered his head in either shame or shyness, I couldn't tell which.

"I said let her go," Simmons ordered again. He took a step towards Pauly.

"Make me."

Pauly shoved Jane hard to the ground. As the rope slipped through his fingers, he cocked his huge fist and fired it at Simmons's head, knocking him backwards.

Jane saw her opening the moment I saw mine. She scrambled to her feet, while I nudged Jessie even closer to the action. Pauly was stooped over Simmons with both fists clenched while a scared-looking Billy stood motionless behind him. As Jane's half-crouched form stumbled towards me, her arms still tied behind her, she managed to side-swipe Billy with her shoulder, knocking him off balance and into the back of Pauly, who toppled like freshly-chopped timber onto Simmons, who was too stunned to protest.

Billy managed to stop his own teeter tottering, but then, just as quickly, he slipped and fell right on top of Pauly.

"Get the fuck offa me!" Pauly screamed.

Billy looked terrified as he tried to untangle his limbs from those of Pauly who was now engaged in a snarling match with a yapping Milah. And I could see the fear of being pecked in Simmons's eyes, as he flailed his arms in the air at Paddy who flew in close circles around his head, cawing at him to yield.

By the time she had reached Jessie, Jane had managed to free her bound hands. She then removed the tape from her mouth, just as Paddy dropped a poop bomb on Pauly's forehead with the pinpoint accuracy of a modern-day bomber pilot.

Taking advantage of the chaos on the ground, I reached down, grabbed one of Jane's hands in one of mine, and swung her up onto Jessie's back behind me. She wrapped her arms snugly around my waist.

"Let's get the hell out of here!" she shouted.

I dug my heels into Jessie's sides and directed her towards a narrow trail at the edge of the clearing, but not before taking one last look at the distraught trio lying on the ground. It would have been a funny scene were it not for the pain and humiliation they had inflicted on Jane to get at me.

Pauly pushed Billy off him and screamed after me, as he wiped bird poop from his forehead with his fingers.

"You're dead, Cagney. You're dead, dead, dead, you fucking bastard!"

Neither Jane nor I bothered to reply and didn't say another word until we had put a half-mile or so between the cabin and us. Paddy flew escort above us while Milah scouted ahead.

"Better give Jessie a rest," Jane suggested. "Horses have been known to run until they drop stone dead."

I heeded her advice and slowed Jessie to a walk until we reached a hill covered by a bed of dying wild blueberries. The muffled sound of revving dirt bike engines in the distance reached our ears and we stopped to look back.

"Look!" Jane cried. "It's Old Tom's. They've set fire to it."

Thick black smoke filled the sky above the clearing and we could see flames dancing across the roof of the cabin while three figures sat on motorcycles, watching the show.

Maybe we should go back." Jane said.

"It's too late for that," I replied. "It won't take long for it to burn to ashes. They probably torched it to destroy any evidence of what they did to you."

"We should report it."

"Who to? The sheriff? He's not going to believe us over his son? I'll tell my grandparents. They'll know what to do."

"Let's get going then. But we'd better walk," Jane added with downcast eyes. "I think Jessie's sprung a limp in her leg."

We dismounted to examine Jessie. She didn't protest as Jane lifted one of her hooves and carefully removed a stone that had lodged itself inside the shoe. Then Jane massaged Jessie's limb gently.

"There you go, beautiful lady," Jane said as she wove her palms expertly into Jessie's muscles and tendons.

Jessie whinnied her appreciation and we began our slow trek back on foot to the farm. Overhead, dark clouds began to steal what was left of the once sunny morning. Gulls circled the sky far below them. I had one hand on the reins and the other on Jane's hand. Paddy flew onto my shoulder.

"Look at all the seagulls," I exclaimed.

"They're herring gulls," she said. You can always tell them by their grey backs and wings, and their black wingtips with white spots. You can't see their legs right now, but they're usually pink. They're telling us we're in for another thunderstorm."

"Their legs?"

"No, silly. Because they're flying so low, picking off insects. When they act that way, it signals a low air pressure area where insects gather. Rain starts falling soon after the gulls start feeding."

All of a sudden, Jane went pale and she started shivering.

"What's wrong," I asked. "You're shaking."

"It just hit me, I mean what could have happened to me back there. Pauly was going to…to rape me, wasn't he?"

We stopped walking. I pulled her close to me and hugged her.

"Let it out," I whispered. "Let it all out."

Tears rolled slowly down her cheeks. Then she started to cry.

I cried in my heart, without tears. I cried for Jane, for Mom, and for the loss of Old Tom's cabin, where I had just begun to feel a little bit more at home.

Chapter 19

JANE HAD NO MORE TEARS to shed by the time we reached the puddle-filled farmyard an hour or so later. I was the first to notice the sheriff's car parked close to the house, its red lights flashing. Milah was barking angrily at Wade and Pauly who were standing still like statues near Billy in front of the sheriff's car. Sheriff Simmons was on the porch talking to Poppy who was half listening while he spoke on the phone. Gran stood quietly beside him.

A tall man with a square jaw and a thick moustache, the sheriff had Wade's eyes and nose. He wore a long, clear plastic raincoat over his cap and uniform of green and gold. He pulled his revolver from its holster when he spied Jane and me. Then he pointed its barrel directly at me. I froze.

"Daniel Cagney. You're under arrest for arson and criminal trespassing. You have the right to remain silent. Anything you say or do can and will be held against you in a court of law. You have the right to speak to an attorney. If you cannot afford an attorney, the court will appoint one for you. Do you understand these rights as they have been read to you?"

Jane looked at me and opened her mouth to say something, but she was gasping and shaking so much that the words would not come out. I squeezed her hand to reassure her.

"It's okay," I whispered. "You don't have to say anything unless you want to."

"Hold on there, Edgar. I just spoke to John Boyd and he said to lay off Danny until you get a warrant from Judge Peters. He's on his way to see him right now to protect Danny's rights. And, by the way, he may ask the judge to withdraw you from the case because your son, Wade, is one of the complainants. If you persist without a warrant, I've instructed John to launch a civil suit against you, personally, on Danny's behalf."

"That shyster, Boyd is always putting his nose where it don't belong. I don't give a shit what he told you. I'm bringing the boy in."

Poppy took a few quick steps forward and stood between the sheriff and me.

"Go right ahead," he said. "But I'll bankrupt you and your family, if you do. And guess what, the law will be on my side. As for Danny, I'm going to ask him to accompany me to see the judge. Between now and then, I suggest you separate those three liars there and get to the bottom of this."

"Why are they're lying and not your grandson?"

"I know Danny. He loved that old cabin too much to burn it down. What's more, isn't it a bit strange that Pauly has what looks to me like soot on his boots, scorch marks on his jeans and stinks like an oil refinery, while Danny's don't? Oh, and as for the criminal trespass charge, that won't hold water in court."

He took a step back and said, "And just how the hell do you figure that?"

"Because the cabin lease expired when Old Tom died and the land reverted back to me, its rightful owner. So, if anything, I could charge those three with trespassing for starters. And I'm sure my insurance company will be interested in what I just told you. That lot could even be charged with making false statements."

The sheriff glanced at the three boys and, in that moment, I knew that he knew retreat was his only option. They lowered their heads and he lowered his revolver.

"Get your asses in the back of that bloody patrol car," he ordered as he holstered his revolver. "We've got some serious jawing to do. And not a bloody word out of any of you unless I say so."

Wade protested, "But Pops?"

"Don't you *Pops me*," he shot back. "Right now you are not my son until I say so. You are a material witness in an alleged crime you reported."

When the boys had plunked themselves down in the back seat of the police car, the sheriff looked at Poppy.

"Looks like I won't be back unless they stick to their story, Tyler. Sorry for the bother," he added, looking at me. "No hard feelings. I was only doing my job, son."

I couldn't help myself. I raised my index finger at him and made sure the boys got some of it. "I'm not your son," I said. "You'll do your job when you get your facts straight."

The sheriff looked at Gran for comfort, but when he found none, he simply tipped his hat and said "Ma'am." He then turned on his heels and made for his car.

As the sheriff pulled slowly away from the house, Paddy flew over the car. He dropped a generous plop of creamy white bird shit on the windshield.

"I think Paddy is saying *poop on you* to the sheriff," Poppy said.

He and Gran laughed at the thought of a young crow standing up to Sheriff "High and Mighty." Jane and I didn't join in.

Chapter 20

GRAN AND JANE WERE DRIVING a pair of weather-beaten rocking chairs to clarity on the balcony while Poppy and I leaned against a corral fence, dealing with my situation.

"Why do you keep on believing in me?" I asked. "Because I'm your blood?"

"Maybe I know you better than you give me credit for," he answered.

"Well, now that you know the real story, are you surprised that Jane didn't speak up when she had the chance?"

"She'll open up when she's good and ready."

I looked over at the balcony and saw Gran stroking Jane's hair. Poppy's eyes followed mine.

"Looks like Gran's special touch is working on her."

"Well now, that doesn't surprise me."

"Me, neither. I think I'll go check in on Paddy."

• • •

Paddy echoed my cawing when I entered the shed. He flew onto my shoulder to grab the peanut I had placed there for him.

"Hey, Paddy, me boy. How're you doing?"

He stared at me and blinked. Then he walked behind my neck to my other shoulder.

"Looking for another peanut, are you?"

"Caw."

"Sorry, I'm all out."

I stretched out one of my arms as far as it would go and then uncurled my index finger to see what he would do. He studied the finger for a few moments and then flew to it to perch there quietly as if it were the branch of a tree. As I watched him, the thought of Mom lying in her prison cell flashed through my mind and I wondered what she was thinking about. Her voice in my head was saying, "When are you coming to see me, Danny? I miss you."

I answered with a decision to do two things. I would go to see Mom on Monday and I would not wait for Paddy to leave the shed for good through the opening in the broken window. I would take him to Paddington Pond to reunite him with his family after I got back from the detention center.

"Hey stranger," the voice behind me declared. "You trying to get away from me?"

"Never," I replied and turned to see Jane standing there. "You okay?"

"Better. I was pretty shook up, but your granny and I had a heart-to-heart. She's good comfort. How about you? You look down."

"I'm pissed about what happened to you and I'm feeling bad having to let Paddy go."

Jane stroked Paddy's back gently with her middle finger.

"Why don't you just keep both of us?"

"You I'm never going to let go. But, it'll be time to release him soon. Maybe the day I go to see my mother."

"Can I go with you?"

"You can come for the company, but they only let family in. You'll have to wait in the car. Before we can go, Poppy has to contact the judge to get her permission because I'm under farm arrest. I'm supposed to stay in the county."

"Maybe I should contact the judge myself and thank her for her wise decision in jailing you so close to me."

We both laughed, but Paddy must have thought what she said wasn't very funny because he flew off my still outstretched finger to a favorite rafter of his, above our heads.

"Danny, you never told me why you were arrested," Jane said. "What did you do exactly?"

"You really want to know?"

She nodded.

"Nothing. I took the rap for one of the gang. I was charged with stealing an old lady's purse and assaulting her. I was there for sure, but I didn't know anything was going down until this stupid bastard, one of the gang, knocked her down. He grabbed the woman's purse and ran. I made the mistake of picking her up to see if she was okay. Then a cop saw me and I made another mistake: I ran. He spotted me the next day as I was coming out of McDonalds munching on a burger. He pushed the burger into my face and handcuffed me."

"Did you tell the judge about the other guy?"

"Are you kidding? That would be ratting someone out. You don't do that in the 'hood."

"Well, if it's an honor thing, why didn't the guy who did it speak up and say he did it?"

"Sammy the Wham Bang? That would take courage and that's something someone like him never had."

"So, let me see if I can get this straight. You take the rap for a big coward like Sammy the Whammer, or whatever the stupid twit's name is, and he's laughing at you behind your back for being a big sucker?"

"Well that's just the way it is."

"Well then, please tell me just one thing. Would he have taken the rap for you?"

My unsure look was all she needed for an answer.

"Then, I rest my case, Your Honor. *This twit* is definitely guilty. Guilty of being stupid in the first degree."

When I tried to put my arm around her shoulder, she shrugged me off.

"Not now, sucker. Right now, I am so angry with you, I could scratch your bloody eyes out. How could you even think to stay loyal to a creep like that?"

She took a deep breath. "I better get on home."

"I'll drive you."

• • •

Jane and I drove in silence until we reached our agreed-upon drop-off point at a bend in the road, a quarter of a mile or so before her house. She leaned over and kissed me on the lips before getting out.

"I thought you were mad at me," I said.

"Oh, I'm still mad at you. Really mad. I'm still crazy about you, too, but you're still a twit for getting yourself into such a mess, with a record and all."

"What're we going to do about the fair tomorrow?"

"How about I meet you in front of the shooting gallery around noon? My dad won't be there that early because he'll be doing some repairs at the church. It's his annual turn to pitch in."

"It's a deal," I replied, blowing her a kiss. "See you."

"See you, sucker," she said, making sure to stress the word "sucker."

I watched after her as she walked away. Before disappearing around the bend in the road, she raised a hand in the air and waved without looking back, just to let me know that she knew I couldn't keep my eyes off her.

Chapter 21

THE FAIRGROUND was jam-packed with people of all ages when I arrived on Saturday. I paid my eight-dollar entry fee and an elderly woman stamped the back of my hands. She was wearing a black, embroidered cowgirl's shirt with fringed pockets, black jeans, and a white Stetson hat with a snakeskin band circling its brim.

"Show your stamp whenever a fair official says *hands up*," she ordered. "You can come and go as you please and there's no charge for re-entry, if you have to leave for a spell."

"Thanks. Can you point me to the shooting gallery please?"

"You can't miss it. It's right next to the Ferris wheel. Follow the gunshots. Next please," she added, waving me on.

Jane was aiming a BB rifle at a moving target of metal ducks when I arrived at the shooting gallery. Pop pop pop went her rifle in quick succession and three ducks obliged by falling over. She did the same again to win a giant stuffed panda, which I just knew I was going to have to lug around for her all day.

"Line 'em up again," she ordered the middle-aged concessionaire. He wore a patch over his left eye.

"Not on your life," he replied, pointing to the sign: *Management reserves the right to admit players. Maximum of one prize per day per player.*

"Sharpshooters ain't welcome. You'll clean me out in no time."

"That's not fair," I protested.

"Life ain't fair, son," he replied, pointing to his patch. "I should know. I lost this in Afghanistan on the last day of my tour."

Jane took the panda from the man and handed it to me. Then, almost as quickly, she took it back and handed it to a little girl who was lined up for the Ferris wheel with her parents. She was decked out in cowgirl costume with toy six-guns in a holster hanging from her waist.

"Here, Sally," she said. "I won this for you. Would you like it?"

"Can I, Momma? Can I? Oh, can I, Daddy?"

Both parents smiled their approval and thanked Jane. Sally took the bear in her arms and hugged it.

"You'll have to leave that toy with us if you want to ride the wheel," we heard the ticket taker tell Sally as Jane and I made for the hot dog stand. "Or pay for an extra seat."

"That was a nice thing to do, Jane," I said.

"Not really. I go to at least two country fairs a year and I always win something. Another stuffed animal I don't need. I'm running out of room. Let's eat. I'm starved. Your treat."

We made our way through throngs of people who seemed to be coming or going from four different directions, After a few minutes, we ended up at Nini's Diner where we both ordered an all-dressed steamed hot dog and home-made spruce beer.

We sat down on a bench to eat. I had just bitten into an end of my foot-long when a hand grabbed my shoulder.

"You gonna share a piece of that dog?" the hand's owner said, as he plunked himself down next to me.

I recognized the tattoo of the black crow's head on the back of the speaker's hand and turned slowly to look up at him. His face was partially covered by a black hoodie.

"Hey, Karate," Bongo said, as he looked Jane up and down. "Who's the broad? Nice pins," he added, focusing on her legs.

Jane gave him another dirty look.

"Hey Bongo," I replied. "I heard on the radio you might be heading north. You guys have got yourselves in a shitload this time. New York and state cops are out for blood."

"That's why we're here. Hey, go take a piss somewhere," he ordered Jane. "I need to talk to your boyfriend here in private. And don't go saying anything to anyone about seeing me, if you know what's good for him."

Jane gave me a dirty look.

"Look, Jane. I'll catch up with you in a few minutes. Meet me back at the shooting gallery. Please!"

"Okay, but I just want to say one thing before I go. Why is it that all this loyalty talk falls on your shoulders? It's plain to see that all he cares about is himself."

"Beat it, bitch!" Bongo ordered.

She walked away, but turned her head a couple of times to look back.

Bongo sat down next to me.

"Here's the story. We need to hang a while before you sneak us across the border to Canada. She can come along, too, if she wants."

"Look, Bongo. You know I'm not even supposed to talk to you. They'll put me away for a year or more if I'm caught."

"Do you think I give two shits about you doing easy time? Your brothers and sister have caught a fucking attempted murder charge, and we need your help. We're talking life, man, not some nothing juvie rap. Remember, you swore an oath to the gang when you joined."

I stood up and glared at him. "Well now I'm unswearing it."

He stood up, too. He was so close that I could smell raw onions on his breath when he spoke.

"No, you ain't. Once a Crow always a Crow, you know that. And, if you don't help, I'll send the Western Union paper to the judge along with my cell phone record of our calls. You ain't got no choice."

I resisted the urge to correct his double negative.

"Here's the shit," Bongo added, pushing his body hard against mine to move me over. "We need some travel scratch. Aladdin, Sammy and Nipper are casing out the General Store in, what's the name of that hick town, Nobody Cares, or something like that. We're gonna knock it off just before closing Monday. Nipper overheard the owner tell the cashier that's when he banks the weekend take. The old asshole thinks it's safer than Sunday."

I gulped when I saw Sheriff Simmons's studying us in the distance. Wade and Pauly were standing near him.

"You better run," I said, looking down. "The sheriff's watching us."

"Meet us in town Monday at five-thirty. Bring wheels and don't be late."

Without saying another word, Bongo disappeared into the crowd. As for myself, I sat down and waited for Jane to come back. After a few moments, I saw the sheriff's boots first, and then Wade's and Pauly's. I looked up to see the rest of them looming over me.

"I see you've decided not to lay arson and making false statements charges against your son and his two sidekicks," I said.

He opened his mouth to say something, but all he could muster was, "I..." when a young boy ran up to him and shouted, "Sheriff come quick. A kid fell off one of the rides. He's badly hurt."

"Point the way, Bobby," he replied. Then he chased after him, barking an order at Wade and Pauly to follow.

"This'll find you later," Pauly threatened, clenching a fist to reinforce his point. "I'm really looking forward to it."

"So am I," I lied.

It was impossible to see the accident from where I was positioned. I learned later that the boy survived the ordeal with little more than a couple of broken bones and a few scratches.

• • •

I got up and walked over to the Ferris wheel. I watched it go around and around like the thoughts in my head. Jane put her arm around me and squeezed.

"Has your Crow boyfriend left you?" she quipped. "What didn't he want me to know about anyway?"

"Nothing."

"What do you take me for?"

"I'll tell you later," I said, hoping that that would satisfy her for the time being.

"Okay, but watch your back! Remember, your stupid Crows got you into this mess in the first place and you never even saw it coming, did you? They'll do it again, if you don't smarten up."

"Want to go on the roller coaster?" I asked to change the subject.

"Not really, I've had enough ups and downs for the day. I'm also peopled out. Let's get out of here."

I took her hand and we made for the gate.

"Leaving so soon?" the admissions lady said. "You'll miss the admissions draw and the chance to win a mountain bike."

Jane shrugged. "Que sera sera."

"There's my grandparents," I said.

We walked over to them as they approached the entrance gate. They were decked out in matching denim dungarees, red plaid shirts, and brown Western boots.

"Where are you two lovebirds off to?" Gran asked.

"We were feeling penned-in by the crowd," Jane said.

"We'll be back a little later maybe," I added, only half-believing my words.

"I hope so," Poppy said. "Maybe we'll all hunt up some grub together when you do."

"That'd be nice," Jane replied.

After we had gone a few paces, Poppy called to me and I turned to face him.

"Oh, Danny, I just got word from Judge Fisher. She's okayed a special visit for you to see your mum on Monday. There's just one catch. Because you're a minor, she is going to join you at the detention center. She wants to talk to both of you at the same time. You and your mum I mean. By the way, normal visiting days are Saturdays and Sundays, so she must have pulled some strings for you."

"Monday's when I take possession of Jake Saulter's truck. I had planned to leave right after doing the transfer.

"That works then."

I thanked him for making the arrangements. Then Jane and I took off on foot.

"That judge really likes to stick her nose in my life."

"Is that a bad thing?" Jane asked.

I shrugged and she didn't push it further.

"So what do you want to do now, Danny?"

"Go see Paddy, I guess. Then we can hang out."

When Jane and I arrived at the tool shed, I was sad to see that Paddy was not there. Despite my calls and caws, I couldn't find him anywhere. I looked throughout the day on Sunday, and again Monday morning after chores. I stopped searching when Jake and Judy drove by around seven in their Volkswagen Beetle.

"Judy and I are going to head off earlier than we planned," he said. She wants to do some shopping before we meet at the DMV, probably afterwards, too. I just wanted to make sure that the truck was running okay."

"Everything's perfect, Jake. Thanks."

When he drove off with Judy, he left me feeling grateful and trusted. He never charged me for that when he sold me the truck, I thought.

Chapter 22

JANE AND I HEADED OFF AFTER BREAKFAST to meet Jake at the DMV. This arrangement worked out well for us since Burlington was on our way to the detention center. As I was driving there, I couldn't stop thinking about Paddy and I wondered what he was up to.

After we made the transfer around 10:30, I thanked Jake again for the great deal.

"Be good to her, son," Jake beamed. "She's been right good to me and I'm happy to see she's found a decent home. Regular oil changes, rust-proofing and tune-ups are her survival secret."

After wishing us a good journey, he walked towards University Mall to meet Judy who had been shopping all morning.

"I really like that man, Jane. I'm glad our paths crossed. He's the real thing."

"He's always been that way ever since I can remember," Jane agreed. "He lights up every place he goes. Even my dad likes him from a distance in his quirky sort of way."

As I coaxed my "new" pick-up south along Dorset Street, I couldn't help grinning at the thought of Jane's dad actually liking someone with a darker skin than his. I made a legal U-turn onto Williston to give me easy access to I-89 South via the Montpelier ramp.

The web map I'd consulted on Poppy's MacBook before starting out that morning had promised me that the entire journey to Vermont's Southwest Correctional Facility would take a little more than another hour, traffic permitting. I used the time to talk to Jane about everything and anything except the robbery Bongo was planning after we got back. She played along with my game of distraction until we were almost within earshot of the detention center.

"Stop!" she ordered. "Now!"

I did as she said and pulled over to the curb.

"What's wrong?"

"Don't try to pull the wool over my eyes. You're holding something back. I can feel it. And, if you don't come clean, I'm going to get out here and hitchhike home."

"Look, Jane..."

"I'm waiting!"

"Okay, you win," I sighed. "Bongo and his gang are planning to knock over the Noburg General Store this evening and they want me to drive them across the border to Canada afterwards."

"What! No way! No effing way!!! They're going to rob the store and you're going to drive the getaway car? That'll make you equally guilty under the law. What if poor Mr. and Mrs. Cumber or Tessa get hurt, or worse, killed?"

"There's more."

She braced herself for more bad news.

"All of them are wanted for the drive-by shooting of a Scars gangbanger last week. They've been on the run ever since."

She smacked the dashboard hard with the palm of her hand.

"Oh, that's just great! You can even be charged for helping them get away. Aiding and abetting, I think it's called. You're going to be a very old man when you get out of prison, if ever. Just don't expect me to be waiting around for you when you get out. Stupid! Stupid! Stupid!!!"

She stopped talking and waited for a reply. When it didn't come, she lowered her voice and said, "What're *we* going to do?"

"I don't know. Can we talk about this on our way back? I need to get psyched up for my mom's visit."

I was expecting her to say something, but she simply sunk back into her seat and sulked. The next sounds I heard were three distinctive caws. Jane looked through the rear window of the truck's cab at the feathery object perched on top of a metal chest in the cargo area. I took my foot off the accelerator and let the pick-up crawl to a stop.

"It's Paddy! How on earth did he find us here?"

"Beats me," I replied. "I'm just as surprised as you are."

I reached up and pulled the sunroof window open.

"Caw...caw," I called to Paddy.

"Caw...caw," he echoed, as he flew through the sunroof opening and landed on my shoulder.

"That's incredible! He's definitely imprinted on you. I guess it takes one crow to know another."

Paddy cawed again when I preened the back of his head gently with my fingers.

"Do you mind bird-sitting him while I visit my mother?" I asked.

She said she wouldn't and we continued our journey.

It took us only about five more minutes to reach the visitors' parking lot on State Farm Road. I was surprised to see that the detention center was laid out more like a farm than a prison. After kissing Jane goodbye and exchanging caws with Paddy, I made my way to the reception area.

A burly, middle-aged female guard with tomboyish red hair asked me for photo i.d. and ran my name against the visitors log. The sign on a nearby wall shattered my early impression of being on a farm:

> *You are entering a correctional facility. All visitors and vehicles are subject to search by Department of Corrections' personnel. Bringing weapons, drugs or alcohol on to this property is a crime punishable by imprisonment, fine or both. Violators shall be prosecuted.*

"Okee-doakie, Mister Cagney. Everything seems to be in order. Judge Arlene Fisher is waiting for you in the next room. You'll have to stay with her at all times, seeing as you're a minor."

She handed me a small plastic tray and told me to deposit the contents of my pockets in it. I passed through the metal detector portal and was patted down by a sour-faced male guard. He handed me a visitor's badge and told me to pin it on.

"All clear," he said to the female guard who had already placed the tray inside a clear plastic pouch, which she then sealed.

"He's clean," the male guard said, pointing to a door. "Go through there. You'll get your belongings back on the way out, unless we decide to keep you, of course."

I didn't laugh at his jailhouse humor. He did.

Judge Fisher was sitting on a chair in the next room when I entered. She smiled and stood up when she saw me. I was surprised to see how short she was away from her courtroom perch, about five feet nothing I reckoned, maybe less. She reached out her hand to greet me like we were old friends. She had a strong grip.

"Hi, Daniel. How have you been doing since we last saw each other?"

"Okay, I guess," I replied, trying to avert her enquiring gaze.

"Your grandfather told me that you have been adapting well to life in the country. I envy you being away from the hectic hustle and bustle of city life."

"I miss it sometimes. The city I mean."

"And your friends, your Crow buddies? Do you miss them, too?"

I shrugged.

"You know, some of them are being sought by the police."

"Yeah, I heard on the radio the other night."

"They were last seen headed your way. I wondered what you would do if they contacted you."

"I wouldn't turn them in, if that's what you mean. I'm no rat."

"They nearly killed a young man in broad daylight. Isn't that a good reason to do the right thing?"

I shrugged again.

She opened her mouth to reply, but was interrupted by the sound of a buzzer and a metal door opening.

There she was in the flesh, holding a pitch-black cat in her arms: Maire Mahoney-Cagney, my mother, looking healthier than I could remember. She wore a drab-grey prisoner's smock. Her hair had returned to its natural brown color and was tied back in a ponytail.

She had put on much needed extra pounds in all the right places and the muscles on her arms told me that she'd been working out. She looked from the judge to me. Then she placed the cat down on the floor and it curled up at her feet. I was the first to break the long silence.

"Hi Mom. You look good."

She toyed with her hair. "You, too, Danny. God, how I've missed you."

She threw her arms around me and cried. I looked over at the judge, hoping that she'd say something to break the ice. She didn't disappoint me.

"Mrs. Cagney, I'm sorry to intrude. I'm Judge Arlene Fisher."

Mom pulled away from me and looked at her.

"The deputy warden told me you'd be here."

"I know. But, there's are things she couldn't tell you. Like the fact that I was the presiding judge at Daniel's juvenile court hearing and I've taken a special interest in his well-being. Since he's a minor, I arranged to be his guardian during this visit. However, I will try to give you as much privacy as I can without, of course, leaving the room."

Mom nodded her appreciation.

"I'll just sit over here out of your way."

The judge did her best to look invisible on her seat on the far side of the room while Mom and I did our best to pack in as much conversation as we could during our one-hour visit. Mom told me that her cat, Dolly, was her dearest friend at the detention center and that inmates had been caring for cats there since 1980. Of course, she wanted to hear all about me and I told her only the good stuff, like "the good life" on the farm. I also told her about Paddy and Jane.

"And what does Abe Calloway think of you dating his daughter?"

"He just *loves* the idea," I scoffed.

"That figures. He never had time for me while I was growing up. Free-spirited females were never his liking."

She asked me about the trouble I had gotten myself in. When I shared that I was taking the rap for someone else, she looked relieved.

"Show me your company and I'll show you who you are," she said.

I looked at her.

"Your great grandma Mahoney used to say that when I was going out with someone that she didn't care for. She never studied psychology, but she sure lived by her proverbs until the day she died."

"Show me your company and I'll show you who you are," I parroted. "Gran said the very same thing to me a couple of days ago."

"You'll probably say it to your own kids one day. It's hereditary."

She took my hand in hers and gave it a reassuring squeeze. Out of the corner of one eye, I could see the judge's face buried in a large book about American juvenile justice and alternative sentencing, leaving me with the impression that she was being true to her promise of giving us the space she'd promised.

"How much more time do you have to serve?"

"Believe it or not, Dolly and I get out Friday week. I just got word before you arrived that the judge in my case shaved my original sentence by a third for good behavior. Taking drug counseling and staying dry for 12 months played a part I guess. And Dolly was a great support, too, weren't you, Dolly?"

Dolly rubbed her body across my leg and meowed, as if to say, "Purr-yup, I did my part."

The electronic buzzer cut our laughter short. The steel door opened and the same guard who had body-searched me earlier told us that our time was up. I found it hard to believe that the hour had flown by so quickly. I promised Mom that I'd pick her up upon her release if the judge gave her approval.

She hugged me and then turned to face Judge Fisher.

"I heard that last part," the judge said. "Permission granted."

"Thank you," Mom said with a smile. "Not only for arranging today's visit, but for watching out for my boy."

The judge smiled back and wished Mom good luck. The guard then led Mom away before we were allowed to exit the room ourselves.

The judge walked me towards the pickup truck. She had a large envelope tucked under her arm. Before we reached the pickup, she stopped and touched my shoulder. I waited for her to speak.

"Whatever you've been doing, Daniel, you keep right on doing it, okay?"

I nodded.

She handed the envelope to me. I fumbled with it, wondering what was inside.

"This is for you," she said. "The deputy warden asked me to give it to you. It's your mother's journal about her life in detention. She wanted you to have it."

I thanked her.

When we reached my pickup, I introduced the judge to Jane and Paddy. I told her that I'd been caring for Paddy and why.

"Believe it or not, I'm not keeping him as a pet. I'm supposed to release him into the wild today."

"I believe you. Besides, he doesn't look caged up to me."

She told us to be good to one another and then said good-bye. Paddy cawed twice, as if to wish her well on her journey. I shouted after her as she was leaving.

"Judge? Judge Fisher?"

She turned to face me.

"Thanks," I managed to say with some effort. So that she wouldn't think I was a total wuss, I added, "...for the card, and for today."

She smiled and turned towards her car, a Suzuki Grand Vitara, four by four, not much younger than my Toyota. I tucked Mom's journal away in the glove compartment and forgot about it for a couple of days. To be honest, I really didn't forget. I avoided reading it for as long as I could. I was afraid of what I would discover there.

On our way home, Jane pestered me with questions about my visit and the robbery the Crows were planning. As for Paddy, he cawed whenever she paused to take a breath.

"Why can't you just turn them in? All it takes is a simple phone call."

"The old crow in me won't let me do that."

"I figured as much. Well, I'll come by your place at four," she said. "You'd better have a good plan to stop your gang by then or this bird will blow the whistle on them, all by myself. Four generations of Cumbers have owned that store and I'll make sure Milton and Millie Cumber won't be the last."

I promised to try and come up with a good plan before we went our separate ways. Paddy and I got home about 15 minutes later. It had been one long day, so far.

Chapter 23

GRAN COULDN'T WAIT to hear all the news about my visit with Mom and I did my best to fill her in. When I told her that she would be released on Friday, next week, her eyes darted all around the living room looking for anything out of place. Then she began making plans for the grand homecoming.

"By the time Gran's done, we'll have to scrounge up a fatted calf, and a ring and a robe," Poppy said

"Oh, never mind him and his biblical scholarship."

They were pleased when I told them how well Mom looked and that she was thinking more clearly than she had in years.

"I really think Mom is determined to make it this time. Oh, and she has someone new in her life who has been helping her. She'll be released with her."

They looked at me with worry in their eyes.

"Relax," I laughed. "It's not a guy this time."

They looked at each other, wondering.

"Her name's Dolly. She's a beautiful black cat. Mom took care of her in jail."

"You," Gran said, stabbing her finger at me, laughing. "I'll get you back for that."

Poppy broke into a belly laugh. He looked happier than I'd ever seen him.

After our chat, Gran started to deliver on some of the many plans that had been popping in and out of her head since I first told her the good news. Poppy, as calm as ever, continued about his day in his usual fashion, but I could see more pep in his step thanks to the lifting of a heavy burden that he had been carrying far too long. Yes, he was happy his lost daughter was coming home and he was hopeful that better times were ahead for the whole family.

As for me, I wished that I had a plan of my own -- to deal with Bongo and the gang. I also wished I could conjure up some powerful words that would lighten my burden as magically as Poppy's had just been lightened by mine.

The conjuror I wished for appeared in the form of none other than lovely Jane Calloway. She arrived riding bareback on Goldie, thirty minutes earlier than she'd said she would, with no apology for being early. I could easily see that she didn't have any tricks up her sleeves because, in spite of the cool temperature, she was wearing a tight white T-shirt over black shorts. A black sweatshirt was knotted in front of her tummy by its sleeves.

Without as much as a "Hey, Danny," she ordered me to saddle up for what would be "the ride of my life." It was. I lusted after her every hoof beat of the way.

• • •

Jessie, Paddy and I chased Jane and Goldie along the trail until we reached a rocky area about a half-mile before Paddington Pond. We tethered the horses to the same pine sapling and sat down on boulders to face each other. I started to say something, but she stopped me.

"Shut up and listen up!"

Paddy cawed in response.

"I know you have this confused loyalty thing with *Bongo the Hood* and his not-so-merry creeps," Jane said, "but I don't. My loyalty is to two hard-working people, Milton and Millie

Cumber, and all the young people around here they give jobs to year after year, in good times and bad. So, with or without you, I'm gonna do everything in my power to stop them. If it's without you, then we're done, you and I, right here and now. The choice is yours, Danny. So, what's it going to be? Your ego or me?"

"Ego?"

"I mean looking good to your so-called friends."

"You know I don't want to see anyone hurt. It's just that I feel like I'm somewhere between a rock and a hard place. I took an oath to stay loyal to them. I told Bongo at the fair that I was breaking it, but I don't know if I meant it."

"All I can say to that is what I said to you before: *stupid, stupid, stupid!* I bet you didn't even tell your grandparents about the big mess you're in."

I shook my head.

"Well, make up your mind. Are you going to stop your *friends* or do I have to do it on my own?"

When I didn't answer, she hopped onto Goldie and started to ride towards town.

"Wait up!" I shouted. I'll go with you."

She kept her head low and looking forward as Goldie broke into a hard gallop towards town. A headwind was getting stronger by the minute, but it was not strong enough to slow her down.

Jessie and I did our best to catch up, but only Paddy was a match for Jane's faster Goldie. Jane was a good two hundred feet ahead of me when she reached town. She stopped there and waited until I caught up. Paddy circled the sky above her.

"You decided to do the right thing yet?" she asked.

"Yes. But, I still don't have a plan."

"I do."

She removed her cell phone from a side pocket of her shorts and dialed a number. I could hear the phone ringing.

"Is that you, *Simmons*?" she asked into the phone.

Paddy cawed angrily when he heard Wade's voice.

"Hey, Jane. I'm glad you called. I'm sorry about what happened at Old Tom's. I was so jealous and things got out of hand."

"It's too late for sorries, you lump of pig shit! I just want you to know that I'm in town with your replacement, Danny Cagney. We've been sitting around thinking what cowards and little dicks you, Billy and Pauly really are. And in about 15 minutes, I'm going to write what the three of you did to me at Old Tom's on the courthouse bulletin board. For everyone in the county to see in the *Noburg Chronicle*!"

"You can't do that! I said I was sorry."

She snapped the cell phone lid closed. Then she and I let our horses walk slowly towards the General Store. The wind was getter stronger and the temperature seemed to be dropping by the second as dark clouds began to move in and blot out the sun. Paddy didn't seem to be bothered by the changing weather. He flew up to the store's roof to keep vigil after we dismounted and tethered our horses to the store's hitching post.

"Why didn't you run your plan by me?" I asked.

"Because you wouldn't stop sitting on the fence."

She removed her sweatshirt from her waist and put it on.

"Hey, you don't have to stick around unless you want to, Danny. It's up to you."

I started to shiver before answering. I think that had more to do with my thoughts than the temperature.

"I don't know how you think this is going to play out, Jane, but we'll do it your way for now."

"Good. Wait here. I'll be back in a minute."

She disappeared into the store and returned a few minutes later with a black marker in her hand.

"You'll get arrested for doing that!"

"We'll see about that. I told Tessa to call the sheriff as soon as she sees me writing."

Jane looked at her watch.

"In about five or ten minutes. Tessa didn't want to get me in trouble, but I convinced her that it was important to me -- and *you*. I think the 'you' part convinced her to do it because her face lit up when I mentioned your name. I think she's got the hots for you."

I decided to ignore her last remark.

"I sure hope this all works out the way you think, Jane."

"So do I."

She made for the courthouse and I followed her. We waited out of sight behind the war memorial for a few minutes. A glass-encased bulletin board, announcing court in-session dates, stood next to the monument.

Paddy, who was now perched on top of the bulletin board, appeared to be reading the information written there upside down. Afterwards, he flew onto the hood of a Noburg town van that was parked on the street in front and then to the top of a Vermont State flagpole to keep watch.

My heart was pounding and, except for Jane's labored breathing and mine, the town was eerily quiet. Paddy broke the silence when he cawed a danger warning.

After several long and apprehensive minutes, we heard the roar of motorcycles getting louder as they approached the town center.

"We've got company," Jane warned. "Looks like all three of them."

I stayed a step behind her as she walked to the front of the bulletin board. She uncapped the marker and began printing large bold letters on the bulletin board's glass face. She then wrote the full names of Wade, Pauly and Billy below the message.

"Are you sure you..."

Her disapproving look cut me off.

Tessa was standing on the porch of the General Store. She nodded and mimed that she had made the requested call. Jane blew her a kiss just as Wade, Pauly and Billy wheeled their motorcycles into an alleyway two blocks east of the store. Their dying engines sputtered, coughed and then fell silent.

• • •

Nipper must've sneaked into town earlier. Like a cautious cat, she poked her head out of an alleyway next to the store to eyeball the street. She made an okay sign with a thumb and finger to signal "all clear" to her fellow Crows: Bongo, Aldo and Tommy. The three marched past her and made their way slowly to the front of the General Store. They looked about them for the slightest hint of danger.

• • •

As Jane's targets got closer to us, I heard Pauly say to Billy, "If you're such chicken shit, frig off home."

Billy hung his head in shame and retreated down a side street.

Pauly shouted after him, "Loser."

Wade and Pauly swaggered towards the bulletin board to read the message while Jane and I stayed out of sight. When they reached the board, Pauly placed a foot on the rear step of the still parked utility van to study the message while Wade stood beside him.

Pauly gritted his teeth and said, "Stupid bitch. I should've put the wood to her when I had the chance."

Wade glared at him and mumbled something I couldn't make out. Paddy answered him, however. He flew past him, landed on the bulletin board once again, and cawed furiously at him. Wade backed away. Paddy then appeared to be reading Jane's message upside down once again, as he walked back and forth:

WANTED
FOR ARSON OF OLD
TOM'S CABIN
AND ATTEMPTED
RAPE OF
JANE CALLOWAY:
**WADE SIMMONS
PAULY PENDLETON
BILLY CROSS**

The three Crows were only a few yards from the General Store when rain started to pour. A police car siren wailed in the distance and got increasingly louder as it got closer to town. The revving of Billy's departing motorcycle added to the mix.

On seeing the police car, the three Crows stopped in their tracks and disappeared down the alley after Nipper. I breathed a sign of relief knowing that the General Store would not be knocked off -- at least not tonight.

Sheriff Simmons pulled up in front of the courthouse just as his son, Wade, was wiping off the water-soluble marker ink from the glass with his jacket sleeve, aided by the fresh rain that had covered it.

"What're you doing?" the sheriff shouted.

"Just being a good citizen, Dad. Someone wrote graffiti on the sign. I'm just wiping it all off."

"Well it's gone now and so's the evidence with it. I got a dispatch that said Jane Calloway was defacing town property. Was that her work?"

Jane stepped out from behind the monument, with me on her heels. Wade and Pauly stared at her.

"I don't see any defaced property. Do you, Danny?"

"No." I took Jane by the arm and we started to walk away. "Let's go, Jane. We'll be late for supper."

Jane shouted back at the sheriff. "Shouldn't you be chasing those gang members the state police are looking for instead of hassling us?"

"I'll be watching you two," the sheriff said. "As for you, Wade, you better hightail it home quick like. Your mother's been looking for you all day. And don't you never have nothing to do?" he asked Pauly.

Pauly shrugged.

"Figured as much," the sheriff said. "Trouble with you kids is you've got too much time on your hands."

Jane gave the two boys the finger as we squeezed past them towards our horses. Pauly returned the favor. Then Paddy did one of his well-practiced flybys. He dropped a bomb of fresh white poop on top of the sheriff's hat as he passed over him. The sheriff didn't seem to mind. He rubbed his chin to help him think.

"What's this you said about those gang members, Calloway?" he shouted " They been around here?"

Jane raised her arms shoulder wide and shrugged.

"Can't say one way or the other. But don't you think you'd be the first I'd tell, if I did?"

We didn't wait for his answer.

As we rode slowly down Main Street, I asked Jane what she thought about what had happened back there.

"It felt good. Very therapeutic. I reclaimed a good bit of myself. Yeah, it felt real good and still does. And Paddy pooping on the sheriff's hat was the icing on the cake, if you can forgive the metaphor."

"Groan. Double groan."

She reached across and pretended to punch me in the shoulder.

"Hey, you. I won the English literature prize in my class last term. So, my metaphor can't be all that bad."

"Okay, if you say so, but icing on the cake? And bird poop? I'd call that poor taste, pun intended."

"Now it's my turn to *g-r-o-a-n*."

We let our horses gallop out of town, leaving our laughter behind. The sun shone down on us through an opening in the clouds and we followed Paddy's long shadow as it flapped its wings ahead of us along the ground until we arrived at the farm. He hovered above the farm gate and cawed. I cawed back.

By the time we rode up to the farmhouse, the clouds had moved on, leaving the sun behind to dry up the mess the rain had made. We had worked up quite an appetite by then. I realized that I was hungry for something else, too: more of that sense of freedom I'd been feeling since we stopped the General Store from being robbed. I told Jane that I was thinking of telling my grandparents the whole story about the Crows, which pleased her. I just hadn't quite made up my mind exactly when or how to do that.

Gran invited Jane to an early supper as it turned out. The occasion gave us the opportunity to talk about the attempted rape and holdup. Poppy and Gran were full of praise for Jane.

"You showed Solomonic wisdom," Poppy said.

"You make me feel proud to be a woman," Gran added. Standing up to those hoodlums like that."

They praised me for backing Jane up. However, I didn't tell them I did so reluctantly, or that I hadn't told them everything. I felt bad about that, but I was scared they'd freak out if they found out that I was supposed to be the getaway driver.

After supper, Jane decided to ride home alone since I still had chores to do. She made sure she didn't head off before giving me a piece of her mind.

"You didn't tell them the whole story, Danny. That's all I'm going to say about it."

"I know. I'm sorry."

Gran stopped Jane, as she was about to turn Goldie's head towards home.

"Jane, as you know, Danny's Mum will be coming home for good next Friday. I would like you to join us when she arrives. I know that you two will just hit it off."

"If it's okay with Danny, I'd love to come."

"I wouldn't say no to that."

"Then it's settled then," Poppy said. "Bring Goldie, too. Maire's crazy about horses."

"So I've heard. I can't wait to meet her."

Poppy, Gran and I waited until Jane and Goldie had disappeared around the bend in the path before doing our respective evening chores. As I walked past the tool shed on our way to the barn, Paddy poked his head out of his broken window and cawed "hello." He made me wonder what hole

Bongo and his gang had crawled into for the night and whether or not they would bother me between now and when I went to get Mom.

While I felt thankful that I was not with them, I had a gut feeling that it would only be a matter of time before they contacted me again.

Paddy interrupted my thoughts. He bombarded me with four rather agitated caws and then flew above the fence line towards the source of his concern. A calf was entangled in barbed wire in the north field and its distraught mother was mooing for help. I heeded her plea and approached with some reluctance when I saw a bull glaring down at me from a hilltop. He was snorting loudly and stomping one of his front legs on the ground. Thankfully, Milah decided to join the rescue party and ran back and forth, staking out an invisible barrier between the big brown beast and me.

"Thanks, Milah." I shouted.

I untangled the barbed wire from around the calf's head while Paddy, who had perched himself on top of a fence post, bobbed his head back and forth and cawed. As soon as the calf was free, it ran to its mother and began sucking on one of her teats. At that moment, I remembered Mom's notebook in my truck's glove compartment and I decided to give it a read after chores.

Speaking of chores, I realized that I was no longer thinking of them as reluctant labor. I was enjoying them. Another surprising revelation on the farm!

Chapter 24

I FLIPPED THROUGH PAGES OF MOM'S JOURNAL. It said "For Danny" on the front cover.

From the very first page, I got more of a sense of where she was at that point in her rehab. The personal thoughts she shared helped provide me with a fresh perspective on my own life – not only where I came from, but also where I was now and, most importantly, where I might be headed.

One section in the journal, in particular, still stands out for me. It focuses on relationships. It's dated Sept. 29, 2007 and, like the first page of other sections, it greets me as if I were right there.

• • •

Good morning, Danny. I'd like to introduce you to some of the characters in my life at Southwest State.

Unlike many of my fellow guards here, instead of barging into my cell unannounced, Sarah Garcia taps politely on my dormitory door for permission to enter and greets me with her usual "Buenos dias, Maire."

For the past four weeks, Sarah has been an active member of my "society re-entry team." She now allows me to address her by her first name when no one else is around – informality I have some difficulty getting used to.

Today, she sits on my favorite chair, the only one in my room, and opens a brown manila folder. I sit on the edge of my cot.

A black Hispanic who escaped by boat from Cuba with her family in the late 1970s, Sarah is four or so inches shorter than my five foot six inches and about 15 pounds lighter soaking wet than my 120. However, as many new and stronger inmates discover early on during their incarceration, size doesn't matter when it comes to Sarah Garcia. She's a black belt in both judo and karate, and she can tumble an opponent in an eye blink when talk fails to make its point.

This morning she tells me that she has some release paperwork for me to look over and sign and that I will get $50.00 gate money, a bus ticket home plus the $263.27 I've still got left in the canteen kitty, minus what I spend between now and release day.

I tell her that I don't need the bus ticket, but I'll take a hundred to buy some gifts for you and my folks. The rest she can transfer to someone who has no coin. I leave that choice up to her. She tells me in a soft tone that I will have to confirm that in writing, of course.

She asks me if I am still on plan when I get out.

I tell her yes. I want to continue my distance education university courses after I play catch-up with you and my parents, which are number ones on my list of scarier to-dos. I stress that I plan to stay clean and sober and a million miles away from your dad's old pals. Oh, yeah, and ride horses until my butt's saddle-sore red.

Sarah toys with the tiny gold crucifix earring that pierces her left ear and tells me she hopes I stick to my plan. She also says she never wants to cross paths with Dolly and me in here again. I tell her that I hear her loud and clear, as Dolly creeps into the room and jumps into the comfort of my lap to be petted.

Sarah stands up to leave and hands me the folder. She tells me in a make-believe bossy tone that I've a little over a week to go and that I should keep my nose clean or it's off to solitary I go.

I thank her for going out of her way to make this place more bearable. She answers that if it were not for the grace of God, any of *the guards could be sitting right smack where I am. She shares that times were tough for her financially before she started here and that she had no real calling to be a prison guard. She says that she promised herself one thing when she passed through the same front gate I'll soon be leaving by: to never lose sight of who she is.*

I can tell you she keeps that promise every day, Danny.

Sarah's walkie-talkie squawks and a broken male voice crackles in and orders her to report to the cafeteria for a code two-seven. It's the current code for inmates fighting.

Sarah dashes off without saying another word. I brush Dolly off my lap and reach for a pen from my desk to sign the release documents and jot down a note about the canteen funds. I slip all the paperwork into an envelope and address it to the attention of Sergeant Garcia.

I feel guilty when I think about Sarah making a positive choice in her difficult life because I had been given so much in my own before meeting your father. I am still coming to terms with my choice to go down the wrong road. I realize now that mine was not a sudden choice; I made it a bit at a time until there was no going back.

I sigh and look around at the four walls of my room. A photo of you, as a 12-year old, and me, around 30, is the centerpiece of my well-stocked bookshelf on the wall above the headboard of my cot. Between us the ever-present silhouette of your absent father stares back at me, reminding me of a different time. A week or so after arriving at Southwest State, I used an artist's knife to meticulously remove his image from the photo. During my time here, I am now so accustomed to looking at the piece of green prison wall replacing it that I can no longer recall what he looks like, which pleases me to no end.

A photo of your grandparents hangs above my beloved bookshelf. Facing it on the opposite wall is a large hazy watercolor of our farm that I had painted from memory six months ago in an art class run by Audrey, a fellow inmate; Millie, my horse, is tied to the hitching post in front of the house, casting a long shadow across the ground beneath an early morning sky. I smile as I appreciate how well I have managed to capture Millie's shiny coat and the twinkle in her right eye that seems to be saying, "I'm ready for a ride whenever you are, my lady."

Audrey, a fellow inmate and one of my closest friends here, pokes her head through my door. She has an Afro hairstyle, but she's as white as they come.

"Let's go, girl," she says in her British accent. "Meeting starts in five."

• • •

All 12 of us sit on chairs in a circle. We leave one chair vacant to make any late-coming inmate feel welcome. The Narcotics Anonymous poster, with its distinctive symbol, occupies a spot on the wall opposite the meeting room door. I find myself reflecting, as I do every day, all the words on it: "Freedom, Self, God, Society, Service and Goodwill."

Margot, a Moroccan Jew, finishes her sharing.

The rest of us thank her.

Dolly, who is a regular attendee at these NA meetings, naps on my lap. Three other inmates have their cats with them this day, too.

Gloria, a full-blood Mohawk, stands and addresses the gathering. She tells everyone that today's a special day for me because I have one year of sobriety. She shares that, as my sponsor, she is delighted at my progress and my commitment to recovery.

Gloria hands me my anniversary cake. I lift it up for all to see before setting it down on the table. I promise a piece to everyone over coffee after. The room is filled with whoops, cheers and whistles.

I share that my name is Maire and that I'm a cocaine addict and an alcoholic. They all chant "Hi Maire," in unison. I thank all of them and Gloria, in particular, for being with me on my journey to recovery this past year. I thank them, too, for helping me come to terms with who I am in the silence of my own heart.

Although I could not see it on the day I was sentenced, I tell them that detention is the next best thing to my NA experience. I point out that the people in this room are the most important people in my life after my own family. I thank them for their encouragement when I am down, and for accepting me where I'm at whenever I screw up, which is often, I know. I tell them that I love them all and that I'll miss them when I'm released. I conclude by thanking them repeatedly.

They thank me in return and applaud when I lift up the cake. I invite them to eat and worry about the calories later.

More applause, cheers and whistles follow.

• • •

These remaining days are the longest I can recall spending at Southwest State. Even the clock hands in my cell seem to conspire by revolving in slow motion, stretching the silent beats between seconds. The hectic pace of the detention center's activities wheel slows to a snail's pace the more I reflect on the aimless journey that had delivered me here and, most importantly, the trials, tribulations and therapeutic healing I continue to experience during my incarceration.

As I stretch out on my bunk after the NA meeting, my palms become clammy and my hands begin to tremble when the prospect of freedom rears its head like an unruly horse. My stomach turns and tears roll down my cheeks. At first, I think that the autobiography I have started reading is triggering these autonomic responses. It's called "Peig" by Peig Sayers, one of Ireland's finest female storytellers. A touching work, the book recounts Peig's life in rural

Ireland and, in particular, her many years scratching out a living and raising a family on The Great Blasket Island in County Kerry. I begin to realize that the book is triggering my own personal memories of scratching out a different kind of living: an unproductive one.

Each flip of Peig's pages is like peeling away another thin layer of onion skin on the road to the realization that I have been in denial far too long, ignoring what really matters in my life, like the true meaning of family and friendships and, most importantly, motherhood. I had traded simple life on the farm for the complexities of the big city for which, unlike Peig, I had not been even remotely prepared.

• • •

"Wow," I said to myself after I closed the journal. "Peig, Mom and I have a lot in common."

Then, in my mind, I saw Paddy perched on Sarah Garcia's outstretched finger and I thought how much those two had in common, too.

For some reason, I had a strong urge to begin writing about my own life and that rattled me.

"Caw, caw, caw, caw," I said out loud to myself.

Chapter 25

WHENEVER I IMAGINED MOM'S RELEASE, I wondered if the most dramatic moment would be when the detention center's gate slammed shut behind her. However, except for seeing her receiving Dolly and an unexpected hug from a guard who, I would later learn, was Sarah Garcia, her departure was, for me at least, no more dramatic than an exit door closing at the local food market.

What surprised me most was the fidgety silence that sat between us as we drove north to the farm; it reminded me of a line in the film, *No Country for Old Men,* when a drug smuggler asked the antagonist, Anton Chigurh, "Do you mind riding bitch?"

I decided to leave well enough alone and let the silence occupy that center spot for as long as it was needed. It broke about 30 minutes into the drive when Paddy, who had flown away for a few minutes, flew back into the cab via the open sunroof when we were waiting for a traffic light to change. He parked himself on the stick-shift console between us and cawed twice.

"What the heck!" Mom exclaimed.

Dolly jumped off her lap and ducked for cover under her legs.

"Mom, meet Paddy. Paddy meet Mom," I laughed.

"Nice to meet you, Paddy," she replied, adding a caw of her own and laughing.

Paddy cocked his head and studied her with one eye. Then, cawing, he hopped onto my shoulder to keep a wary eye on the road ahead.

"You've trained him well," Mom said.

"Not really. He just tags along and does whatever he wants."

"All the same, you must be doing something right for him to behave like that."

"I guess."

She reached over and patted my leg.

"Thanks, Danny."

"For what?"

She managed a tiny smile and then looked out the passenger side window at busy farmers on tractors as they bailed hay for winter under a lightly clouded autumn afternoon sky. I thought I saw a tiny tear roll down her left cheek as she looked at a scene that was once so much part of her earlier life.

"Red sky," I said. "It's going to rain soon."

"Ah, ah! Your grandma's been sharing some of her meteorological secrets, I see."

Now it was my turn to return a smile with no talking back. I did so without taking my eyes off the road, which was a good thing because a tractor-trailer nearly hit us after cutting us off on our left. I pumped the brakes and turned the truck slightly to the right without honking.

"Good driving," she said. "You didn't even get mad at him for cutting in."

"No point. He wouldn't have noticed anyway."

"Grandma's not the only one rubbing off on you up at the farm, is she?"

This time I really wanted to say something and opened my mouth to do so. I wanted to tell her that she was imagining things, that there was no way I was like my grandfather, and that we were from two totally different worlds, he and I, but the lie stuck, like phlegm, in the back of my throat.

Paddy answered for me. He cawed three times softly before flying out through the opened sunroof.

"Look," Mom said. "Who needs one of those new GPS gadgets with him around? He's flying ahead of us, leading the way."

"He's been doing that a lot lately," I replied.

• • •

Mom's eyes filled with tears as soon as we turned into the driveway. Dolly sat on Mom's lap and purred in response to being petted.

"Nothing's changed," she said when she saw the house. "Except for everything looking smaller. It's as if time has stood totally still since I left."

"In some ways it has," I said.

"Scary. Now you're really beginning to sound like your grandfather."

My impulse to protest disappeared when Poppy and Gran appeared in the doorway. Gran ran with open arms to greet us, with Milah at her heels. Poppy seemed to be making a deliberate attempt to take his time.

Mom opened the door and got out with Dolly in her arms. She looked down at the ground when Gran opened her arms wide to greet her.

"Come, come, Maire. No need for that now. Let me see that beautiful face of yours. Welcome home, my darling daughter. How I've missed you! Is this Dolly?"

"Mom, I..."

She stood up straight, sobbing and shaking, clutching Dolly to her breast with both hands for security.

"You're home now and that's all that matters."

I decided to let them be and went around to the back of the pickup to get Mom's suitcase. Milah and Paddy must have decided to stay out of the way, too, because they joined me there. Milah crouched beside me when I removed the lone suitcase from the cargo area and Paddy perched himself proudly on my shoulder like Long John Silver's parrot.

"Welcome home, Maire," I heard Poppy say. "You look good."

As I walked towards the house with Mom's case in hand and Paddy still perched on my shoulder, Poppy, Gran, Mom and Dolly were locked in a hugging foursome. Milah looked up at them, wagging her tail. Paddy decided not to come in the house and, when I entered, he flew off towards the tool shed.

• • •

Mom couldn't stay still for long all evening. Although she answered my questions, she asked few of her own and she made no effort to fill in the time gaps that Gran and Poppy seemed anxious to bridge. Instead, she explored every nook and cranny of the house -- from basement to attic.

I can't explain why, but I felt compelled to watch her explore from a distance.

I watched her rub her palm up and down an antique glass bottle and then stare at the wall in front of her. I wondered if that action would conjure up a succession of old memories or trigger *could've, should've, would've* wishes. As for me, it conjured up a fleeting, unwanted image of Aladdin "the Magician" Forlini drawing a Crows' tag on the elevator wall of my apartment building the first day I met him.

Mom turned her attention to the dining room table. When she walked her fingers around its edge, I wondered if she were regretting the many meals she'd missed there in the company of those who loved her.

When she rocked back and forth in the cane-back rocking chair beside the fireplace, I wondered if she were recalling the times Gran rocked her to sleep when she was a little girl.

When she switched on the light above the painting of her horse, I wondered if she were daydreaming about earlier carefree rides along country trails.

When she put on an old winter coat and pulled it snugly around her without buttoning it, I wondered if she were thinking about the times that she had felt the bitterness of physical, emotional and spiritual cold during wasted years.

When she looked in the hall closet and slid coats and jackets along the coat hanger rail, I wondered if she were regretting many missed opportunities to go out and enjoy herself.

She noticed me staring at her from the living room doorway.

"You've been watching me, haven't you, Danny?"

" I, er... I guess. I wanted to make sure you were okay."

"You've never stopped watching out for me, have you? You've been my caretaker for so long. It should have been the other way around."

"I'm not complaining."

"Neither am I. I'm glad you were there. Things could've turned out worse for us, you know."

"Supper's on the table," Gran sang from the kitchen. She walked towards the dining room with a plump roasted turkey on a serving platter.

"Let's catch up, you and me, after supper," Mom whispered. "There are things you need to know about me and I need to know about you."

"I've been reading your journal. It explains a lot already."

"I hope so."

My thoughts drifted to Jane. Whenever I heard the phone or a distant cowbell ring, I wished that she would ring the doorbell. After all, she had promised to come and meet Mom.

Gran prepared an amazing meal with all the trimmings of a Thanksgiving Day feast, but Jane's absence curbed my appetite. I ended up picking at my food and moving it around on my plate. Thankfully, the conversation was light and cheery, with no mention of bad days. Mom was anxious to catch up on what neighbors had been up to during her absence. Gran and Poppy told her who had died, married, had children, divorced, or moved away. She was especially interested in what her many old flames were up to. Gran was pleased to fill her in.

After dinner, despite Mom's protests (not mine), Gran and Poppy insisted on doing the cleanup. They ordered Mom and me to the front porch to put our feet up.

We plunked ourselves down in the two-person love seat, which hung from the wainscoted balcony ceiling. An unusually warm westerly breeze for that time of year blew softly against us as we rocked back and forth. A white partial moon shone above the roof of the tool shed beneath a star-studded sky.

The light was on in the shed. I could see Paddy's silhouette pacing back and forth behind the broken window. Then, suddenly, he stopped moving. I got the impression he was looking our way.

"Paddy likes to keep an eye out for you, doesn't he?" Mom said.

"I suppose."

"What is it? You look troubled."

"Oh, I was just wondering where Jane was. And whether or not you think things would have turned out differently if -- you know -- the sperm donor hadn't shown up at the farm one day?"

"Sperm donor?"

"What else would I call him? He sure never acted like a real father or husband, did he?"

"Which one do you want me to tackle first?"

"Huh?"

"Real father or real husband."

I shrugged.

"I haven't figured it all out yet. But, I'll let you know when I do."

She took a deep breath.

"Who am I kidding? I already know the answers to both questions. Except for the gift of you, I wish I'd never met him. What's more, except for a very brief few weeks when he dried out, when you were about five I think, he was a terrible husband and father. The stress was more than you and I should have had to bear -- especially you. That doesn't mean that I have not accepted responsibility for my own actions. I wasn't exactly the model mother, was I?"

"I never blamed you."

"Maybe you should have."

"Well I didn't and I don't."

We stopped talking for a few minutes and tuned in to what Mom called "a mélange of night sounds": random wood knocks and cracks, falling branch thumps, cricket chirps, squirrel chatter-clacks, geese honks, cow moos and distant dog barks. I fixed my gaze on the woods about 200 hundred feet west of the house when I heard what sounded like a bird scream. It seemed to be firing a question at us.

"What the heck was that, Mom?" It sounded like *Who-cooks-for-you, who-cooks-for-you-all?"*

"A barred owl. They're quite common in these parts.

"Amazing," I said.

"They're good predators to have around. They help keep the rodent population under control."

I closed my eyes to see what other sound I might hear, hoping one of them would be Jane's voice. The next one I heard was the raspy call of my own name, "Danny, Danny."

"What?" I replied without opening my eyes.

"As your grandfather would say, I'll be a monkey's aunt," Mom said.

I opened my eyes slowly and saw Paddy perched on the balcony rail.

"Danny, Danny," Paddy said, staring at me. "Caw, caw, Danny, Danny. Caw, caw."

Poppy gloated from the doorway. Gran was standing beside him.

"I told you that crows could talk like parrots, didn't I?" he said.

"He's one smart bird," Gran said. "It's darn right uncanny just how smart he is. Almost human, if you ask me."

The clanging of a single cowbell interrupted our conversation. It was coming from the front of the house and grew louder. We finally spotted its owner: one of Poppy's prized Holsteins. It had escaped from one of the enclosed pastures. Milah jumped into action and waited for a signal to round her up.

"How would you like to help Milah get Bessie to the barn, Danny?" Poppy asked. "I have to head down to the south pasture to check on some bullocks."

"Sure," I said, whistling at Milah. "Let's go girl."

I hurried towards the barn while Milah ran on ahead and barked at Bessie's heels, herding her towards me. She was a gentle milker with patches of rusty red and white all over her back and sides, and a lazy, swaggering walk. She obeyed every one of Milah's corrective barks and pretended heel snaps. Milah showed that she was not the least bit intimidated by her charge's mountainous size.

Bessie entered the barn and made for the first open stall. I locked her in for the night after filling her water and hay troughs to keep her contented.

I was just about to leave the barn when I heard Milah bark, then growl. I walked to the tack room, where Poppy kept his bridles, saddles, horse blankets, ropes and other farm "this 'n' thats." I slid the door open cautiously, hoping that the intruder wasn't a big barn rat.

You can imagine my surprise when, for the second time in a few days, I saw Jane Calloway sitting on the floor surrounded by her captors, except they weren't Wade, Pauly and Billy. No, this time, they were Crows to a fault: Bongo, Aladdin, Sammy and Nipper. Their hair was messy, and their jeans and boots were caked with red clay. The three guys had beard stubble on their faces and Nipper wore a sad look on hers.

Milah barked louder.

"Tell her to shut the fuck up or I'll shut her up for good," Bongo threatened. He pulled out his gun to reinforce his point and aimed it at Milah's head.

"It's okay, Milah," I said calmly. "Good girl, sit."

She sat down at my feet just as Paddy flew in and landed on my shoulder. Instead of his usual double caw, he made one drawn-out one. Bongo lowered his gun and stuck it in his belt.

"Looks like all the crows are here now," Bongo laughed.

"You okay, Jane?" I asked. "Did they hurt you?"

She shook her head. "No, at least not yet. I'm sorry, Danny. They grabbed me at the front door when I arrived for supper."

"We got no reason to hurt her," Bongo said.

"Then why'd you bring her here?"

"To find out what you and everyone else was up to since we saw you in town, except the bitch wouldn't tell us. So, you'll have to. What was that fuck-up with Deputy Dawg and those locals in front of the store all about anyways?"

I shrugged.

"It's a small town. The sheriff keeps tight control over it, I guess. He knows you're going to spit on the sidewalk before you even think about doing it."

"You want me to believe that? I'd be awfully pissed if I found out you had anything to do with setting us up, Karate. That wouldn't make you a brother any more, would it guys?"

"Nope," Aladdin and Sammy replied as one. Nipper shook her head.

"You can't stay here, Bongo," I said. "There's an arson investigation under way and the sheriff is sure to come back here to ask questions. Someone burned down the old cabin in the woods after you guys were there."

"Well they can't pin that on us. Those fuckups who messed up our action in town Monday did the torching," Aladdin said. "We saw them do it."

"Why are you even talking to these assholes, Danny?" Jane asked. "They're only out for themselves."

Nipper bent over Jane and raised her hand to strike. Her breasts almost flopped out of her tight V-neck sweater.

"I'll smack her fat mouth shut for her," Nipper volunteered.

Paddy had other plans. He made several quick danger caws. Then flew off my shoulder onto Nipper's and pecked hard at her scalp. Bongo pulled his revolver out of his belt and pointed its barrel at Paddy who continued to peck at Nipper, making her scream.

Milah had plans of her own. She leapt at Bongo and knocked him over. When Bongo hit the floor, the gun discharged and the bullet whizzed by Jane's head, passing through the tack room wall. The next sound we heard was what I could only describe as a frantic, high-pitched moo-and-a-moan. It was followed by a heavy thud.

"Bongo!" I shouted. "You bastard. You shot Bessie!"

I belly-flopped onto Bongo and punched him several times in the face and head until Aladdin and Sammy pulled me away.

"Let's get the fuck out of here." Sammy whimpered as he helped Bongo to his feet.

"Not before I finish them."

Bongo spat through bloodied lips. He kicked Milah hard in the stomach. When the poor bitch yelped and curled up to lick her wound, Bongo aimed the barrel at me and curled a finger around the trigger.

"Danny!" Jane shouted.

Paddy cawed furiously at Bongo, warning him. Bongo ignored his warning and squeezed the trigger. But the trigger jammed and clicked. He squeezed again and again, but still the gun didn't fire. I felt wetness in my groin and, for a brief moment, thought that I'd been shot there, until I realized I'd pissed my pants.

Frustrated and angered by his failure to whack me, Bongo hurled the gun at my head.

"Fucking lucky bastard!" he shouted.

I ducked and the gun flew past me, ricocheting off the far wall onto the lid of a tack box, where its only remaining bullet fired with unintended accuracy through the barn wall and into, as I found out moments later, the back of Nipper's calf, as she ran away. She screamed in pain.

Still swearing, Bongo chased after Aladdin, Sammy and Nipper who, by now, were all well beyond the confines of the barnyard fences. I picked up the gun and ran outside. Jane ran after me.

I saw Nipper dragging her left leg as she limped after Bongo who had almost disappeared into a thick stand of maple and brush.

"Help me, help me!" Nipper screamed again.

Paddy cawed up a storm as he flew after the Crows.

Poppy headed towards us in his pickup to check out the gunshot he had heard from the south pasture. Mom and Gran had not heard the shot because they'd been listening to music back in the house and had the volume control set too high.

"Help me, Bongo!" Nipper pleaded. "I'm bleeding like a fucking pig!"

"It's every Crow for himself!" he shouted back.

"Danny," Poppy yelled through the pickup window as he drew closer to me. "What have you done? Put that gun down!"

It was the first time that I had ever heard him raise his voice to me.

"He didn't do anything," Jane shouted in my defense when Poppy stepped out of the pickup. "The gun went off when the Crows gang leader, Bongo threw it at Danny. Danny just picked it up."

Poppy walked over to me.

"What were they doing in the barn anyway?"

He didn't push me for an answer when I lowered my head. He placed his hand on my shoulder and said, "That's okay, Danny. Sorry for accusing you before."

I managed a weak smile and handed it to him.

"You'd better take this, Poppy. I bet the sheriff would love to catch me with it."

"I bet he would, too, so there's no money in that bet. Hey, where's Milah? I thought I heard her yelping."

"She's been hurt. We left her in the barn."

"How, and how bad?"

"I think she could've cracked a rib when the Crows leader, Bongo, kicked her," said Jane. "He's a coward."

"Let's go get her," Poppy said with an urgent tone. "We'll take her to the house and patch her up."

When we started walking towards the barn, Jane nudged me and asked, "Did you tell him about Bessie?"

"Bessie?" Poppy said with a quick tilt of his head.

"She was..." I said.

He gave me a worried look when I couldn't finish my sentence.

"What about her?"

• • •

Poppy looked sad when he saw Bessie lying in a pool of blood on the floor of the barn, but he never said a word. He knelt down to stroke her neck, shaking his head. I left him with Jane and went into the tack room to get Milah who was whimpering. I cradled her in my arms and she stopped.

When Poppy, Jane, Milah and I were leaving the barn, Paddy flew towards us. He landed on Poppy's left shoulder and cawed four times slowly, as if to offer his condolences. Poppy opened his mouth to acknowledge him, but said nothing.

• • •

After we returned to the house, Milah brought out the maternal instinct in Gran, Mom and Jane. They fussed over her and whispered words of encouragement.

Paddy didn't enter the house, however. As soon as we reached the front door, he flapped his wings and took flight from Poppy's shoulder.

As I watched Paddy fly north, a silly thought sprang into my mind. I imagined Paddy landing in the pasture to break the sad news about Bessie's passing to her surviving Holstein family. In spite of all that had just happened, that thought made me smile, just a little.

"You won't have to worry about the sheriff," Gran said to me. "I called the Vermont State troopers. I'm waiting for someone to phone me back."

"No!" I shouted. "The Crows'll think I'm a rat."

Mom placed an arm around me.

"I used to think like that. You're no rat. They are, the whole pack of 'em. If they kill someone, you don't want the victim's blood on your hands, do you?"

She gave my shoulder a reassuring squeeze when I shook my head.

Gran's cell phone rang.

"Hello. Yes, this is she. No, no. Not Baloney... Mahoney... M-a-h-o-n-e-y. Mahoney Farm. You can't miss the sign. We're about five miles from Noburg. No, no. Not Snowburg, Noburg. N-o-b-u-r-g."

She flapped the phone lid closed. "The state police are on their way. Imagine calling me Mrs. Baloney."

Jane and Mom smiled. Poppy didn't; his thoughts were elsewhere. So were mine.

• • •

A few minutes before the police arrived, I saw Poppy sitting on the five-bar gate to Bessie's pasture. I was surprised to see that he was smiling as his eyes scanned it for memories. I climbed up and sat next to him. Paddy perched on the gatepost and cawed.

"You okay, Poppy?" I asked.

He put his long arm around my shoulders and hugged me.

"I will be. Thanks for asking."

I forced myself to smile as I searched carefully for my next words.

"What's on your mind, Danny? You look like you're dying to say something. It's about your Crows, isn't it?"

"They're not my Crows anymore, but yes, it's about them. I want to tell you the whole story."

"I know," he replied, hugging me. "I know you do."

Chapter 26

HOLDING BONGO'S DISCARDED GUN in a sealed plastic bag under her left armpit, Lieutenant Irena A. Kobernick, a tall, strong-looking woman in her mid-forties, flipped the black leather cover of her notebook closed and thanked Gran, Poppy and me for our assistance. She said that she would swing by later that morning to talk to Jane who had promised to stop by.

Kobernick was the last Vermont State Trooper to leave. I watched as she drove her patrol car away from the house towards the road with lights flashing, but no siren blaring. She seemed in no hurry to catch up with her half dozen or so subordinates who had combed the farm earlier in search of the Crows. Judging by all the competing siren wails, they were chasing after their elusive prey in different directions like the persistent hunters they were.

As senior officer on the scene, Kobernick supervised the search of the Mahoney farm. She insisted on removing Bessie's carcass for an autopsy to recover the spent bullet. She enlisted the services of Iain Kerr, a local contractor, to transport it to the nearest vet's clinic outside Noburg.

Poppy's eyes filled with tears as he watched Bessie's lifeless corpse dangle from a harness attached to Kerr's backhoe shovel and then descend slowly into the back of his truck.

"She was the most contented of the herd," he said. "An old friend I enjoyed seeing first thing every morning. I'm going to miss her."

When Gran wrapped her arm around Poppy's waist to comfort him, tears welled up in my own eyes. My once fellow Crows would count that kind of "wuss-fit" a weakness.

That night, I tossed and turned in bed, wrestling covers and wakefulness at the same time. I'd been fighting on the wrong side of everything far too long. I kicked the blankets and sheets. I squinted at the aerial photo of the Mahoney farm on the far wall and, in that instant, I knew. I made up my mind that, whatever happened, I was not going back, not to the Bronx, not to the Crows and, especially not to my old self. There was only one problem: I hadn't a clue how I was going to manage all that.

"Jane will help me sort it through," I whispered.

Then I remembered what an old friend of Poppy's had said to me when he discovered that I was both a Mahoney and a city boy the week after I arrived at the farm. I was standing with Poppy and Gran outside the chapel after Sunday service.

"If you stay around here long enough, son, this place'll stick to you, like flies to flypaper."

"Or a boy to a crow," I whispered to myself.

I wondered how much longer Paddy would stick around me. I realized that I was having a harder time letting him go than I had thought I would, and that I had broken my promise to set him free, so far at least.

Chapter 27

SHORTLY AFTER CHORES THE NEXT MORNING, Jane drove by in her father's pickup and met me outside the tool shed. She was gift-wrapped in a tight pair of blue jeans and a white turtleneck sweater.

Paddy watched us from the broken window. When I told her that Lieutenant Kobernick was going to come by later to take her statement, she told me that she'd already given her one at the farm entrance.

"Good. That leaves more time for us. Come here, Jane."

"Why?" She inched towards me, without smiling.

"This is why."

I pulled her gently towards me and kissed her, softly at first, then passionately. We hugged each other without saying a word for two to three minutes. Then, all of a sudden, she pushed me away.

Paddy poked his head through the hole in the broken window and cried, "Caw, caw, caw."

I imagined him saying, "Speak up girl!"

Jane smiled at Paddy's intrusion. She stopped smiling when she turned back to face me.

"We both have a lot on our plates right now, don't we?"

"We'll get through it."

"I think we're going to have to do more than just get through it."

"Meaning?"

"Being even more careful when we meet."

"Any more careful and we'd be invisible! What brought all this on?"

"I had another big fight with my dad last night."

"About what?"

"About you! He threatened to *pluck you out*."

"Pluck me out?"

"He was quoting the bible. Mathew 5:29 to be exact: 'And if thy right eye offend thee, pluck it out, and cast it from thee'."

"What brought that on?"

"He was reading the Good Book and it spoke to him, I guess. That's what he does. It led to a screaming match about you. He wants you plucked out of my life, period!"

Paddy hopped out of the broken window and flew onto my shoulder.

"As I've said before, no bloody way. I'm going to keep you in my life whether he likes it or not."

She put her arms around me and hugged me.

"I have to go. Ma's not feeling well. I think she's stressed out about dad and me. I promised to pick her up at the clinic in half an hour."

"Will you call me later?"

"As soon as I can."

Paddy and I watched her drive off. As the pickup disappeared from view, I felt angry. I clenched my fist and looked around for something to hit with it. The remaining glass in the shed's windowpane caught my eye and I punched all of it out with one strike. Paddy didn't like that one bit, judging by his caws of protest and his flight from my shoulder to the sanctuary of the nearest tall cedar. He rested on the topmost branch for a few minutes to stare down at me before flying off towards Paddington Pond.

"Hey, Paddy!" I shouted after him. "Come back. Please come back."

I felt tears welling up in my eyes and I reached up to wipe them away with the still clenched fist I had used to punch out the window. I stopped when I realized my knuckles and my eyes were drenched in my blood.

• • •

"You are one silly, silly goose," Gran said as she bandaged my hand. "I hope you learned your lesson."

I thought about answering her, but I bit my lip instead.

"So, what's the rest of the scoop on you and Jane?"

"I don't know any more than I told you. I just don't understand women."

"I assure you the feeling can be mutual."

I took a deep breath and said, "Gran?"

"Yes?"

"What should I do about Jane and her old man?"

She slipped the first aid kit into a kitchen drawer.

"Give her time. She'll make sense of everything when she's darn good and ready. Yes, time's the best healer. You'll need lots more of it for him though."

Gran lifted a lunch box off the kitchen counter and handed it to me.

"This is for you and your mum. She wants to go riding with you. She's out saddling up Jessie and Lightning right now. I think it will do the pair of you the world of good."

I was about to protest that I wasn't in the mood, but Gran stuck an index finger in each of her ears.

"I can't hear you," she sang. "I can't hear you."

Chapter 28

I PUSHED JESSIE hard to keep up with Mom, but Lightning was just too fast for us. He sure lived up to his name as his hooves chewed up mile after mile of trail, leaving behind a cloud of dust in his wake for Jessie, Milah and me to swallow. We were unable to close the gap until after Mom tugged on Lightning's reins and pointed his head towards a side trail I'd never noticed before. She waited there until we reached it.

"Your grandfather and his father used to hunt partridge and pheasant on this old hunting trail," she said. "It's a bit rocky in spots, so be careful."

Jessie's nose was almost touching Lightning's rump as we trekked slowly along the trail.

"Where does it lead?"

"Old Tom's, eventually. The trail twists and turns, and it has lots of challenging hills. It's great for cross-country skiing, if you know what you're doing."

"There's nothing left to see at Old Tom's," I protested. "Except for charcoal."

"Are you sure about that?"

I said nothing more until we reached Old Tom's clearing.

In spite of the cool autumn air, it was truly a fabulous morning. The sun was shining in an almost cloudless red sky. I could hear the faint calls of whip-poor-wills as they lay in their well-camouflaged nests of decayed leaves after a busy night of foraging. I could also hear squirrels chattering happily to each other from somewhere among the trees while a woodpecker tapped a familiar tune on the bark of an old maple beside me.

"Tat-a-tat. Tat-a-tat. Tat-a-tat-tat-a-tat."

I looked up and was glad to spy the tapper, one of my favorite birds: a red-bellied woodpecker, with its distinctive red cap and, of course, red belly. I used to see them quite often during winter visits to New York's Central Park. Milah barked at the sight.

Another familiar sound reached my ear: the cawing of a solitary crow as it flew overhead. I didn't have to wonder long if it belonged to Paddy because he swooped down and landed on my familiar left shoulder.

"Hey, Paddy," I said, pleased to see him.

"Caw, Danny. Caw, caw, Danny," he replied.

I reached into the inside pocket of my jacket and retrieved some Trailmix.

"Want some, Paddy?" I asked.

I placed my upturned palm under Paddy's beak and he grabbed the treat. In doing so, he knocked a nut off and it landed on my shoulder, next to his feet. Then he did something that surprised the heck out of me. He picked up the nut in his beak and touched it gently to my lips. When I opened my mouth to accept his gift, he cawed once, leaving me speechless.

And there we all were, the seven of us, Lightning, Milah, Jessie, Paddy, Mom, Jane and me, plodding along rather quietly, closing in on the charred skeleton of Old Tom's cabin, absorbed by our own thoughts and expectations. Yes, as far as I was concerned, Jane was right there with us, too, maybe not physically, but there, nevertheless, keeping me company in my daydream.

The only thing recognizable from my last visit to Old Tom's cabin was the potbellied stove that had warmed its tenants and visitors over many years, excluding the four foreign Crows who wouldn't have had a clue how to light it. The once proud-looking chimney was now a heap of stones on the scorched ground next to it.

Mom and I dismounted and tied our horses loosely to nearby trees so that they could lower their heads and munch freely on wild grass. I followed Mom and Milah past the charcoal heap to a hump of dead Scotch pine branches a few steps away.

"Give me a hand," she said. "Help me clear away this brush."

When we had moved branches, leaves and pine needles away, I was surprised to see a metal trapdoor with a pull ring. It was about 20 x 20 inches. The color of its faded rust-paint reminded me of the red-bellied woodpecker's belly.

"What's down there?"

"You'll see. Grab hold of that ring and pull it up. Careful though, it's pretty darn heavy."

With Paddy still perched on my shoulder, I straddled the door and pulled it up slowly. When it was fully open, I peered into the pitch-black darkness, wondering what surprises lurked there.

Mom pulled a four-inch penlight from a pocket of her jeans.

"This'll help shed light on the situation."

She switched on her penlight and aimed its strong beam at the hole below, making the darkness disappear.

"You'd better follow me down," she said. "I'm familiar with this place. You're not."

She made her way down the wooden ladder. I followed closely behind her, without Paddy, who had decided to fly off for some reason, and Milah who had run off into the woods after who knows what. When I reached the hard-packed soil floor below the last step, Mom cautioned me again.

"Stay put for one more sec."

She held the penlight between her teeth. My eyes followed its beam to a hurricane lamp hanging from a beam a few feet ahead. She lifted up the lamp's glass and struck a match, touching its flaming head to the waiting wick. She then adjusted the flame, and then lit another nearby wall lamp before blowing out the match. She switched off the penlight before returning it to her pocket.

"Let's keep the trapdoor open, Danny, until we make sure the ventilation pipe is clear."

I looked around the earthen chamber, which was about half the size of my bedroom back at the farmhouse. Neatly arrayed on shelves were woodcarvings of ducks and other wild animals. They were all wrapped in clear plastic to protect them from dampness.

"Who carved all these?" I asked. "They're amazing."

"You can't guess?"

I looked into her eyes and knew.

"He did?"

She nodded her head. I picked up a duck carving and examined it. Its fine detail made it look so lifelike.

"Why did he hide them away here?"

"I don't think he believed enough in his talent to sell them. Self-confidence was never one of your father's redeeming qualities. Anyway, in between selling drugs, he hid out here and carved away. I think it was one area of his life, as private as it was, that he felt in control. You may find this hard to believe, Danny, but he never ever did drugs or booze down here."

"Did he dig this place out all by himself?"

"No, he just stumbled across it one day. Poppy thinks a survivalist could have built it back in the early sixties during the Cuban missile crisis. It was stocked with all sorts of provisions when he found the place. If you look around, you'll still see some of them."

On unpainted barnwood shelves, I saw jarred and tinned food next to really old medicine bottles – all with faded labels, some with glazed and crackled finishes. It was like being frozen in time a half-century ago. Old newspapers and magazines were arranged in neat piles on top of a table made of half-inch-thick bamboo poles that had been tied together with rawhide strips. A rain barrel, coopered with a padded wicker seat, was tucked under the table.

"Look at that rock in the wall there, the one with Doug's initials etched into it."

"That sounds a bit weird."

"What?"

"It's been a long time since you referred to him by name."

"It has been, hasn't it?" She said, wincing as she did.

I concluded that the rock was not a natural formation because it had chisel marks on its sides. Its almost perfectly square shape intrigued me and I wondered what was behind it.

I traced shapes of the "D" and the "C" letters slowly with a finger, coaxing memories of my father. I then removed the rock from its resting spot in the hard clay wall and laid it down carefully on the ground. I looked at what was waiting for me in the cavity the extracted rock had left behind: a plastic box, a little bigger than a shoebox.

"What's in it?"

"I've no idea."

"You mean you've never looked inside yourself?"

"No. He was a man of many secrets."

"That's an understatement."

She shrugged and opened her arms wide.

I lifted out the box and opened the lid slowly. A shiver crept up and down my spine. I could feel the hairs on my arms standing to attention as I wondered what was inside.

"Oh, my God!" Mom said.

I lifted out three bound volumes, each individually sealed in clear plastic. I unwrapped them, one by one, before opening any of them. Mom brought a hurricane lamp a little closer.

The first volume was a personal diary covering the last 12 years of my father's life.

"He must've come back here the week before he died," I said.

"What makes you say that?"

"The date of the last entry."

"Wow, I never knew that. I want to read that later, that's for sure. What's that book about?"

I opened its cover.

"It's a scrapbook of old photographs, newspaper articles, birth and death notices," I said. "They're all about the Cagney family."

I flipped through the scrapbook's pages. One section shocked the heck out of me. It contained a series of articles on child abuse at an orphanage run by so-called Christian brothers, and the criminal investigation and trials of the accused that followed.

The names of the victims were not mentioned in the articles, but I quickly concluded that one of them had been none other than Doug Cagney himself. That's because every mention of a "victim" or "alleged victim" had been crossed out and replaced with my father's own name in bold capitals, printed in red ink.

The one thing that stood out in my memory from the brief mentions of his past was the name of the orphanage he had attended: *Mont Clonmel*. It was located across the border in Québec.

I stared at Mom.

"You knew about it, didn't you? The abuse?"

She nodded.

"Why'd you never tell me?"

"He asked me not to. He didn't want anyone else to know."

"But it helps explain so much," I protested. "His anger. Drugs and booze. His treatment of you and me."

Instead of answering, she pointed to the third volume. It provided the escape we both needed at that moment. It was a near-complete portfolio of Canadian 25-cent pieces, dating from the 19th to the 21st century.

"Where did he get all these?" I asked. "They're in great condition."

"I know he liked to check his change for dates. He used to toss ones he liked into a small wooden barrel he had stripped down for that purpose, but I never knew he was a serious collector in any way. It's a real surprise, considering we could have sold them many times over I bet -- just to eat."

229

I read a small card inside the back cover and showed it to Mom. She handed it back to me after reading it. I placed the portfolio of coins on the bamboo table and read the message again:

To Danny, from Douglas Cagney, your dad.

These Canadian coins are for you. I've been collecting them since I was a boy. I've bought and traded them over the years, but never sold any.

I hope you find the missing ones. I never could.

Your Dad, Doug Cagney

"Strange how he spelled out his name. Did he think I didn't know who he was for crying out loud?"

"Maybe he did that in case someone else found them. They're all yours now. I hope you cherish the gift and the thought."

"What did he leave you, Mom, besides bad memories?"

She closed her eyes to hide from the impact of my question. She opened them again when we heard the war cries of Paddy and Milah.

"Paddy and Milah are upset about something, Danny. Let's go see what. We sure don't want someone to bury us down here."

"We do," Bongo jeered. "Good thing Aladdin saw you turn down the trail back there."

I looked up at our worst nightmare in the flesh: Bongo, looking quite pleased with himself. He was squatting on the ground, holding Paddy firmly between his two hands, ignoring his caws of protest and Milah's barks. I could see someone's legs next to him.

I rushed to the ladder and started climbing. As soon as I reached the second rung, Aladdin shoved Milah down and she crashed against my chest, knocking me off the ladder.

Fortunately, for her, I had broken her fall and she was not injured. Fortunately, for me, Mom had managed to reach out and cushion my fall before my back hit the ground next to the coin portfolio, which now lay there.

Mom helped me to my feet and petted Milah who was barking up at Bongo and Aladdin.

"I'm sending Aladdin down," Bongo said. "Don't do anything stupid or I'll rip your bird's fucking head off. Now move away from the ladder and keep that bitch of a dog away, too."

Mom and I backed away from the ladder and she commanded Milah to do the same. Aladdin, cocky as ever, climbed down and looked around the chamber when he reached the floor.

"Hey, Karate. I like your old lady. She don't look much older than you. Maybe I should do her a favor while I'm here."

I raised my fist and lunged at Aladdin, but stopped when he pulled out a switchblade and pointed it at me. Paddy cawed at him from above.

"That's better. Now what do we have here?"

He picked up the coin portfolio and used the tip of the knife blade to flip open its cover, ignoring Milah's barks and Paddy's caws.

"Leave that alone!" I shouted. "That's my dad's."

"He's dead, ain't he? He don't need it no more, so now they're ours."

"You son-of-a-bitch!"

"Ain't that the fucking truth?" He sneered. "She was one bitch alright, and a street hooker to boot. I was her *acci-dent*."

"Hurry up, Aladdin," Bongo shouted down. He was still clutching Paddy. "There's a chopper coming. Could be cops."

"See you, sucker. Caw. Caw," Aladdin smirked.

231

He climbed up the ladder with his prize.

"Close that trapdoor," Bongo ordered when Aladdin reached the top. "Let's roll that big mother of a rock over it so they can't get out."

"I don't want no part of this," I heard Nipper shout.

"Who the fuck cares what you think, big tits?" Bongo replied.

"But they'll die down there!"

"So, what's your point?"

"You don't have to do this," Mom shouted. "You've got what you want."

"That's right, Mummy," Bongo scoffed. "But, we don't need no witnesses."

I scrambled up the ladder again. Just as I reached the opening, Bongo tapped my head with the sole of his boot, sending me back down. Thankfully, I managed to keep my hands gripped around the ladder's rails, which helped minimize the impact of my forced descent.

"Danny, are you okay? " Mom asked.

She bent down to examine my head. I was grateful for her soft touch as she rubbed the spot where I had been kicked. Milah tried her best to pacify me, too, by licking my face. My vision was blurred, but I could make out Paddy staring down at me from the trapdoor opening. His head bobbed left and right between Bongo's hands that were still clutching him -- as if he were thinking, "Should I do this, or that?" Then, suddenly, he stabbed his beak into one of Bongo's fingers.

"What the shit?" Bongo yelled, letting go of Paddy. "The bad ass black bastard has gone and smurfed me. My finger's bleeding like a fucking fire hose!"

Those were the last words we heard. We watched the ladder being pulled up, followed by the hard closing of the trapdoor and the eerie, grating sound of the promised rock rolling onto it. Then there was silence, except for Paddy's rapid, but muffled cawing and Milah's growling at our now invisible assailants.

"What're we going to do now? No one'll find us down here. We've no way out."

"Says who?" Mom replied.

I gave her a disbelieving look.

"We're going to get out the Ali Baba way," she said.

"What?"

"You know. Like Open Sesame."

"You're losing it, Mom."

She smiled, then reached into a side pocket of her jeans and pulled out her cell phone.

"It's your grandfather's." Gran asked him to lend it to me before we left. She wanted me to call her and let her know what time we'd be back. Let's hope it works from down here."

The cell phone signal was, in spite of Mom's numerous attempts to connect, too weak to fly beyond the crackling static and Paddy's muffled caws.

"Try Jane," I suggested and told her the number, which I had memorized, thankfully, the day before. "She lives closer."

Mom got through, but there was still a lot of static on the line when she did.

"I think I hear Jane's voice, but I can't be sure."

"Tell her where we are anyway. Maybe she can hear us."

Mom did as I suggested and hung up.

"So, since it looks like your 'Open Sesame plan' didn't work, what now?"

"We can start by blowing out one of the lamps to save precious oxygen. Then we'd better think of some way of getting more air down here just in case."

She pointed to something in the chamber's cemented ceiling. I walked over to it.

"It's just an old pipe," I said. "And it's blocked with dirt."

"That used to be a ventilation shaft."

Mom lifted the glass of one of the hurricane lamps and blew out the flame. I searched the chamber for anything to help us escape. I was about to give up when I fixed my eyes on the table. I grabbed hold of it and used the largest blade of my Swiss army knife to slice through the tough rawhide strips that bound its bamboo structure together.

"What are you doing?" Mom asked me.

"The poles," I replied with excitement.

"What?"

"Bamboo is hollow inside. If we shave off some of the ends, maybe we can attach them together to make ventilation tubes."

"Good thinking," she said.

In about ten or 15 minutes, Mom and I had managed to carve, pull, twist and cajole three poles together -- a foot longer than the length we needed to span the seven-foot distance to fresh air above. We then repeated the operation with a second set of three I had freed from bondage -- in about half the time.

"What's your next bright idea?" she asked.

I found two tiny medicine bottles on a shelf and used my teeth to extract their dried-out corks.

"Here. Plug one of these corks into one end of the pole to seal it. I'll do the same with mine."

When we had finished capping the poles, I told Mom to press one corked tip hard against the earth that was blocking the ventilation pipe.

"Grip tightly and don't let go," I ordered.

I then picked up the rock I had extracted earlier and used it to hammer the end of the bamboo tube repeatedly until its tip had broken completely through the ground above. Thankfully, the soil was only packed hard into the first foot of the pipe.

"We're through," I shouted.

I moved the pole back and forth to widen the air tunnel it had made a bit more. I then removed it and uncorked it, hoping that the second one would be as easy. It wasn't. It took me dozens of attempts to bore through the second time, as I seemed to hit a rock with every bang of my stone hammer. Finally, however, I managed to set the two uncorked bamboo air tubes firmly in place in case we needed them to breathe later.

"Good job, Danny."

"You, too."

Milah seemed to enjoy our upbeat spirit. She ran circles around us several times and then collapsed on all fours, panting.

Mom said something but I was too focused elsewhere to hear. I was scanning the chamber's contents for something to help us bridge the gap between the floor and the trap door when my eyes fixed on the wide barnwood shelves along the walls. Two of them looked to be at least 12 feet long and a good inch thick.

"Perfect!" I shouted.

"What?"

"Help me clear away all the stuff on the shelves and you'll see."

After we'd removed all the items and placed them carefully on the floor next to the far wall, I easily lifted two loosely mounted shelf planks off their brackets. I then placed them back-to-back and set them upright on an angle between the floor and the trapdoor.

"Wish me luck," I said as I crawled on all fours up the makeshift bridge. The wood was dry and brittle from age.

"Be careful."

"Why do mothers always say that?"

"Because we care?"

When I reached the top, I pushed hard against the trapdoor, but I couldn't budge it. The rock on top was too heavy.

"I need to dig my feet into something to give me leverage."

Mom answered by crawling up behind me until her shoulders made contact with my boots. She wrapped her arms and legs tightly around the two planks.

"Dig your feet into my shoulders and push away!"

I did as I was told and, slowly but surely, I managed to push the door open this time -- inch by inch. I heard the rock roll away when I had opened the door half way. When I had opened it completely, I heard a creaking sound, and then another one.

"Get off quick, Mom. The planks are cracking! Get out of the way, Milah!"

Mom slid down and I followed her. Milah sat down a few feet away.

When I reached the ground, I grabbed the planks, one after the other, and placed them on the floor to examine them. Both had splits in them around the middle.

"Looks like we got off just in time, Danny."

"Well, they're no good to us now and I don't see any more long enough to help us out of here, do you?"

"We'll think of something."

I looked up at the trapdoor opening. It was a rectangle of cloudy, but welcome autumn sky.

I thought Milah was as pleased as Mom and I were to be breathing easier until I realized that she was barking at the distant claps of thunder rolling towards us.

"That's all we need," Mom said. "A thunderstorm with us down here, standing at the bottom of what could soon be a well. We need an exit strategy and quick. And this won't help," she added holding up Poppy's cell phone. "The battery's deader than dead."

"Did you tell Poppy or Gran where we were headed today?"

"Not exactly. I did say that we *might* head towards Paddington Pond. I wasn't any more specific than that. I think we're on our own for now."

"If we hadn't busted up the table to make the poles, we could have used it to gain some height."

"We'll just have to sit it out. Dad and Mom are sure to come looking for us when we don't return."

But sit we couldn't. The thunderclaps were getting louder and more frequent as they drew closer, signaling a violent thunderstorm. I was afraid that heavy rain would soon pour into the chamber.

While it wasn't noon yet, the sky was now as dark as night. To make matters worse, a strong wind blew cold air, leaves, branches, and even soil down upon us. We began to miss the protection of the trapdoor we had worked so hard to open, but we knew there was nothing we could do to close it. Then the wick of the hurricane lamp flame flickered and died, leaving us in total darkness. Mom switched on her penlight but its battery was now too weak to give off much light. I felt around the chamber for the hurricane lamp that we had turned off earlier, but could not find it among all the items we had removed from the shelves when we made our makeshift bridge.

• • •

What we didn't know at that time was that another piece of the drama was unfolding four or five miles away as the crow flies. A familiar black messenger flew into the family farm to alert Poppy and Gran in his own tongue. When he arrived, they were standing in front of the porch in their yellow, hooded ponchos, enjoying the lightning show and waiting for the rain to fall.

"I wonder what's got into Paddy," Poppy said. "At least I think it's Paddy."

"He sure is cawing up a storm, isn't he?" Gran replied. "Pun intended," she added, following a powerful thunderclap and another lightning flash directly above the farmhouse.

Paddy flew around and around in circles above them and every time he arrived at their southernmost points, he screamed, "Caw… caw… caw… caw, Danny." He repeated this message five or six times.

"Well, now we know it is Paddy and he sure is trying to tell us something," Poppy said. "Let's start walking towards him the next time he starts cawing."

When Paddy arrived at the southern point of his next circular flyby, Gran and Poppy walked in that direction. After cawing twice when they did, he swooped towards them. As he flew past Poppy's head, he screamed, "Caw… caw… caw… caw…Danny." He then flew slowly south, maintaining an altitude of a dozen feet or so above the ground.

"Before she left this morning, Maire told me that she and Danny might go to Paddington Pond and that seems to be the direction Paddy's heading. I'm going to phone her."

Gran reached into her poncho pocket for her cell phone and tapped an automatic dialer button. She reached the recorded voice of an announcer who told her that her call couldn't be completed.

"I can't get through. My intuition tells me that something's terribly wrong."

"Maire could be out of range."

"Any other time I'd settle for that. But that's one smart bird and he sure seemed worked up about Danny."

The roar of a pickup caught Gran and Poppy's attention. They watched as Jake Saulter's new pickup truck appeared in the laneway and pulled up outside the house, bringing heavy rain with him. He rolled down the window. He was wearing a green rubber poncho with its hood up.

"Hey, Lee-Ann and Tyler. What's up? You two look like you've lost your best friend."

When Poppy and Gran told Jake about Paddy's strange behavior, he apologized for his poor choice of words and offered to drive them to Paddington Pond. Poppy accepted his kindness and locked up the house.

• • •

Around 1:30 p.m., the sky directly above the trapdoor opening was night black, except for the lightning that flashed across it -- again and again. Deafening thunderclaps and heavy rain followed the flashes. Then rain cascaded into the underground chamber at such a fast rate that it was up to our ankles in less than a minute. A few minutes later, the water was almost up to our knees and Milah's tummy, and climbing.

"At the rate it's coming down, we'll be able to swim out soon," I said.

"And, if it stops too soon, the three of us could drown down here," Mom replied.

Milah stood beside us, whimpering. Occasionally, the poor mutt barked at the thunderclaps. I grabbed Mom's hand and held onto it.

"Why is it filling up so fast?"

"Probably because the land around the shelter is on an incline, I guess," she said.

"Some shelter," I scoffed.

We felt helpless. We knew that the storm was very much in charge now -- not us. The rain continued to pour down on us, and soon it was up to our waists. Then, in what seemed like no time at all, it filled up to our necks, and Milah was dogpaddling in it.

Mom stood on her toes to gain extra height. We wrapped our arms around each other for support. A short while later, we found ourselves treading water to avoid swallowing it.

"We'd better pray that the rain doesn't stop," Mom said. "At least we're getting closer to the exit."

Her words must have jinxed us because, soon after she spoke them, the rain did stop, leaving us nowhere else to go. It was now a case of treading water for dear life or sinking below the water line and drowning.

We were feeling colder and more exhausted the more we tried to stay afloat.

"I love you, Danny," Mom said weakly. She was shaking, and her eyelids were heavy. "I needed to say that because I don't think we've much time left."

"I love you, too, Mom, but I'm not giving up yet. Please hang on!"

"We need a miracle…I'm so cold."

I never prayed before, but I found myself screaming to God in my mind for that miracle. I didn't know it then, but it was flying our way.

• • •

Jake Saulter kept his eye on the trail ahead while Poppy kept his on Paddy, their navigator. The pickup's headlight beams kept him in view, as he flew above the trail towards Paddington Pond, and then past it. Gran was sitting on the pickup's front seat between the two men. While the wipers were set to high speed, they were having a hard time beating the heavy rain off the windshield.

"You'd better make a left at the 'Y' and head for Old Tom's," Poppy said. "That's where I think Paddy's going."

They could hear Paddy cawing excitedly between thunderclaps the closer the pickup got to Old Tom's. When they arrived at the clearing, they saw Paddy swoop towards the underground shelter, screaming, "Caw, caw, caw, caw, Danny." He repeated this action several times until Jake wheeled the pickup closer to the underground shelter.

• • •

Milah barked when she heard Paddy's cawing. A moment later, Paddy swooped past the shelter's opening.

"Mom, it's Paddy," I shouted.

I shook her to keep her awake, to make her listen and to give her hope.

"How can he help us?" she whispered weakly. "He's only a bird."

I shook her again.

"Listen! I hear the sound of an engine. It's getting closer."

Paddy and the engine grew silent. I strained my ears to hear more. Seconds seemed like long, agonizing minutes as we waited, not knowing how much longer we could hang on. Then, in an instant, I knew that we'd be okay. A flashlight beamed down on us from the trapdoor opening and I heard a familiar voice shout, "Over here, Tyler! Over here!"

Milah barked more excitedly.

"Jake! Poppy! Mom and I are in deep water and she's getting colder and weaker. I don't know how much longer she can hold on."

"We'll have you out in a minute, Danny," Poppy yelled. "Lee-Ann, call 911. Tell them we'll need an air ambulance."

"Hurry. I think Mom's passed out. She's really cold."

Paddy flew down through the opening, screaming, "Caw, caw, Danny!" Finding no place to land, he cawed three times and flew back through the opening.

"You can thank your bird for helping us find you," Jake said. "But, more about that later. Let's get you out of there first. Hey Tyler, give me a hand with the winch. It's housed in the box on top of the front bumper. Just press the starter button and I'll guide the cable down to them.

"Okay."

"A heli-ambulance is on its way!" Gran shouted. "They said to keep them warm to prevent hypothermia."

The hum of the winch motor was music to my ears. Jake, as he promised, lowered the cable down to us. It had a loop at the end.

242

"Is it strong enough to pull both of us up at the same time?"

"You bet," Jake said.

"Give me a bit more cable then. I'll put my foot in the loop and hang onto Mom while you winch. Then I'll go back down and bring Milah up the same way."

I held onto the cable with one hand and wrapped my free arm snugly around Mom.

"Pull away," I shouted. "We're ready!"

While Jake guided our ascent, Poppy raised Mom and me inch by inch until we cleared the opening of our near tomb. I was delighted to lay my eyes on my grandparents and Jake.

Despite my protests, Poppy would not let me go back for Milah. He went down to get her himself.

Chapter 29

POPPY, GRAN, MOM, AND I continued to chat about the day's events long after Jake had gone home. Jane rang around ten the next morning, about an hour after mail carrier, Elton Aycock had delivered the news of our ordeal to her house along with the mail.

"Are you all right? I've been worried sick about you since I heard what happened. I had to wait until my dad went to town to call you."

"We tried to phone you from the shelter around lunchtime, but all we got was static."

"I remember getting a call about then, but I couldn't hear anybody. Can you pick me up? I'll wait for you at Four Corners?"

"I'm on my way!"

I hung up without saying goodbye.

I stepped hard on the gas pedal of my pickup and didn't realize how fast I was driving until Lieutenant Kobernick passed me about a mile from the farm and signaled me to pull over.

"You got a train to catch?" she asked. "Step out of the truck please."

I got out and leaned against the fender.

"I was on my way to see you about last night, so I'll overlook the speeding this time. So, what gives? I don't want to rely on Elton Aycock's hearsay for my report. He's been blabbing your story all over the county and it's getting saltier with each telling."

She recorded every detail of what I could remember in her notebook -- except one.

"And?"

I looked away.

"Come on. I need names, dammit. Were they the same idiots who burned down the cabin? I've got the fire inspector and the insurance company breathing down my neck for results on that one. Or was it your Crows? Come on, Danny. Cough up. No sense protecting scumbags like that."

"I'm no rat."

"They're the rats. They could've killed you and your mother. Tell me everything about the fire and everything afterwards or I'll have to bring you in as a material witness."

"It was them. It was the Crows."

"Their names? I know you used to run with them."

"I only saw Aladdin and Bongo, but I heard Nipper talking and Bongo called out to Aldo."

"Nipper's the girl, right?"

I nodded.

"She tried to talk Bongo out of shutting us in, but he wouldn't listen."

"Okay, now what about the fire? I've already spoken to Jane Calloway about it, so your story had better match hers."

I filled her in on all the details.

"And the sheriff didn't follow up any more on this afterwards?"

"No," I replied.

"He was, as usual, protecting his son. Okay, that's all for now. You drive more careful-like, hear? And call me, if you remember anything else."

I nodded and resumed my journey after she made a U-turn and sped off in the opposite direction.

I kept pretty well to the speed limit the rest of the way to the crossroads. Jane waved when she spotted me and I flashed my headlights to acknowledge her. When she got in, she wrapped her arms around me and kissed me on the lips.

"Let's go somewhere where we can be alone," she said.

"I want to give you something."

Following her directions, we pulled into a side road and parked in a secluded grove of poplar. She began to unbutton her blouse slowly.

"Are you sure you want to do this?" I asked and she nodded.

Paddy was my witness to how wonderful a first time it was. He must have followed me from the farm and was perched on the side of the cab, peeking through the rear-view window. We concluded with a long kiss of appreciation and, when our feathery voyeur cawed his approval, Jane and I cawed back, then laughed.

I was naïve to think that our euphoria would last and Jane was the first to dispel it.

"What're we going to do, Danny?"

"About?"

"Everything. I'm terrified about what your gang might do to you and your family. And I'm scared about what my father may do to you, especially if he finds out what we just did. He'll want to send us both to hell."

"I wish I had all the answers. What I do know is I've totally made up my mind on one thing. I'm not going back to the city. For the first time in my life, I have felt secure and at home somewhere – in spite of everything that's been going on."

"And how do I fit in to your happy country plan?"

"Do I really have to spell it out?"

"Yes. I need to hear it."

"You're the main reason I feel I belong here. If you weren't here, I probably wouldn't be."

"Then, if that's true, why don't we just run away together? We can always come back when we turn 18."

"And go where to do what? How would we live? And don't forget, I'm under a court order to stay here."

She stopped talking and pouted instead. I caressed her cheek.

"Don't sweat it," I said. "It'll work out, one step at a time. By the way, what's your father doing in town?"

"Selling cattle at market. He'll be haggling for best prices all morning, if I know him."

I turned the key in the ignition.

"I'm going to drop you off at Four Corners. Can you come by the farm this aft?"

She nodded. "Where are you going?"

"There's something I have to do myself. I'll tell you all about it later."

"Tell me now," she said.

"Can't," I replied, managing a quick smile. "It's a surprise."

Chapter 30

PADDY WAS PERCHED ON MY SHOULDER as I watched Abe Calloway from a safe distance. He and a fellow farmer, a toothless old man, wearing a ragged straw hat and dirty dungarees, spat into their respective right hands. They then exchanged firm handshakes while a young bull, the object of their negotiation, chomped away on dry hay in a pen.

"Fare you well with him then, Dickie," I heard Abe say as he accepted the money. He stuffed the bills in his back pocket without counting them. "I'm sure he's got lots of good seed in him for your heifers. Remember, I get the first calf as part of the deal."

"I hope your bull's smarter than the blockhead you sold me in '89, Abe," Dickie answered. "It took forever for him to figure out what to do with his plumbing. As sweet Jesus knows, I had to bring in an older bull to show him where to put it."

"Come on then, Dickie, you old complainer, you. Didn't he end up delivering you three prizewinners before you had him ground up?"

"That's true. Just wish he'd been quicker on the draw from get go, if you know what I mean. I'll be seeing you," he added. "Oh, and don't forget to write up the bill of sale before end of day. I don't want you to have me arrested for rustling."

Abe laughed. "That's not such a bad idea then."

Because I had never even seen Abe smile before, his laughter came as a surprise.

Dickie chuckled back and then walked off towards the Auctioneer's Palace, which was anything but regal; it was really a monstrous old barn in disguise.

Abe turned and walked in the opposite direction. When he had gone about 15 yards, a rough-looking young man bumped into Abe and stuck his hand into the back pocket of Abe's jeans.

While I never gave it a passing thought at the time, I had noticed the bumper watching the bartering seconds earlier. He wore a baseball cap and its peak was pulled down so low, it almost completely covered his face.

"He's after Abe's money, Paddy," I said.

Paddy responded with a low, gargled caw.

"Get your hand out of there!" Abe cried.

He pushed the bumper away and half-ran down a long alleyway between rows of weathered wooden sheds and barns, yelling, "Help, help!"

The bumper chased after Abe. Paddy flew after the bumper and I ran after them all. I lost sight of the two men for a moment when they disappeared around a bend in the alley. After I passed the bend, I saw the bumper stooping over Abe who was facedown on the ground, bleeding and groaning. He had Abe's money in his fist. He turned when he heard Paddy's agitated cawing and swung wildly at me when I arrived on the scene.

I brushed Paddy away and charged the bumper, knocking him to the ground. He was scrawny and he looked like he was strung out on something. He tried to fight back, but he was no match for me. And he was no match for Paddy who cawed and pecked at his throwing arm when he tried to hit me a second time. I put him in an arm lock and pulled him to his feet.

"Let me go!" he screamed. "You can have the money."

"Hand it over first!" I ordered.

I had to relax my grip to grab the money from him and he took advantage of that moment to kick one of my ankles and run off through the barn's doorway. I was in too much pain to run after him. When Abe looked up at me from the ground, I could see that he was in pain, too.

Paddy flew back onto my shoulder.

"You!" he said. He coughed up a mixture of phlegm and blood, and spat it on the ground at my feet to let me know that it was a present for me. "You in on this, too, then? I see you have my money."

"It wasn't me, Mr. Calloway," I said. "I came here to talk to you about Jane and me, and I saw that guy attack you."

He got up slowly and took a step towards me. He stopped when I adopted a defensive position and Paddy cawed at him to back off.

"You expect me to believe your made-up story? I've nothing more to say to the likes of you then, young fella. You can tell your made-up story to the judge."

"The boy is telling the truth," a man shouted at Abe from the doorway of a nearby barn. He wore a market official's badge on the lapel of his wool jacket. "I saw and heard everything while I was doing a safety check on the foals. He and that crow of his may have just saved your life *and* your money."

"I don't believe you."

"You can believe the moon's made of blue chicken shit for all I care, but it's the gospel truth. *And* you can count on me to swear to that in open court."

Abe looked up at the sky and said, "Sweet mother of Jesus, what am I going to do with this constant thorn in my side?"

The official looked at his watch.

"Well, I'd best be going. I've lots more stalls to check before my day's done. If you need me as a witness, son, ask for *The Saint*. The name's Santino Starnino, but folks call me *The Saint*."

He waved good-bye and went into another barn across from us.

"Here's your loot," I said to Abe. *"Every dollar of it!"*

He counted the bills before stuffing them into his back pocket. Then he stared at me -- and at Paddy.

"You said you were coming to see me," he said without a word of thanks. "What's on your mind then?"

"Jane."

"Look, I told you before to stay away from her."

"Well, I'm not going to. And that's that. We both want to be with each other. You can either accept that and the fact that I will treat her well, or you can try and keep me away until she's 18, and then she can do whatever she damn well wants -- with or without your blessing."

He walked away but, when he reached the first paddock, he stopped, turned and rubbed his chin. He just stood there for a couple of minutes and stared back at me. Then he retraced his steps, wiping blood from his face with an old handkerchief.

"You've got balls bigger'n the bull in my pasture. I'll give you that much."

"Does that mean you're agreeable to me seeing Jane then?"

"Agreeable? Not on your unholy life! But, as the Good Book said about Jesus, if it's to be, then it's to be then. Mind you, you court her proper. Hear? No hanky panky stuff and have her home at a decent hour. And you make sure she keeps the Sabbath. I've no never mind what you do about your own soul. I do about hers. Those are my rules then. Hear?"

"Can we shake on it?" I said, spitting into my right palm, knowing that the no hanky panky bit was going to be my biggest challenge.

He chuckled. "I suppose you can't be all that bad if you're Tyler Mahoney's grandson. You could be a worse'un then."

He spat into his right palm, too, and we exchanged handshakes; his was soft and hesitating while mine was firm and more determined than ever. Paddy sealed the agreement with his signature caw.

"Are you going to report what happened here?"

"I'll think on it some. That robber will get his comeuppance whether I do or not -- in this world or the next."

"Abe, better hurry!" a middle-aged woman shouted. She was wearing a green blazer with an official-looking yellow ribbon in her lapel. "Margie Wainright's prize rooster is about to hit the block."

"I thought she'd get him on early," he replied, looking at me squarely in the eyes again. "I've had my eyes on that critter for a spell."

"I hope you get it," I said.

"Tell the auctioneer to choke his hammer 'til I get there then," he shouted at the official.

I watched Abe waddle off after her, his oversized Wellingtons making sucking sounds in the wet mud as he approached the building. He now looked less scary than he did in the image of him that I had stored in my memory since our first encounter.

On my way back to the parking lot, three Holstein calves looked up at me from their pen. The largest one bellowed "mm-mawwww" to me. A *For Sale* sign hung on the gatepost above its head. Their caretaker leaned against the gate. He was about 20 years old, decked out in matching blue denim jeans and shirt, with a cowboy's hat hanging from its loop around his neck.

"How much for one of your calves?" I asked him.

"Two hundred or best offer."

"The best I can do is $150," I lied.

"There's no use haggling with you then. Take your pick."

"No, you pick out your best one."

"That would be the one in the middle. She was born with an extra teat and she's been fattening-up faster than the other two, even though she's not the biggest of them yet."

"Can you deliver?" I said, counting out the money. "I'll give you half now and half on arrival"

"It's an extra $50 for local delivery within 15 miles. Where to?"

"Tyler and Lee-Ann Mahoney's farm."

"Mahoneys?"

I nodded.

"I'm their grandson."

"No delivery charge then. I can't charge blood. Tyler's a first cousin of my mother's and we're only two farms over. You're Maire's boy?"

"Yes," I answered. "Danny. Danny Cagney."

"Robbie McGrath. I guess that would make you and me second cousins, I suppose. Is the calf for Tyler?"

"Yeah. His prize breeder was killed yesterday."

"So I heard. Terrible business that was. Hey, what's the bird's name?"

"Paddy," Paddy replied. "Paddy."

"Well, I'll be," Robbie said. "That's the first time I've ever heard a crow talk. Didn't know they could. I'll drop the calf off after I close up this evening."

"That'd be great. I'll have the money ready."

"No hurry. If you're there, okay. If not, you can drop it off whenever. Tyler or Lee-Ann will tell you where."

We shook hands and I hurried over to the parking lot. I was feeling anxious to tell Jane my good news.

• • •

I met Jane back at the farm as planned and she could hardly believe her ears when I told her. She peppered me with questions, expecting me to spice up my encounter with her father even more, but I insisted on reporting the event exactly as it had transpired.

"If I told you anything else, I'd only be making it up, and what would be the point in that?"

"I'm just so happy it turned out the way you say it did. I guess I'll see how well when I get home."

"And I'll be there with you when you do. We don't have to hide our relationship anymore."

She took my hand in hers.

"Danny?"

"Yes, Jane."

"Only two to go."

"Two what?"

"Problems to solve."

I looked at her inquisitively.

"The Crows and the locals," she said.

"The cops'll take care of them."

"And if they don't?"

"We'll just have to see *then*, won't we?"

. . .

Robbie McGrath – true to his promise -- delivered the calf around sunset when Poppy, Paddy and I were putting the farm to sleep for the night. Poppy found it hard to find his words when he told Gran later, but his smile and his nod told me how much he appreciated the gift.

"You'll be dirt poor, if you keep that up," he managed to say.

"Money's not everything," I replied. "By the way, I made peace with Abe Calloway at the market today, and now Jane and I are an official number."

"How in heaven's name did you manage that?" Gran asked.

I shrugged my shoulders.

"Must've taken some convincing," Mom said as she stepped off the porch. "I've never known Abe to change his mind about anything before."

"Well he did and that's all that matters, I guess. He isn't exactly thrilled about the situation, but at least he didn't chase me off with a gun."

Chapter 31

A FEW NIGHTS LATER, I was lying in bed fighting sleep, reflecting on what Jane had said when I told her that I had made peace with her father. She had hit the nail squarely on the head concerning the cards I had been dealt and the different hands I'd played since my last court session with Judge Fisher. However, while things seemed, on the surface at least, to be coming together, two wild cards were left in the deck: the four Crows and the Wade Simmons trio. As hard as I tried, I could not get them out of my mind, even when I finally fell fast asleep.

• • •

They were all waiting for me in a black-and-white dream. All of them, except Billy Cross, were laughing and pointing at me as I flew with Paddy in the sky above a winding, frozen river.

Suddenly, Billy appeared naked and shivering, flying in formation with Paddy and me. He looked down at the ice, pointing at the others. They were dressed in soldiers' uniforms, shooting bullets from rifles at us.

Paddy was the first to be hit and fall from the sky. I flew down fast after him and had just caught him in mid-air when a bullet from Bongo's gun struck me in the chest, sending me crashing, nearly unconscious, through the thin ice, still clutching Paddy to my chest.

The strong current dragged Paddy and me down river towards a roaring waterfall. Paddy cawed frantically for me to do something to save us, but I was too weak and dazed to act. As we were being swept over, Paddy flew away from me. I was screaming and thrashing my arms in desperation when I saw the angry maelstrom and jagged rocks waiting for me downriver. I breathed a sigh of relief when a fisher's net captured me and unseen hands pulled me slowly upward, landing me on dry ground in front of my grandparents' farmhouse.

"You're lucky Paddy came to get me," Billy Cross whispered hoarsely. "You could've drowned or frozen to death. Here, I'll help you out of that net."

I thrashed my arms and legs to break free of the net and woke up punching, kicking and screaming at the sheets and blankets covering me on my bed. Paddy cawed at me from his cage on my dresser.

• • •

I realized I'd been dreaming when I woke up to Paddy's cawing. I thought that Billy Cross, the least of the Wade Simmons trio, might just be the trump card I needed to beat the wild cards in the deck I'd been dealt. While he was not the smartest of the bunch, I had the feeling he could, nevertheless, provide useful intelligence, if I handled him just right.

Chapter 32

I DECIDED TO TAKE THE BULL BY THE HORNS and not wait for another chance meeting with Billy Cross, in my sleep or otherwise. I called Jane for directions to his family's lumber mill and rode out on Jessie the next morning after chores. Paddy and Milah tagged along for support. I followed Milah who seemed to know the way, although, true to form, she explored both sides of the roads and trails en route. Paddy roosted quietly on his favorite perch, my left shoulder.

The hum of a circular lumber saw provided the first hint that we were closing in on our destination. It reminded me of Robert Frost's poem, "Out, Out." I knew the lines well because I had to memorize every stanza in junior high. I found myself reciting a few lines now:

The buzz saw snarled and rattled in the yard
And made dust and dropped stove-length sticks of wood,
Sweet-scented stuff when the breeze drew across it.
And from there those that lifted eyes could count
Five mountain ranges one behind the other
Under the sunset far into Vermont.
And the saw snarled and rattled, snarled and rattled,
As it ran light, or had to bear a load.

At least the Vermont setting's right, I thought. I wondered if Billy Cross would just snarl at me when I began rattling his cage, which I was determined to do, no matter what.

The sawmill was set in a clearing in Grand Isle County, between the Green Mountains to the east and the equally majestic Adirondacks to the west. The first person I spotted there was a man I took to be in his fifties. He was wheeling a trolley stacked with fresh lumber to a waiting truck, which he loaded up. Except for his wrinkled skin and a slight limp, he was almost a twin of Billy, complete with his crop of carrot-red hair and pointed chin. A Dorian Grey in the flesh.

I tied Jessie's reigns around a birch tree and hid until the man had driven past me with his load of lumber before moving closer with Milah and Paddy. When I entered the sawmill, the saw was no longer snarling and rattling. Billy was sneezing as he swept sawdust from the knotted pine floor.

"Was that your old man, Billy?"

Milah wagged her tail, hankering for a pat from Billy who ignored her. Paddy cawed "hello," but Billy didn't pay him any attention either. He stopped sweeping to wipe snot from his nose with a long, slow swipe of his sleeve. He had a black eye, and a band-aid on his left cheek.

"What're you doing here?" he stammered.

"I just want to talk to you."

"'bout what?"

"I think you know what."

"I've got nothing to say to you."

"Why? You afraid of Wade and Pauly? Did they do that to you?"

He lowered his head when I pointed at his face.

"They've been real busy since you torched Old Tom's."

"The cabin fire was Wade's and Pauly's idea. I didn't know they was going to do it until they started burning it. I've been trying to stay away from them ever since, but they won't let up."

"I'm not here about the fire."

"Then what?"

"I need you to tell me what they're up to - as far as Jane and I are concerned."

"I dunno."

He lifted the broom as a warning to back off when I took a step towards him.

"I think you do know, Billy. And I'm not leaving here until you tell me."

"I'm no squealer!"

"Just tell me what they're up to and I'll leave you be. I give you my word that I won't tell anyone you told me."

"How do I know I can trust you?"

"You don't, but you can because I've been in your shoes before. I know what it's like - always being pushed around. It's no fun, is it?"

"You can say that," he said with teary eyes.

"So, what are they up to, Billy? Tell me!"

He looked about him to see if anyone was listening to our conversation. He then switched on the dust collector above the saw to muffle what he was about to tell me.

"The sheriff is mad as all hell at you and your grandfather for making him look bad in front of Wade and everyone. He started looking into your background and found out you belonged to the gang the state police and the FBI have been looking for. He decided to get you. He's gonna make Wade look like a hero and rich at the same time."

"How's he plan on doing all that?"

"Wade and Pauly are going to be the ones to turn your gang in, with the sheriff's help."

"So, how's that going to make them rich?"

"The reward. There's $25,000 on each of 'em. The sheriff can't claim it himself because he's a public servant or something, but Wade and Pauly can because they're civilians.

The sheriff's going to get 50 thousand, Wade and Pauly 25 each. They promised ten and a getaway car to the Crows in exchange for their help in getting you, but they don't intend to give it to them."

"And how do I figure in all this?"

"They plan on setting you up, so that you'll get caught with your gang. The sheriff says you will then be sent to reform school to serve out an earlier sentence."

"He's a real piece of work, isn't he?"

"Who?"

"The sheriff."

Billy shrugged and I turned on my heels, pretending to leave.

"Are you really going to keep this between you and me?"

"I said I would, didn't I? But, I warn you. The insurance investigators are sure to come and see you about the fire. Don't lie to them for your own sake. You'll be screaming a lot louder than that saw of yours, if they put you away for something you say you didn't do."

"They know about me?"

"They know everything and more."

"But, what if Wade, Pauly and the sheriff find out I've squealed? I'm no match for them."

Billy looked terrified and I have to admit I felt a little sorry for him. He scratched at the band-aid on his cheek. If he was guilty of anything, it was poor judgment in hanging around with the likes of Wade and Pauly. I guessed he had nowhere else to go.

"Tell the fire investigators you'll cooperate, if they keep you out of it."

I had one last question for Billy.

"How will Wade and Pauly know where to find the Crows?"

"They already have. The sheriff got word they're holed up at Guildford's."

"Guildford's?"

"An abandoned copper mine near the Canadian border. All that's missing is for you to be brought there. I guess they're waiting for the right moment."

"Wait a minute! Bongo's not stupid. How did Wade and Pauly get him to play along?"

"Wade got him to promise to burn down your grandparents' barn as part of the deal for helping them get away. They're going to blame that on you, too, along with the fire at Old Tom's."

"When's all this supposed to happen?"

"I dunno. First chance they get, I guess. I heard my dad say that the sheriff was complaining he's been hard up for cash since his divorce. So he's pretty motivated."

"Thanks," I said. "I'll see you around."

"I'm sorry about all this," Billy said. I thought he really meant it.

"We'd better watch our backs from now on guys," I said to Paddy and Milah as we made for Jessie.

Paddy cawed while Milah just looked up at me and wagged her tail.

As I rode off on Jessie, that feeling of being watched overcame me once again. The trouble was, when I scanned the trees and the sky, I could see no other crow. I shuddered. Then I squeezed my thighs against Jessie's sides, sending her into a fast gallop towards home. Paddy flew ahead of us all the way there, cawing occasionally as he did.

Chapter 33

ABE AND JANE APPEARED LIKE GHOSTS during several quick lightning flashes while Poppy, Jake Saulter and I were talking about the Crows and the sheriff's gang on the porch. They stepped out of their pickup, wearing near-matching clear plastic rain suits and hats. He nodded to Jake, while she exchanged a warm hello with all of us.

I had already told Poppy about my meeting with Billy and my promise to keep his name out of it. I knew that I could count on him to do the same. I also told him more details about the Crows since their arrival in Noburg and how torn in my gut I felt. He listened without passing judgment.

Unlike Poppy and Jake Saulter, who were both clutching over-and-under 16-gauge shotguns, Abe was armed with a lever-action Winchester 30-30 rifle this time; it was tucked loosely under his arm; and he had a belt-full of cartridges running across his chest on a 45-degree angle, from left shoulder to waist.

"It's a wet one then, Tyler" Abe said to Poppy, ignoring me. "Jane tells me you and the boy got some trouble then, and that she was threatened."

He held up his rifle proudly.

"Me and ole Mathilda are here to help you out. Where you want me to set up?"

"Anywhere beyond the barn, I guess," Poppy replied. "No sense being inside if they manage to set it on fire."

"You think they'll do that?"

"We have reason to think they will."

"What about your stock?"

"I left them out in the fields. The state police are on their way. The FBI, too, I think. They were called in after the Crows gang crossed the state line. They'll have to take the long road here because the main one's washed out between the bridge and Noburg. I've sent Lee-Ann and Maire over to Owen McLaughlin's place to play it safe. I'm thinking maybe Jane and Danny should go, too."

"I'm staying," Jane piped in.

"Me, too," I replied. Poppy nodded my decision.

"What about the mine then?" Abe asked. "Jane tells me they're dug in there."

"Not any more. The state police said they've cleared out, which means they could be on their way here."

"You'd better stay in the house then, Jane," Abe said.

"Okay." she answered.

"Danny should stay here, too," Poppy said. "He doesn't have a gun."

Abe gave me a worried look, then turned and walked towards the barn without saying another word.

"Abe, don't shoot anyone unless you have to," Poppy shouted after him. "And be careful we don't catch each other in a crossfire."

Abe didn't answer and continued walking.

"I'm coming along with you, gun or no gun," I said to Poppy. "I know these guys. You don't."

"Will you be okay by yourself, Jane?" he asked.

"Don't worry about me."

"That's my girl! Lock the doors and stay close to the phone. You can keep Milah with you. If you need to reach me, use the house phone to call my cell."

"I don't know your number."

"Use the automatic dialer function. Same for Jake." He paused for a moment and then continued. "Maybe I should program your dad's number, too."

"He wouldn't have answered," Jane said.

"Oh?" Poppy replied.

"He doesn't have a cell. He thinks phones should have wires and rotary dials."

"Hmm. Well, Jake, do you mind staying close to Abe then?"

"Sure thing," Jake replied. "I won't mind, if he doesn't."

I kissed Jane before she went into the house. Then Poppy and I walked cautiously to the opposite side of the barn, hugging a footpath along the edge of the woods.

The rain was heavier now; it felt like pin pricks on my skin as it fell. Poppy and I camped out under the sloping roof of the woodshed, which had three walls and an open side facing the barn. We crouched behind neatly stacked cords of aging firewood, watching and waiting, until three state police cars pulled into the farmyard with lights flashing.

"How stupid can they be?" Poppy asked. "They're going to scare them all off, if they haven't already. We'd better go talk to them."

• • •

Lieutenant Kobernick insisted that the police had no choice but to show up with lights flashing.

"Our first priority is for your safety," she said, as her five male subordinates began searching the area with flashlights. "If we scared them off, all well and good. We'll get them soon enough. Our gang's bigger'n theirs."

She turned quickly on her heels and removed her gun from her holster when she heard the sound of a branch breaking behind her.

"It's okay, Lieutenant. They're with us," I said. "Meet Abe Calloway and Jake Saulter, our neighbors."

Abe and Jake walked up to us and nodded to the Lieutenant. She re-holstered her firearm and looked at theirs.

"I'll assume for now you've got permits for those fire sticks. Just don't go getting vigilante-like and trigger-happy. We want to bring them in one piece, if we can."

We all waited on the porch for the other five officers to complete their search, drinking fresh coffee that Jane had brewed for us. When the officers returned, there was a sixth man with them. He was handcuffed and cursing. He was wearing a long oilskin coat and a cowboy hat with its rim pulled down over his brow.

"Dammit it to hell, Mahoney. Tell them to get these effing cuffs offa me!"

"He says he's the local sheriff," the oldest of the officers volunteered. "But, he has no ID on him and he was packin'," he added, holding up the magnum for all to see.

"You know him?" the lieutenant asked.

"Unfortunately, yes," Poppy replied. "He's the local sheriff all right, at least in name. Sheriff Edgar Simmons."

"Any relation to Wade Simmons?"

"His father."

"Well now. Well now. Isn't this a blessing? We were going to talk to you tomorrow about the arson fire at the cabin in the woods. Looks like we can do that tonight and save some shoe leather. Tell me, *Sheriff* Simmons, what are you doing on the Mahoney farm? I assume you have permission to be here...or you have a warrant?"

"I'm here on police business and I have reasonable cause to be," he answered cockily. "I got a tip from an informant that there were people running around with guns. Looks like my info was accurate."

"Oh yeah, so why aren't you in uniform then?"

He rubbed his chin with his handcuffed hands.

"I'm...er... undercover. I got the call after I got home and changed."

The lieutenant frowned and shook her head in disbelief. Then she turned towards Poppy and winked.

"Mr. Mahoney, if you don't mind, we'll take *Sheriff* Simmons in for trespassing on your land."

"I don't mind one bit."

"I'll sue you all to hell," the sheriff protested.

"Hey, Jimmy!" the lieutenant said to the older male officer. "You want to Mirandize the sheriff please before he starts counting his suing money?"

Jimmy nodded and pulled the sheriff by the arm towards his waiting car.

"You have the right to remain silent..."

"You can skip the rest of that shit. I'm the law for crissakes. Just get to the part where I can call my goddamned lawyer."

The officer ignored his request and kept on reading the Miranda statement.

Chapter 34

LIEUTENANT KOBERNICK might just as well have read the farm its rights, too, because it became unusually silent for the rest of the night. She posted one squad car out of sight on each of its four sides while Jake, Poppy, Abe and I stood sentry on the porch in two-hour shifts. We jokingly appointed Milah lookout-in-chief due to her superior hearing. Paddy nodded off beside me on a bench during my watch and returned to my room with me when it was over.

Lieutenant Kobernick showed up the next morning for coffee and told us that the sheriff had been released due to lack of evidence.

"Who was the judge?" Jake asked.

"Kingston."

"That figures. His hunting buddy."

"The first thing he did out the door was ticket my car for parking illegally."

"Sounds like something he'd do, but not for long I hope."

"Oh?" the lieutenant asked.

"I'm trying to convince Jake Saulter to run against Simmons next year. I think he has a good chance of beating him. A lot of people are fed up with the way Simmons runs things around here."

"Good luck, if you do," she said to Jake.

"We'll see," he said. "I don't know if the county's ready for a black sheriff."

"They weren't ready for Bass Reeves in Indian Territory over a century ago. He was as black as they came and he turned out to be one of the finest U.S. deputy marshals the Wild West ever saw. He even arrested his own son for murder, winning the respect of blacks and whites alike for his fairness. And the famous Hanging Judge Parker, who first pinned a tin star on him, thought there was no one else quite like him."

"Sounds like you're one of them there history 'buffers' then," Abe said.

"You betcha. Nineteenth Century Oklahoma Territory's my favorite period."

"So where do we go from here, Lieutenant?" Poppy asked.

"We'll keep looking for the Crows gang. They're bound to slip up sometime. What's more, it's going to get mighty cold around here soon. That won't make it any easier for them. Of course, there are lots of empty summer cottages to hole up in at this time of year. Anyway, let me know if you see anything suspicious and I'll keep you posted at my end."

She walked to her car and I followed her with Paddy on my shoulder.

"Lieutenant…?"

She waited for me to finish my sentence.

"If I tell you something important, will you promise not to ask me for my source?"

"I'll do my best to," she replied. "Unless it's about a crime you committed. I'd have to read you your rights first."

"No, it's not about something I've done. It's about something I heard. If I tell you, you cannot pressure me to reveal my source. I gave the person who told me my word."

"You've got mine then. No pressure."

I recounted what Billy had told me at the sawmill without mentioning his name.

"Too bad you or your grandfather didn't tell me all this sooner."

"I asked him not to say anything just yet. He was just respecting a confidence. I was secretly hoping that you would catch the Crows and find out yourself. Then, when you arrested the sheriff, I thought he'd spill his guts to save himself and his son."

"Fat chance of that. He lawyered up right away. He knows his own rights all too well, and he uses them to his advantage."

"Will you be able to do anything with the information I gave you?"

"It'll help us refocus our efforts, but nothing you told me would stand up in court. It's only hearsay."

She thanked me and got in her car. Before driving away, she held out her upturned palm to Paddy through the open window. He seemed pleased to see the tamari almonds she had placed there for him.

"Caw," he said before pecking off the nuts, one by one.

"Caw to you, too, my friend. What's his name?"

"Paddy," I said. "He was injured and I've been nursing him back to health. He'll be going his own way soon."

"Well, Paddy, keep your beak clean or I'll be coming for you."

"Caw," Paddy answered. "Caw…caw…."

She drove off, cawing and laughing.

Chapter 35

THE RAIN REFUSED TO LET UP for the next three days and nights. It transformed the farm into a lake of muck that stuck to our boots like globs of porridge wherever we walked. Poppy and I did out best to go about our chores normally, while Abe and Jake continued to patrol the farm with their firearms ready for action. Gran and Mom returned from the McLaughlin farm earlier and joined Jane in the house.

The State Troopers continued to patrol the perimeter of the farm until midnight of the third night. Lieutenant Kobernick called while Poppy, Paddy, Milah and I were keeping watch on the porch. She said that she had been ordered by her captain to direct her men to other duties due to a possible sighting of the Crows 20 miles away.

After the call, Poppy remarked that Paddy and Milah had been unusually fidgety all evening.

"I wonder if they know something Kobernick and her captain don't," I said.

"Meaning?"

"Well, you know, animals are well known to act up before a natural disaster. Maybe they're warning us to be careful."

All of a sudden, Milah sprung up like a just released jack-in-the-box from her crouched position. She craned her neck and tensed her ears. She remained in that frozen state for about thirty seconds and then lay down, exhaling an exhausted sigh. She didn't move when Abe and Jake showed up from doing their rounds.

"I think we can call off our watch," Poppy said. "Looks like the Crows have been spotted a good piece from here."

"You sure that's a good idea?" Jake asked. "Abe and I saw a couple of what did you call 'em, Danny, you know, gang symbols."

"Tags," I answered.

"Yeah, that's what you said they were. Drawn big as you like on the barn door and a window. Sneaky buggers must have snuck up when we dozed off because they sure wasn't there before."

"I'd second that then," Abe said, patting his Winchester. "Wished we had seen 'em then. We wouldn't be having the same conversation then."

"I'm sure," Poppy replied. "Let's call it quits for now anyway. I can always call you, if need be. I'm sure your families will be glad to have you home."

"Well, I'll stop by around noon tomorrow then," Abe said.

"That time suits me, too," said Jake, yawning. "It'll be good to lay my head down on my own pillow and get a lie-in in the morning."

Poppy shook hands with the two men and thanked them. Abe looked at me, nodded and almost smiled. Then he turned to face Poppy.

"No need to wake Jane then," he said as he made for his pickup. "I'll leave her in *your capable hands*, Tyler. She'll be good company for *your missus*."

He left without saying another word. Jake raised two fingers to offer us a peace sign as he walked to his truck.

"What do you think of Abe Calloway now?" Poppy asked as we watched the two men drive away.

"I dunno. I can't quite figure him out yet. He's a crossword puzzle with no clues."

"You can say that again. Let's tuck in for the night."

I held out my arm for Paddy to hop onto it from his perch on the veranda rail.

"Caw," Paddy said. "Caw, caw."

Chapter 36

THE NEXT MORNING, I woke up from a deep sleep to what I can only describe as a "cawcophony" of crow calls. At first, I thought I was dreaming. I rubbed my eyes to focus better. When I saw that Paddy was not in his cage, I presumed he had flown out the bedroom window, which I had left partially open all night to let in fresh air. I got up and went to investigate.

As I was walking upstairs, I had another urge to start journaling again the way I used to before joining the Crows, and the feeling grew with each step. "After all," I thought, "there'd just been too much going on at the farm since I arrived to rely only on my memory."

The caws were more deafening when I reached the porch. Everywhere I looked – on every branch of every tree, on the roofs of the farm's barns and outhouses, under buildings – I saw crows, crows and more crows. There were hundreds and hundreds of them, all looking my way, or at least Paddy's way because there he was, perched once again on the veranda rail, like a preacher in his pulpit, waiting for the noisy applause to die down so that he could speak. Milah engaged in the conversation, too. She ran back and forth in front of the house, barking at the black congregation until, suddenly, like the abrupt final beat of an Irish bodhrán drummer's music-stopping tipper at a seisiún, the cawing erupted into total silence. This silence -- not the commotion -- drew my grandparents, Mom and Jane outside to witness the screaming murder for themselves.

Paddy waddled back and forth along the rail, his eyes fixed on the muted murder. He uttered a staccato caw pattern I had not heard before. A crow perched on the topmost branch of the tallest tree, a cedar, broke ranks and cawed back to him. Paddy responded with a throaty sound that I imagined was a stamp of approval for the decision that the lookout had just made. Then he flew onto my shoulder and stared at me without another caw. I was about to say something to him when squadron after squadron of crows took to the air in silence, flying off as suddenly as they had appeared. We all watched until some wing-flapping stragglers had faded to nothing in the morning sky.

"Wow!" Mom exclaimed.

"Wow is right," said Jane.

"In all my years, I've never seen the likes of that," Poppy said.

"I have," Gran remembered. "I was ten at the time. I was staying with the Collins family over in Montpelier. My mother was in hospital having Ellen, my youngest sister. Mr. Collins, a kindly man who would give you the shirt off his back, was shot dead by a careless hunter one autumn morning. A short while later, hundreds of crows crashed his wake. They took to the trees and mourned his passing in respectful silence for several hours. Then they flew off as mysteriously and as silently as they had arrived."

"Why would they do that?" I asked.

Gran shrugged. "No one knows for sure, but some folks claimed it was because old Archibald, Mr. Collins, was good to them. Unlike other farmers who would use propane gas cannons to scare birds off their land, he had a fondness for our black-feathered friends and they for him. He would leave out heaps of corn kernels for them to feed on in winter and, in return people say, the crows left his precious money crops alone."

Gran's fascinating story made me wonder whose wake these crows had just attended. Were they mourning a member of their own Corvus brachyrhynchos family or a member of my Homo sapiens family? Or both?

We soon found out. Poppy and I found a dead crow when we went to do the evening milking; it was hanging by its neck from a tree branch not near the barn. A short while later, Paddy made his own grim discovery in the woods at the edge of our farm. We could hear his alarming cawing from the farmhouse, and then Milah's barking.

• • •

Lieutenant Kobernick told us that Hudson Cross had confirmed that the victim was his son, and that he had not seen him since he had gone fishing early that morning. The body had been tied to a tree and showed clear signs of a savage beating. A Crow's tag had been carved into his forehead.

She asked me when I had seen Billy last, but I knew that she already knew the answer.

"I bet Billy Cross was your source. Am I right? The one who told you that you were going to be set up by the sheriff? No sense protecting him now, is there, since he's dead."

"Yes, it was Billy."

"And would you testify to that in court?"

"Would I have to?"

Her yes nod triggered a knot in my stomach. The knot got worse when two FBI agents showed up later that evening to question us.

I repeated the information that I'd already given to Lieutenant Kobernick, adding little else to move the story forward. They seemed satisfied with that. They said that they were still concentrating their search area 20 miles south, where the Crows were last reported seen.

As the two FBI men were leaving, I had an unsettling thought: "If I hadn't been arrested and sent to my grandparents' farm, the cops would be out there hunting for me, too."

Chapter 37

"HEY, KARATE," the whisperer said, as I was nesting the last of the hens' eggs in the basket after the FBI were long gone.

I froze and Paddy, who was flitting about the henhouse, cawed boldly at the source of the intrusion.

"It's me. Up here."

I looked up at the loft and saw Nipper staring down at me. Strands of straw hung from her head and face, giving her a ghoulish appearance.

"You scared the hell out of me," I shouted.

"I didn't mean to."

"Who's with you?"

"Nobody. I'm hiding out, like, from Bongo and the others. Like, I didn't know where else to go."

"Why?"

"I just told you. I didn't, like, know where else to go."

"No. I mean why are you hiding from them?"

"Because of the way they treat me? Like, always whompin' and trying to, like, pussywhack me. Especially Bongo. He's like out-a-control, man, and getting worser every day."

Her use of words like "whomping" – which means humiliating talk in gang speak – made me realize how foreign that language sounds in a world of green and open space.

"Like that drive-by back in the city. Man oh man, I didn't know Bongo was going to, like, you know, go do something crazy like that. I mean, when he locked you and your old lady away in that hole, well that was just no way any cooler, man. I wanted him not to do that, too. But, like, he was traveling in his own head, as usual."

"Yeah, I saw that. So, what do you want from me?"

"You gotta help me. Like, I'm scareder than a scaredy-cat. He knows you got free from the hole in the ground, and he's worked up as hell about that. So he's like after you, too."

"I know someone who can help you. I trust her."

"Who?"

"She's a cop."

"Cop? No way. I ain't no rat."

"You got a better idea? If your story holds up, she'll help you. Or would you rather do hard time for something you didn't do?"

She sat up and brushed the straw from her face and hair with her hands to see more clearly.

"Like, you really trust her?"

"Yes."

"Okay then, I guess. Hey, I'm sorry."

"For what?"

She shrugged.

"Like, I never treated you right," she said. "I know that. I just don't know why."

"Forget about it."

"Okay. Hey, can you, like, get me something to like eat before I meet that cop? Like, I haven't eaten since yesterday morning. I'm cashed out, but I can like pay you this way, if you want."

Having said that she peeled up her sweater slowly until she had bared the bottom part of her breasts.

"No need to do that. I've got a girl."

"She, like, doesn't need to know. I'm only trading."

"Yeah, but my bird and I would know."

284

She looked from me to Paddy, who flew from one rafter to another.

"Stay put," I said. "I'll be back in a few minutes with some grub."

"You're the first," she said when I reached the door.

"First what?"

"The other Crows wouldn't have, like, passed up a chance to do some freaking with me."

"I'm not a Crow anymore."

Paddy flew onto my shoulder and cawed at her.

"And come to think of it, I don't think I ever really was a Crow. What do you say about that, Paddy?"

"Caw," Paddy replied ever so softly. "Caw."

Before Paddy and I had taken two steps together, we saw Jane outside the henhouse window.

"I heard everything," she said. "You turned down a good offer."

"No I didn't."

"Oh?"

"It wasn't a good offer." I grabbed hold of her hand. "I promised to get her something to eat. She's hiding out from the Crows."

When we reached the porch, she kissed me gently on my cheek and squeezed a tiny smile from one corner of her mouth.

"When we get the food, do you mind if I give it to her?"

"You staking your claim?"

"Something like that. That Crow in the shed is just going to have to lay her eggs in another nest."

Chapter 38

LIEUTENANT KOBERNICK PLACED NIPPER in the front passenger seat of her cruiser. She told Poppy and Gran that, until a higher authority contradicted her decision, she was going to treat Nipper as a victim and a material witness rather than an accused.

I nodded to Nipper as they drove off, while Jane gave her a frown to take with her on her journey.

The next morning, Judy Saulter dropped Jake, Abe and Jane off for breakfast on her way to work. She had picked Abe and Jane up after the radiator of Abe's pick-up truck had overheated about a mile from the farm.

As Gran topped up everyone's coffee, the lieutenant called Poppy. The two of them spoke for about ten minutes, which kind of surprised me because I'd never seen Poppy stay on the phone for more than a minute or two. He called telephones "necessary nuisances" that should be used "like Earnest Hemingway said adjectives should be used. Sparingly."

Poppy returned to the kitchen after the call and leaned against the fridge.

"It seems your Nipper friend has been opening up to Lieutenant Kobernick like they were old friends."

He said that the lieutenant had broken the rules by letting Nipper sleep over at her place on the previous night. She confirmed what Billy Cross had told me the day before he was killed. The sheriff was indeed driving a plan to arrest the Crows and implicate me as an accomplice.

Jane squeezed my hand.

"The state police are trying to decide whether or not they have enough evidence to charge the sheriff with conspiracy to commit a felony or two," Poppy said.

Mom asked him if Nipper had revealed where the gang was hiding out.

"No. All she knows is that Wade and Pauly were to take the three Crows to a cabin. She has no idea where. But the lieutenant believes they may have changed their minds about that hideout since Nipper flew the coop. There's nothing else to do now but sit and wait until the two gangs -- the Crows' and the sheriff's -- show their hands.

"Well, we'd best get outside and keep an eye on things then," Abe said.

"I agree," Poppy said, as he went over to the gun cabinet to get some ammunition.

Chapter 39

AS EVENING WAS GETTING READY TO WELCOME NIGHT, I walked away from the house towards the road with Paddy who had hitched another ride on my shoulder. On our way, we met Abe with his Winchester 30-30 tucked under his arm, its barrel aimed harmlessly at the ground in front of him. The rain was lighter now.

"Where are you two off to then?" he asked, clearing thick phlegm from his throat and spitting it at a rock.

"Caw…caw," Paddy said, staring at him.

"I was feeling penned up and thought I'd go pick up the mail for Gran."

"Well then, I'll walk with you. No sense in taking chances with godless riffraff about. Ole Mathilda here will send them all to hell then, if we see 'em."

Abe stroked the underbelly of his rifle with his free hand.

As we made our way towards the main gate, I felt an uneasy silence marching between us. He broke it when we had only about 50 feet to go.

"So, you doing good by my Jane, then?"

"I'm treating her right, if that's what you mean, *then*."

He didn't seem to notice that I had ended my sentence sarcastically with his favorite and much overused word. I couldn't help myself even though we had made peace at the fair ground.

"Fair enough then. Fair enough, I suppose then. She comes from good Christian stock, you know. She don't need *nobody* putting fancy ideas in her head to make her otherwise, hear?"

Paddy bobbed his head. He gave me the impression that he was trying to make sense of every word that came out of Abe's mouth.

"Good luck!" I whispered.

"Hmm!" He cocked the lever of his rifle. "You get the mail then. I'll stay out of sight over here and keep watch while you do then."

He crouched behind a wild raspberry bush and I left him to fetch the mail. As I closed in on the mailbox, that same old feeling of being watched returned to me.

Paddy, perhaps sensing my discomfort, flew to the top of a tall maple to keep an eye on me, too. When he cawed, I waved at him and made a faint attempt to caw back, but rain drizzled into my mouth, making me gag.

The erect flag on the mailbox told me that there was mail inside. I peeked in and retrieved a few bills and a junk mail package, addressed to Gran, with the "you've got a better chance of being hit by lightning twice" promise of $5,000 a month for life.

I dropped one of the bills. As I stooped to pick it up, Paddy cawed a warning. The intruder was a woman. She was driving a large septic tank cleaning truck. She downshifted the vehicle to a crawl and it shuddered into the laneway. She nodded and smiled as she inched the truck forward between Abe and me. I was relieved that she was a "friendly" and paid no attention to the black van parked at the roadside 100 feet or so away from the lane.

As the truck was passing Abe, the driver of the van stepped on the accelerator and drove it at high speed towards me. It stopped abruptly and its two rear doors burst open.

Two males, wearing black balaclavas, jumped out. They grabbed me and shoved me inside. It all happened so fast that I didn't realize what was going on until they had hopped in and closed the two doors behind them. Abe and Paddy did. Through the rear windows, I could see Abe hobbling as fast as he could towards the road and Paddy flying after me, cawing frantically for my assailants to stop. The last I heard from the kidnapping scene were the three shots Abe fired into the air.

• • •

"Step on it, Aldo," Bongo ordered.

"What about the speed limit?"

"Who in fuck's name is going to pull us over? The sheriff? Not bloody likely."

Aladdin and Aldo removed their balaclavas while Bongo pinned my shoulders to the metal floor.

"Let me up!" I shouted. "Let me up!"

"Shut your face," Bongo commanded. "You're in no position to complain, traitor."

"Ready?" Aladdin asked.

"Tie and gag him," Bongo ordered.

Aladdin used a chord to tie my hands behind my back and strips of oily rags to gag and blindfold me. As he adjusted the blindfold, he didn't notice a frayed section covering my left eye. It let me peek out the rear windows and see Paddy still flying after us. That piece of good news immediately evaporated, however, when it was replaced by a taunting thought that I whispered as best I could into the gag, "Forget about him. He's only a bird. He can't do anything to help you, can he?"

Chapter 40

ABE WAS NEARLY BREATHLESS when he returned to the house, as Poppy would recount to me much later in my story.

Mom and Jane were already on the porch when Poppy and Gran came out to join them. Jake came running from the barn.

"We heard rapid fire," Poppy said.

"A van," Abe stammered. "A van. I saw the tail end of two of 'em. They took the young lad!"

Gran gasped and brought a hand to her mouth.

"Who?" Poppy asked.

"Couldn't tell," Abe replied. "Their faces were masked then."

"I'm going to call the police," Gran said and dashed inside to do so.

"Well I'm not going to wait around for them to come and waste my time asking questions and more questions," Poppy said. "We need to do something and fast."

Jane walked to the far end of the porch and looked south, searching the sky.

"I can understand your haste," Jake said. "But the police have more resources than we do. They can cover more territory. Besides, we've no idea where they took him."

"I wouldn't be so sure of that," Jane said.

We all turned and fixed our eyes on her.

"The dirty clothes they were wearing may provide a clue."

"I don't understand," Gran said.

"The other day in the barn, when Bongo shot Bessie! The gang's jeans and boots were all covered in red clay," Jane said.

"I think I know where she's going with this," Jake piped in.

"Me, too," Poppy said.

"Well I'll be," Abe added. "Sweet Mother of Jee-sus, I think she's hit the rusty nail on the head with a hammer."

"Lake Onek-wen-hTessa," Poppy said.

"Would someone fill me in?" Gran demanded, making no effort to mask the desperation in her voice.

"Lake Onek-wen-hTessa. That's Mohawk for *Lake Red*. It's about 18 miles from here. You remember, Lee-Ann. I went fishing there with my dad before he passed."

"Oh, yes, come to think of it. I do."

"You should see the red soil all around it now," Jane said. "It's redder than ever."

"Yes. It's as red as a Canadian Mountie's uniform," Abe added. "It's the only place around here that's got clay like that. It sticks like cow shite to everything that touches it then."

"Well, what're we waiting for?" Jake said.

"Abe?" Poppy asked.

"You betcha. Count me in."

"Me, too," Jane said.

"There's only room for three of us in my pickup, Jane," Poppy said. "And it looks like heavy rain's heading our way. No sense getting you all wet in the back."

"You stay put then, Jane" Abe replied. "You and Tyler's missus can fill the police in."

Poppy whistled when he got into the pickup and Milah hopped into the back. Jake sat in the middle seat between Abe and him. He made a quick U-turn. As the truck passed the house, Jane sprinted after it and, to Milah's delight, jumped into the cargo section and rolled under a plastic tarpaulin, seconds before the storm turned ugly again.

Chapter 41

WHEN THE STOLEN VAN was only a minute or two from its intended destination, my blindfold slipped further down, giving me half vision in one eye. I saw Bongo drive off the road and descend about 500 feet through heavy rain on a steep muddy track, which was so deeply etched with tractor tread marks that the van's front wheels negotiated the twists and turns without much help from the steering wheel. We wove our way around a large lake until we reached a one-story fieldstone cottage.

"Welcome to *Lake Onek-wen-hTessa*," Aldo said awkwardly after we all got out of the van..

"What stupid school-of-mudder-fuckers did you go to, Aldo?" Bongo said.

"Huh?"

"Why did we blindfold Karate?"

"Huh?"

"The answer, shitface, is because we didn't want him to see where we were taking him to. You might as well take the fucking thing off now 'cause it don't make no rat shit of a difference."

Aldo removed the blindfold and shoved me hard against the wall of the cottage.

"I'll break your balls for this, Karate."

"Promises, promises," I tried to say, but the gag muffled my vowels and it came out as "Prmsess, prmsess."

Aldo cocked his arm, but Bongo grabbed it before he had a chance to fire his fist at me.

"Time enough for that later. Let's keep him in one piece for now. We don't want to have to carry him."

We were about to go inside the cottage out of the rain when Aladdin shouted.

"Look! Someone's up there."

"Shit!" Bongo shouted.

He ducked down and ordered us all to do the same. I knelt down on the ground slightly behind them.

High up on the ridge, I saw two headlights. The left was fading in and out. I remembered that on my first visit to Noburg that Gran had complained that she'd been after Poppy to fix his; so, if it was his truck up there, I wondered how the heck he could have figured out where we were so quickly. Then I found out how.

Paddy flew right past my eyes silently -- behind the backs of the Crows.

"What the fuck?" Bongo whispered loudly. He rubbed the back of his neck. "What was that?"

"I didn't see anything," Aladdin replied.

"Me neither," I lied in my thoughts.

As the headlights began their slow descent towards us, the Crows were frantic.

"Let's get the fuck out-a-here!" Aladdin yelled.

"What about Karate?" Aldo shoved me, pushing me a few steps forward, but I managed to keep my balance.

"Bring him along!" Bongo ordered. "He's our *ass* in the hole."

"What about the other two assholes, Wade and Pauly? They said they'd meet us here. Maybe it's them coming."

"They have dirt bikes, not cars, stupid. They'll just have to find us, won't they? I'm not sticking around here to do fucking time."

Bongo led the way down a narrow footpath towards the lake. He spotted a battered aluminum rowboat tied to the wharf.

"You can drive this shitbox." Bongo said to me.

When I made no move towards the boat, he gave me a quick backhand across my face, causing my gag to slip down below my mouth.

"Untie him and the boat, Aldo," he ordered. "Oh shit, the coins! They're in the van. Go get 'em, Aladdin."

As the two Crows were doing what they were told, Bongo turned to face me again. He removed a black rubber band from his wrist and a catapult arm from his back pocket. He married the two parts together and placed a small ball bearing, about the size of a pea, in the patch.

"In case you get any bright ideas, Karate. This is for you."

He then pretended to fire the missile at me.

Bongo sat in the stern after fastening the packsack to his back. He told Aladdin and Aldo to squeeze into a seat in the bow.

When the pickup's headlight beams reached the cottage, the rain stopped, Clouds moved away across the lake, leaving behind a full moon.

We were soaking wet as we pushed off from the wharf. I rowed south with my back to Aldo and Aladdin. I kept my eyes fixed on Bongo who appeared uneasy to be on a foreign element like water. I hugged the shoreline, ignoring his orders to pull harder.

"If you think you can do better, be my guest."

"Watch your mouth," he shouted. "Or I'll shut it for you for good. Faster!"

I toyed with the notion of telling him everything the cops knew about his connection to the sheriff and that we were all being set up, but decided not to.

I could see the pickup on the wharf in the distance. Its nervous headlight had burned out completely, while the more confident one beamed its light across the glassy lake, searching for us.

"We have to go out more," Aldo said.

"What for?" Bongo asked.

"The water's too shallow and rocky. We'll get stuck if we don't. His oars are already dragging bottom."

"They'll spot us if we go out more," Aladdin said.

"I know that, stupid," Bongo scoffed.

"We've no choice," Aldo yelped as the keel scraped one submerged rock after the other.

"Take us out!" Bongo shouted. "But not too far."

"Why? Can't you swim?" I quipped, cawing like the Crow I once was.

When he glared at me and, once again, pretended to fire his catapult at me, I decided to give in – for the time being. I kept the boat within 100 feet or so from shore and away from the headlight's beam.

As I rowed, I thought about Jane and wondered if she were back at the wharf with Poppy. I also thought about Paddy. I wondered what he had been up to since I'd seen him flying past me on shore. I cawed to him and I thought I heard a faint caw in reply.

"Shut your fucking mouth!" Bongo ordered. "Or I'll shut it for you right now."

Then I saw a black speck grow larger as it moved across the moon. It mutated into a welcome sight of feathers and flesh: Paddy himself. Cawing, he circled a few times before executing a bomb dive. As he had once done to the sheriff, he dropped poop on the three crows as he swooped by. Then he circled above the boat and landed on my left shoulder. He fixed his eyes firmly on Bongo.

"Fucking crow shit," Bongo complained, trying to wipe away the white poop from his hair with his fingers. "You called him here, didn't you?"

Bongo stood on weak legs to strike out at Paddy. He backed off and sat down when Paddy surprised him with several rapid warning caws and threatening pecks.

"That bird's fucking nuts!"

"Nuts about me, you mean," I replied. "Leave him alone and he'll leave you alone."

"I'll leave you and him alone for good when we get where we're going."

I knew that he meant what he said, if only to show Aldo and Aladdin that he still had the balls to deal with me.

The voices of Poppy and Jane traveled from the wharf to our ears. Milah's barks did, too.

"Danny, Danny!" they shouted in unison. "Danny, Danny!"

"Poppy! Jane," I shouted back. Paddy cawed.

"I'm warning you," Bongo said. "Shut up!"

"It's time to say goodbye to you morons," I said.

I stopped rowing, stood up, and spread my feet apart. I began to wobble the boat from side to side until its two gunnels lapped the lake surface a few times. Paddy stayed on my shoulder for the duration of the seesaw ride, cawing encouragement.

"What the fuck're you doing?" Bongo screamed. "Sit down dammit. You'll sink us!"

"That's the whole idea," I shot back.

"I can't swim," Aladdin shouted.

"None of us can," Aldo yelled back.

Bongo gripped the gunnels with both hands and dropped the catapult into the water. I watched it float away.

"I can swim," I said, smiling. "Come on, Paddy. We're out of here!"

I released the oars, stood on my seat, and dove off, tipping the boat and the three Crows into the lake in the process. Paddy must have decided that he didn't want to get wet and flew off my shoulder before I broke the cool water.

Bongo, Aladdin and Aldo were now in a state of panic. They flailed their arms in their desperate attempts to reach the upturned boat.

As I treaded water, watching, Aldo and Aladdin managed to reach the boat by sheer luck. Bongo was too far away from the drifting boat. To make matters worse for him, the pack on his back was getting heavier by the second; he was sinking.

"Help!" he shouted, spitting out water. "Help!"

I didn't want his death on my conscience. I knew what I had to do, even though I knew that he'd never do the same for me. He was already choking on swallowed water and I knew that he could easily drown both of us in his panic if I tried to help him. I grabbed one of the floating oars and reached it to him. Paddy circled overhead, cawing.

"Grab the oar!" I commanded.

I pushed the oar and its no-class passenger to the upturned boat. He latched onto the craft like a suckling to a breast. Aldo and Aladdin were trembling too much from the cold and fear to pay their respects upon his arrival.

I pulled the packsack off Bongo's back, one strap at a time, but he was too preoccupied with his survival to protest. I slipped it over my own shoulders and swam as fast I could to shore while Paddy flew above me, cawing encouragement.

"We'll get you!" Bongo shouted as loud as his quavering voice would let him.

When I reached shore, I was almost breathless. When I got to my feet, I looked back at the three Crows kicking the water with theirs, propelling the boat slowly after me. I began to shiver and wished I could get out of my wet clothes before the temperature dropped any more.

I followed a trail that I hoped would lead back to the wharf until I was startled by the sound of a breaking twig, then the sight of two dark figures on the trail ahead. The one on the left spoke first.

"Hello, Cagney," Wade Simmons said. "Me and you still got a score or two to settle."

Pauly was massaging the knuckles of his right hand with the palm of the other for my benefit. "Don't forget me, jerk-off, I've got a present here for you, too."

I was still trying to catch my breath after my fast swim. Because I felt too weak to run or fight, I slipped into the woods and hid behind a large tree. Then I heard leaves rustling and the click of a gun hammer behind me.

"Freeze!" the sheriff ordered.

He rammed his gun barrel into my back and patted me down, checking for a concealed weapon. He then removed the packsack from my back and was delighted to discover the coins inside..

"What now, Dad?" Wade asked.

"We'll see. We better get a move on. He's got people out looking for him. Here, you hang on to these with your life," he added, handing him the packsack.

I heard splashing water and coughing. It was coming from roughly the same spot where I had reached shore.

"Looks like his three girlfriends have arrived just in time," the sheriff quipped. "Perfect. My car's parked about a mile and a half southeast of here. We'll take them all there. Then you'll do the citizen's arrest thing."

"The state police know all about your plan," I said. "You'll never collect a penny of the reward. Billy Cross spilled his guts."

"Billy's dead. So, anything they got is pure shit. Now, I've just about had all I'm going to take from you and your gang."

"They're not my gang anymore," I said.

"They will be by the time we're finished with *all of you*."

For the second time that night, despite Paddy's protests, I was gagged. By the time Bongo, Aldo and Aladdin had dragged their bodies out of the water and reached us on the trail, I found myself being escorted against my will once again -- into the night.

I tried to make eye contact with Bongo. I wanted to warn him that he was about to be double-crossed, but the gag muffled my words.

"He tried to fucking drown us," Aldo shouted. "Let me at him."

"Me first!" Bongo shouted even louder. He was shivering

He lunged at me, but the sheriff got between us.

"Not now. We've got to put some distance between us and his grandfather's group. I spotted them back at the cabin."

"It won't be fast enough for me," Bongo replied.

Paddy cawed repeatedly as he flew in circles above us.

The sheriff shoved me forward. I lead the way southeast along a winding, moonlit trail. Bongo, Aldo, Aladdin, Wade and Pauly followed us in single file.

"I'll fix that fucking black bastard," the sheriff bragged, looking up at Paddy.

"You racist," I mumbled through the gag.

The sheriff picked up a stone from the ground and hurled it at Paddy. Thankfully, he missed.

"Caw, caw, caw, caw, Paddy," I tried to scream through the gag.

Paddy flew off before the sheriff's second missile had a chance to hit its mark.

I shivered with each step I took. I was afraid that I would freeze before reaching the sheriff's car. I knew that I had to do something quickly.

I studied the moonlit trail ahead and the woods on either side of it with the urgency of a student cramming for exams at the last minute. My mind raced faster than my feet, as I looked left and right, up and down, looking for any vantage point that might help my escape. I was beginning to give up hope when the sheriff shouted at me to be careful.

"There's a gully ahead where the trail narrows. Stay to your right or you'll fall."

The trail ran dangerously close to the edge of a lava-rock cliff. I had to place more weight on my left foot to compensate for its downward slope. I saw the steep gully, which looked to me like it had been carved out of the rock eons ago. Near its bottom was a narrow stretch of wet, red soil that ran all the way down to *Lake Onek-wen-hTessa*.

I glanced back over my shoulder and saw the sheriff about three feet behind me, his eyes fixed on the ground. As I passed a giant oak tree, which hid me from view for a few seconds, I whispered, "It's now or never."

Without a second thought, I inhaled a full chest of cool air and leapt off the trail into the gully, landing hard on my back.

"Fucking hell!" the sheriff roared.

He fired his revolver twice. The bullets ricocheted off boulders on either side of me as I slid on my back towards the lake. I was completely at the mercy of gravity and the bumpy terrain under me. I prayed that I would not run into anything as I slid, rudderless, through the darkness. Thankfully, the sandy patch leveled out eventually and I slowed to a complete stop just shy of the lake.

I caught my breath between beats of my pounding heart. I scrambled to my feet and assessed the mess I was in. My legs and back were scraped and sore, the seat of my wet jeans was torn and plastered with red soil.

Somewhere, not far from me, an owl screeched as it hunted for prey of its own and my thoughts turned to increasing the distance between my own hunters and me.

I noticed the two oars first; they were floating on the water near the shore. The bow of the upturned rowboat peeked out at me from behind a small pine tree that was growing sideways out of the rocks and almost kissing the moon's reflection in the lake. I waded over to the boat and, with some effort, managed to right it, emptying most of its water. I retrieved the oars and climbed aboard.

The voices on the ridge were even more distant and muffled now. I could not tell if the sheriff and the others were still headed in a southeasterly direction or northwest back to the stone cottage.

To stay out of sight, I hugged the shore while rowing as fast as I could towards the wharf. The boat no logger scraped the lake bottom due to its now lighter load. I was spurred on by light coming from the cottage in the distance and I used it as a beacon of hope to guide me.

The light didn't guide me for long, however. I saw the dark figure of a man crouching above me on a huge boulder as the boat passed. It was the sheriff. He dropped into the boat and pulled my hair from behind.

"Even flinch and I'll shoot you where you sit, you son-of-a-bitch!"

He stuck the tip of his gun barrel into my back. It hurt.

"Pull in over there," he ordered, pointing to a sandy spot ashore.

When we got out of the boat, he made me push it away from shore and toss the oars in different directions into the darkness of the woods.

"Follow that trail there and stay the bloody hell on it this time!"

When we reached the top of the cliff, Wade, Billy and the Crows hurled insults and taunts at me. I answered each one with silence, which seemed to piss them off even more.

Paddy and Milah didn't remain silent, however. Although I could not see them, he cawed four times from above and she answered with an equal number of barks from beyond. While I longed for the company of these two loyal friends, I was encouraged by the fact that they were at least close by.

Chapter 42

I NOTICED THE SILENCE FIRST. It was my second opportunity to do so in as many days. My abductors were oblivious to it. It occurred just after we had made our slow descent down the mountain and it lasted for a few minutes until it was pierced by hundreds of caws above us.

I looked up and saw Paddy cawing encouragement to hundreds of flying crows. When the last straggler flew past ten minutes later, I felt deserted and alone.

"Not far now," the sheriff said. "My car's parked just ahead."

Thompson's Glade was a square-mile island, a nature's stage of wild flowers and green grass, surrounded by old forest, and tonight the full moon was lighting the set like a giant floodlight.

"Look there!" Pauly shouted.

"What?" Wade replied as he stumbled over a rock and swore.

"Jesus," the sheriff said.

We watched an amazing show unfold. Hundreds of silent crows occupied every branch of a huge elm in the middle of the glade ahead. There were so many that they looked like a colossal black spaceship, pointed at the sky, primed for lift-off.

Like the murder at the farm two days earlier, this one remained eerily quiet -- until we got closer to the tree. Suddenly, they erupted in a fit of threatening caws and flew directly at us with all the precision of air show pilots, almost touching the tips of each other's wings. Paddy was among them, but he broke formation. He flew onto my shoulder and cawed at them.

The murder, to a crow, must have heeded Paddy's caws. Its members split into two streams as they flew by Paddy and me. I felt safe under their flapping wings.

My kidnappers were not fortunate enough to have a protector like Paddy, however.

Paddy's crows attacked my former Crows first, then the sheriff, Wade and Pauly. They took their prey so completely by surprise that no one had a chance to fire a gun or a slingshot in response. At Paddy's prompting, the birds swarmed over the gang, drowning out human screams and pleas to stop their painful pecking with their constant cawing.

Suddenly, Poppy, Jake and Abe appeared in the glade, with Jane and Milah right behind them. On Poppy's signal, the three men fired into the air, scaring the crows away in different directions. Paddy had other plans. He perched on my shoulder, surveying the damage inflicted upon my enemies who now lay on the ground bleeding from their heads, faces and hands. Abe and Jake rounded up dropped weapons.

Wade was on his knees, groaning. I placed my foot on his back and pushed him face down. I then pulled the packsack off his back for the second time that night.

"You won't need this where you're going, Wade."

"Traitor!" Bongo yelled.

"Coming from you, I take that as a compliment. Caw...caw...caw," I added for good measure.

"It's okay, Danny. I'll keep an eye on them," Abe said, surprising me by calling me by name for the first time. He pointed his Winchester at Wade and Pauly. He then ordered them to sit with their hands on their heads on a carpet of green moss. Jake aimed his gun barrel at the three Crows, prompting them to sit and imitate the other two.

The sheriff was sitting on a tree stump nearby, rubbing his wounds. Before Abe and Jake reached him, he stood up, staggered and aimed his revolver at me.

Blood streamed from the sheriff's eyes and he blinked several times to focus. Poppy dropped his firearm and tried to wrestle the handgun away from him, but he was not strong enough to do so. Jane and I ran to help him. We stopped running when the sheriff pointed his gun barrel at Poppy's chest.

"Back off or I'll blow a hole in him!" the sheriff warned them.

Paddy didn't pay attention to the sheriff's words. He flew at him and dug his claws into his face. The sheriff screamed and tried to hit back with his gun. Milah decided to join the fight, too. She jumped up and bit the sheriff's wrist. His hand jerked upwards and his gun fired harmlessly into the air, just missing Paddy who was now flying towards me.

Poppy pushed the "outlaw" sheriff down. He then cuffed him with his own handcuffs.

"You and your accomplices are all under citizen's arrest," Poppy announced.

I hugged Jane and kissed her on both cheeks. Abe managed a tiny smile; he put it away when the rest of us noticed it.

In the distance, sirens wailed and, the louder they got, I could almost swear that I could hear hundreds of wings flapping approval.

Poppy waited a few seconds after the sirens stopped wailing, and then fired three slow shots into the air. About ten seconds later, he nodded to Abe to do the same.

"That'll bring the police our way," Poppy said. "Then we'll be done with this lot."

Paddy may have had the final say, however. He cawed and flew off towards the approaching police, perhaps to lead Lieutenant Kobernick to the glade, just to make sure that she didn't get lost along the way.

• • •

In response to Mom's request for privacy the next morning, Lieutenant Kobernick ordered her troopers to keep the press and swarms of curious onlookers well away from the farm.

I stayed close to Mom all that day because she seemed to be having a delayed reaction to our near death in the underground shelter, as well as my more recent kidnapping. I guess I was still acting like an enabler, and I was afraid that she would start drinking or doing drugs again. Thankfully, however, she didn't then, and she hasn't since.

While the cops were successful in keeping intruders off the farm, they could do nothing about the hungry paparazzi, who chased after Abe and Jake for a story or a photo when Judy Saulter drove them home for a well-deserved rest.

When Jane insisted on staying behind with me, Abe didn't object. Neither did Paddy who blinked approval while perched once again on his favorite shoulder.

During supper, Poppy brought up a conversation he had with Lieutenant Kobernick.

"She said that your friend, Nipper, has agreed to testify against the Crows in exchange for immunity. And Pauly ratted on Wade and his father in exchange for a reduced sentence."

"There's more good news," Mom said as she slid the local newspaper across the table to me.

There was only one photo on the front page and it was a blow-up of Paddy. He looked proud perched on my shoulder. The headline boldly proclaimed his role in the capture of the six felons:

PADDY THE CROW
HELPS CAPTURE 2 GANGS.
AIDED BY MURDER

We all applauded and cheered when Paddy hopped onto the newspaper and bowed his head to admire his photo.

"Caw," he replied. "Caw… caw… caw."

Crowlogue

PADDY STAYED CLOSE TO ME until the following spring when another crow, whom I presumed to be a female, flew into the farmyard as I scratched a bow across the strings of Poppy's fiddle. The visitor caught Paddy's ear and eye. This didn't take me totally by surprise as, many times during the previous winter, I had thought that nature would one day come calling to draw him away from me.

At first Paddy seemed to be trying hard to resist the temptation to leave, as he should have with Missy, the name I decided to give her. When she beckoned to him from a nearby tree, he would fly to her. They would preen one another's feathers and talk crow there for a few minutes. He would then fly back to perch on my shoulder and gaze back at her longingly. Each visit and departure made me feel that, through no fault of his own, Paddy had reduced me to an even tinier spot in the corner of one brooding eye.

This wrestling match between friendship and courtship lasted from morning until evening when Paddy flew off with Missy in silence towards Paddington Pond, leaving me with a heavy heart. When the two of them returned together the next day, Paddy did his best to communicate with me in new caw patterns I could not decipher. Then, without further notice, he flew off with Missy to begin a new chapter in a life that no longer included me.

I never saw Paddy or Missy again. But, whenever I walk or ride around the countryside, alone or with Jane, I can't shake that same old feeling of being watched and cared for. In fact, whenever a crow caws now in my presence, I make sure to caw back -- just in case the cawer is Paddy, Missy, or one of their beautiful offspring.

References

Bird references:
Reader's Digest, "North American Wildlife: An Illustrated Guide to 2,000 Plants and Animals, 2012. © Reader's Digest, 2012.

The Vermont Fish and Wildlife Department web site: http://www.vtfishandwildlife.com

Poem reference:
Robert Frost's poem, "Out, Out," 1916.

Mohawk language reference:
http://www.native-languages.org/mohawk_words.htm

Song reference:
Sheryl Crow's Everyday Is A Winding Road. ©1996 A&M Records.

CrowNotes

Made in the USA
Charleston, SC
07 May 2013